The Ruby Seat
by Joseph Rector

ISBN 9781938467684

Published by

◤ köehlerbooks™

210 60th Street
Virginia Beach, VA 23451
212-574-7939
www.koehlerbooks.com

Publisher
John Köehler

Executive Editor
Joe Coccaro

Cover: Camp Arden, one of the last traditional camps that remains intact in the
Adirondack Park. Photo by © Joseph Rector. Author photo by © Nancie Battaglia.

In memory of my grandmother

Eva Rector,

and my first true friend,

George Penfield

Visit the author's website at
www.josephrector.com

THE RUBY SEAT

A NOVEL

JOSEPH RECTOR

VIRGINIA BEACH
CAPE CHARLES

When the wind is busy in the branches,

the trees mingle and converse among themselves.

But when the forest becomes still,

the trees talk to God.

Prologue

The flashlight flickered along the winding downhill path, its golden beam gliding over black tree trunks, rutted gray rocks and spooky white birch. When the old man reached the lake, he clicked the light off. Moonlight glimmered off the water as did the millions of stars above. The sweet smell of new leaves, mixed with fragrant balsam, wafted through the soft June air. Cyril tried to focus on the moment and concentrate on the peaceful, starry night with its cool air when without warning his eyelids slammed shut as the tormenting visions returned uninvited: a white house being consumed by orange flames; the endless screaming of a child; his own hands covered in blood; a noose hanging high in a pine tree.

Cyril's frantic eyes snapped open and he roared into the silent night screaming, "STOP! NO MORE!!" When the last echo rounded the lake and ceased, his head tilted back and he whispered pleadingly to the glittering sky, "Please ... please."

The flashlight slipped from his hand and landed without a sound in the soft sand. His chin dropped to his chest, and as he watched the tiny waves carrying the moonlight to his feet, he tried with all his might to remember her voice, her perfect smile, but it was no use; it was too long ago. When a barred owl broke the stillness and hooted from across the lake, Cyril looked up and searched the faraway blackness. A whole-body shiver threw him off balance, causing one foot to land in the water. Not caring, he stepped in with the other, turned and slowly reached down with a strong, wide hand and picked up the light. His weary eyes found the moon-reflected panes of his solitary home, and with slow marching steps he walked back up the hill, where once again he would stand vigil staring out an east window waiting for the sun to return his great faith.

Chapter 1

Eva threw open the bedroom door and hauled two bulging suitcases onto her bed. In heavy handfuls she stuffed her clothes into a tall rickety chest of drawers that stood crooked in the corner. Scurrying around the little room, she savored the familiar smells of the little cabin, even though they were a mixture of cool, stale air, mothballs and a hint of propane gas. Her heart was dancing in her chest; she was so happy to be back at camp, but most of all she just couldn't wait to see him.

The whole summer, she marveled to herself. *I can't believe it! We're finally here!* Eva closed the tight-fitting drawers as quietly as she could, but when she jammed the empty suitcases under the bed, her mother's voice echoed down the hall.

"Eva, I hope you're putting your clothes away neatly."

"Um ... yes, Mom," Eva called out drearily, accompanied by her standard scowl. "I'm almost done."

After giving her room an approving nod, Eva flipped her baseball hat off the doorknob and dashed into the kitchen, almost bumping into her mother. Ann took a step back and began fidgeting with an envelope in one hand and a card in the other.

"I'm all done. I'm going down to Cyril's. Okay?"

While Eva stood tall with an ear-to-ear smile, she watched her mother's questioning frown dissolve. Eva knew that when the rapid blinking started, followed by a nervous smile, her mother would give in without questions. And so the blinking began and Eva smiled even wider.

"Alright, you can go," Ann said, peering suspiciously over Eva's shoulder toward her bedroom. "I know you're excited. I am too. But remember, when you get back I'll need your help getting the camp cleaned up and ready." Ann's eyes fell to Eva's pants. "Eva, haven't you got a better pair of jeans to wear. Those are so old and full of holes."

"No, you know these are my favorite. Why does it matter?"

"Oh, I don't know Eva. It would just be nice to see you in something besides those jeans and that green sweatshirt for once." Ann let out an exhausted breath and walked toward Eva with her arms held out. "Now, you be careful on your way."

"Mom, I'm not five years old!" Eva scolded.

Eva avoided the oncoming hug by dashing around the small kitchen table and making a beeline for the front door. Her hands were busy tucking her long red ponytail through the hole in her baseball hat, when her mother yelled, "WAIT! Eva, please sign the card. I need to get it in the mail tomorrow."

In mid-stride, Eva spun around to face her mother. Her eyes narrowed and her arms crossed tightly against her chest. "I won't write anything on that stupid card, and I'm not signing it. He doesn't care about me or anyone else and you know that!"

Eva held her ground, scowling at her mother's sad expression. Just as Ann lifted the card toward her daughter, Eva adjusted her hat, turned and long-stepped through the tiny living room, across the porch and through the squeaky screen door. On the top step she stood for a moment, thought of her father and then slammed the rickety door.

Eva's new hiking boots hit the ground with a hard thud, clearing all three porch steps at once. She sprinted across the front lawn and halted at the edge of a barely paved, narrow road, her eyes scanning and searching, trying to remember.

Where is it? she asked herself impatiently. Eva's brown eyes squinted as she studied the Adirondack foliage—pine, balsam, maple, birch and beech. When she spotted a tiny green apple, she smiled in relief. She crossed the road, not losing sight of the gnarled, twisted branches of an old apple tree that formed an arched entrance into her secret world—a narrow downhill path that led to Cyril's lakeside home.

Eva never shared her love for camp and Cyril with anyone. At school, she felt very much alone, having very little in common with anybody. Early on, she tried to fit in, but most of the time her so-called friends seemed a million miles away. They talked and gossiped nonstop. It drained Eva listening to the false nonsense. For as long as she could remember, she loved coming to camp more than anything. Each year that passed, the beauty and peace of the mountains seemed to provide a permanent lone-happiness that nobody could take away. But she often thought, *Why isn't anyone in this school like me or just a little like me?* And she also thought, just as often, *Why am I so different?*

Two thoughts buoyed Eva: First, in a few short years she would be attending forestry school at Paul Smith's College located in the heart of the Adirondack Mountains, where Eva knew for certain she would not be an outcast. To graduate early she had been taking extra classes throughout high school. Cyril was her second saving grace. He never failed to evoke a broad smile. She didn't know why she was so drawn to him. She just knew he was different from any other person she had ever met, and someday, somehow, she was going to live just like him, in the solitude of the mountains, away from the hurt and frustrations of the world.

Eva ducked under her archway and entered the green-shaded summer woods. Stopping for a moment under a great pine tree, she joyfully sniffed in all directions, drawing the much-missed aromas of sun-warmed pine, balsam and cedar deep into her lungs. Even the layers of decaying leaves and moss on the forest floor smelled wonderful. She set off on a cheerful trot, pushing the small branches aside, which, over the past year, had grown into her narrow trail. The pathway was made with Cyril's help when she was seven years old. It was well used, easy to follow, and just four minutes of fast downhill walking to Cyril's tiny lakeside cabin.

About halfway down, Eva gasped and skidded to a halt, sending small pebbles rustling through the dry leaves. Her right hand found a thin maple branch that kept her upright while the other was frozen in midair. While trying to hold her breath, her terror-filled eyes frantically searched in every direction. The barking was echoing so loud it sounded like wolves were surrounding her. Her heart was thumping in her ears and goose bumps were creeping up the back of her neck. And then, with a sigh of relief, her grip loosened as she remembered the dogs—the witch's dogs. *But why do they sound so close?* she wondered. With wide eyes still scanning, Eva's neck jerked instantly to the right when an old woman's piercing yell broke over the howling, which quickly turned to faint whimpers and then silence.

Eva's breathing began to slow down when she reminded herself what Cyril and her mother had said about the witch. Cyril simply called her Harmless Hazel. Ann called her the lonely Bus Lady. But to Eva she had always been *that witch* who lived in a dumpy old bus with a bunch of mean dogs. Eva had seen the bus only one time. When she was five, her father had taken her by the hand and marched her, half-dragging, through the woods to show her there was nothing to be afraid of. Crying and hugging her father's leg, the one-time trip terrified her and left permanent, clear visions of the witch's hideout—bus number 176 was dirty and faded yellow with patches of green mold running halfway up the sides. The windows were greasy and dark and most were cracked. A few gray branches and a thick layer of brown leaves covered the top. The tires were half in the ground and the bus leaned to one side and seemed stuck between a huge tree and a boulder as wide as the bus.

Eva shivered remembering her darkened outline on the camp road, slightly bent, wearing layers of shawls that hung like dark rags over her long, dirt-smeared dresses. A knit cap of uncertain color was pulled down to her eyebrows, leaving her black matted hair hanging in clumps about her shoulders. But mostly Eva remembered her sharp nose and the two top teeth that seemed to be the only ones she had.

Eva's mom would repeatedly say, "Eva, you can't judge anyone on their looks or where or how they live." But Eva couldn't be swayed, and when her mind was made up on something it was set in stone. Eva was sure of one thing: She was very afraid of that witch and never wanted to have a run-in with her or her wolf friends. She tried to calm herself by envisioning the bus door slamming shut and all the dogs sitting upright in their vinyl seats, looking out the cracked windows. The thought gave her comfort and a brief smile. As Eva's eyes wandered through the still woods her terror slowly receded. With one last look toward the bus, Eva bravely raised her chin, smiled and thought, *Cyril wouldn't be afraid.* She then lunged forward and sped down her path, leaving the maple branch whipping back and forth.

When glimpses of a burgundy-painted roof began to appear through the soft light-green foliage, Eva's strides lengthened and then stopped abruptly. Smiling, she wiped her brow and pulled off her hooded sweatshirt, tying it around her waist. Just beyond a framework of a dozen slender birch trees she was relieved to see all was well. All was the same. Her happy eyes roamed over a little stream with a single-log bridge leading to Cyril's little green camp with wildflowers on one side and several ranks of firewood on the other. The weather-washed building sat on a high bluff, its many large windows glistening on the eastern side.

The large panes were still without curtains Eva noticed, remembering Cyril once saying, "I like to feel outside even when I'm in." His home looked smaller this year as Eva took in the camp's broad, unobstructed lake view. Eva scanned the sandy shoreline, peering at Cyril's old row boat. Her smile grew even wider remembering all the times Cyril had rowed her up and down the lake in his wooden guide boat. For a moment she could feel the caned seat beneath her and the boat gliding atop the smooth, silvery water with barely a sound. From the beached boat her eyes followed a long path of sun sparkles dancing on the water that connected the boat to the other side of the lake, where on the opposite shore Whiteface Mountain rose massively into three sharp peaks.

Her eyes darted back and forth from the cabin to the lakeshore, looking for any sign of movement. Just when she thought he wasn't home, a door creaked open and a tall, thin man took up the entire entrance. But all Eva could see was his big smile.

She dashed down the hill and cleared the log bridge in one long leap, shouting "CYRIL!" as she landed. She ran the rest of the way and fell into his open arms. His woolen shirt was soft and held a familiar camp and balsam smell she loved so much. She held on tightly until he slowly pulled away and held her by the shoulders at arm's length.

"Eva! My goodness. You're a half a foot taller. I've missed you so much! Come in and sit down," he said, ushering her toward the porch. "Your rocking chair hasn't moved an inch and has been waiting just for you."

"That witch's, I mean Hazel's dogs, I forgot about them. They really scared me. They sounded so close."

"I heard them too. They don't bark very often but I do know she keeps them chained up. As for Hazel, I've never seen her fly by my camp on a broom," Cyril said, looking up at the sky with a quick grin. "I know she's a bit strange, but I've never known her to be mean or harm anyone and she's been there for many summers, just keeping to herself."

As they walked back toward the camp, Eva glanced up at Cyril and was relieved to see that he still looked the same. In fact, to Eva, he never seemed to change. His full head of snow-white hair was always combed and neatly trimmed. He was wearing the same clothes as always—a clean wool shirt buttoned to the top, loose-fitting cotton pants and big leather hiking boots that glistened with a fresh coat of polished wax. But then her smile fell briefly when she looked at his hands. *Those scars,* she thought. *I guess they'll never go away.* She had always wondered what caused the ugly jagged lines that crisscrossed the back of his thick, strong hands. Several summers ago she had asked her father about Cyril's hands, but he had said in his usual flat tone, "It's none of your business."

With a swift, fading smile, Eva went up the three small steps and sat stiffly on the edge of her rocking chair. She had something on her mind and had been practicing just how to say it, and she wanted to get it out of the way as quickly as she could. She looked out across the lake and fidgeted with her compass while Cyril whistled and rocked back and forth. When she felt his eyes, Eva glanced quickly at Cyril and said to her feet, "Well, um, you know everything's different now. My dad's now where he belongs; and it's good, because now he can't hurt anyone anymore, well, at least not until he gets out. But I'm ... it doesn't matter to me anyway."

Eva felt like a huge weight was lifted from her. Relieved, she erased it from her mind and slumped back in her chair.

Cyril's chair stopped rocking and he sat forward.

"Eva, I'm so sorry for all that you've been through. I can't even imagine how you must feel." As his hand reached out for hers, Eva stood up, took a few steps and grabbed the edge of the two-by-four window frame and stared out over the lake, waiting for his questions but hoping to answer none.

"Cyril! Look!" Eva said, pointing. "It's a bald eagle! Do you think it's Charlie? I thought you said he was gone. It sure looks like him!"

Cyril shot out of his chair, grabbed the door handle and motioned Eva down the steps. Neither of them said a word as they bounded down the gently sloping hill toward the shoreline. Eva got there first and had to skid to a halt before bumping into the bow of Cyril's rowboat.

"Is it? Do you think?" Eva asked excitedly. She stopped watching the bird's flight and fixed her eyes on Cyril.

"Could very well be Charlie. There aren't many bald eagles around, but I've not seen him since last summer. That's odd," Cyril said, rubbing his chin. "Maybe, Eva, he's welcoming you back. I think animals know and understand more than we give them credit. Their minds are open and receptive, not all cluttered like our busy brains," he said, smiling down at her.

They watched the dark bird take three powerful strokes against the blue sky and then glide for hundreds of feet, leaning and tilting, its white head sparkling in the full sun. The eagle suddenly careened toward them, and while holding its sharp left tilt, it circled downward toward the water like it was spinning down an invisible spiral staircase.

"Watch this!" Cyril said, inching forward.

Eva thought Charlie was going to land in the water but at the last second it dipped its talons into the lake and magically pulled a fish from the shiny surface. The eagle reared up, flapping powerfully, and flew directly across the lake toward a towering pine tree.

"Wow!" Eva said. "He caught a fish and look at the size of it! How can it carry something that big?"

"Eagles are powerful birds. Faraway they don't look that big, but their wingspan can be six feet or more. Well, my dear Eva, lunch is served. Charlie's all set! Are you hungry?"

"No," Eva replied, shaking her head and turning away from the lake. "We ate in the car, just before we got here. I had one of Mom's most excellent egg salad sandwiches—yuck! Yellow paste smeared between two pieces of wheat bark! She says the wheat is good for my colon. I don't care about my colon! I like white bread, but she's a nurse and as she always says, 'You don't know what I've seen.' Honestly, I don't ever want to know what she's seen!"

Cyril laughed but Eva frowned and shook her head thinking of her mother.

"Well," Cyril began through a few chuckles, "I don't know about your mom's sandwiches, but she makes the best dinners I've ever tasted."

Eva thought hard of something else to say—anything to keep her father out of anymore conversations. "I was hoping we could go on your hike today. Do you still take your long hike?"

"Yes we can. And yes, I still take my walk every day or almost every day. It keeps me in good shape; I don't know what I'd do without it."

"Do you still do it in the rain and snow and sometimes at night when the moon is out? That's really spooky. Don't you ever get scared?"

"I only go at night when the moon is full or near full, and only with snow on the ground. The woods are quite bright and so beautiful and peaceful, but no, I'm not afraid of being alone in the woods. Remember what I told you about being alone?"

"I remember what you said but I don't like being alone in the dark. It's just scary. But I'd go with *you*. I wouldn't be afraid then."

"Well, I haven't done my walk today—I saved it just in case you wanted to go. I'll get my pack basket and we can stop and tell your mom on the—"

BAM!!

Cyril's front door flew open and a strange little man Eva had never seen before stood teetering in the doorway, glaring blankly ahead. He seemed even smaller in his rumpled over-sized clothes that made his feet and hands disappear. Greasy clumps of spiky black hair rose from his head—more on one side than the other—and just above his huge stained eyeglasses, swirling tufts created one long eyebrow. Eva thought he was going to fall when his legs suddenly bowed and locked against the doorframe.

"Good afternoon, Datus. I hope you slept well," Cyril said in a booming, pleasant voice, which echoed off the camp and back down to the lake. Datus scratched his butt and grumbled something about the bright sun before turning to go back inside.

"Just a minute, Datus! I would like you to meet Eva," Cyril

added quickly, just before the door slammed shut.

Datus turned sharply and then slowly grabbed his head and moaned painfully. When he raised his other hand, his elbow banged off the door casing. "Dangit!" he mumbled. Wavering, he squinted back in their direction. "Oh, hiya there. Ahhh ... Cyril talks a lotta ya," Datus said gruffly. He pulled his long shirttail up and peered down at them. He then bent over and looked at his dragging pant cuffs. "CYRIL!!! WHAR IN TARNATION ARE ME CLOTHES!! ... AND WHY AM I WEARIN' YOURS!!?"

Staring at the furious little man, Eva sidestepped toward Cyril until her shoulder bumped into his arm. Cyril patted her shoulder and looked down into her wide, questioning eyes. His familiar smile that she loved so much told her that everything was okay. When she was a little girl she told her mom that Cyril had magical blue eyes that sparkled whenever he looked at her, but only her and no one else.

"Of course, I'm only guessing, Datus, but I think your clothes are on your dock or somewhere near your camp," Cyril offered. "You're wearing mine because you arrived here around two a.m. very wet, and ... well, quite naked. Not a stitch of clothing, not even your wedding band."

Datus looked out at the lake while rubbing his ringless finger. A blotchy red color started creeping up his neck and flushed his entire face. His mouth twisted up and he yelled down from the porch in a broken, gruff voice, "Might drown, dangit!! You know that Cyril! It's all gotta come off, everthin', or I don't float right!"

Datus rubbed his globelike stomach while beadily staring down at Cyril. As the scarlet glow was draining from his face and returning to its usual shade of pasty white, Datus mumbled in just above a whisper, "I'm ... I'm sorry. I ... I don't member las' ... I'll git ta home an brin yer stuff back tomorah. I gotta go."

Datus took off his glasses and wiped them vigorously on his shirtsleeve. Holding them at arm's length, he squinted through them, shaking his head and grimacing.

"I tried to clean those last night!" Cyril shouted. "But that dark spot would not come off."

"Seagull shet," Datus stammered. "Got bombed while sleepin' on the dock ... yesterday, or ..." Datus scratched through his unruly hair and frowned. "... Think it was yesterday ... what the hell day is it?!"

"Tuesday," Cyril reminded him.

Sunlight glinted and sparkled off his trembling spectacles as Datus stared down at them. "Stupid bird!! Musta eaten some kinda purple glue. Won't budge, tried everthin' 'cept kerosene!"

Shakily clearing his throat, Cyril said, "Flossie was here very early this morning. She was a bit frantic of course, but quite relieved that you were here."

Datus took a deep, labored breath and looked as though he was shrinking into the ground. While fuming through an array of colorful words, he crammed his dirty glasses back on his face.

"I bes git ta home. The sooner the screamin' gits done, the better," Datus said wearily.

As Datus clomped down the stairs with his chin bouncing somberly off his chest, he put his back to the cabin and gingerly swayed toward home, shoeless and cursing.

Confused, Eva looked at Cyril and mouthed the question, *Screaming?*

Cyril grinned at Eva, but before he could say anything, Datus stopped and leaned heavily on a large paper birch tree. He half turned around and yelled directly at the white bark of the tree, "Don' worry, Cyril! I'll brin' ol' Floss inside so's the whole lake don't have to lissin to her yellin'!"

Datus took three or four more steps and vanished behind a

stand of springy young pine trees.

Before Eva could say anything, Cyril said, "Well, you've met Datus. He's a lot nicer when he ... ah ... feels better. He and his wife, Flossie, have been at the lake now since last fall. They bought that little red A-frame, just around the first point. They're pretty quiet except when Flossie reprimands Datus about one thing or another. Why, on a still day, her voice carries clear across the lake."

Eva looked up at Cyril quickly, then crossed her arms and glared at the spot where Datus tottered through the pines.

"He drinks all the time, doesn't he? I can tell!" Eva said sharply. "He didn't remember anything about last night!"

"Yes, Datus does drink often and I think you're right about him not remembering anything about last night."

"Why did you let him stay with you? It's his own fault about last night. Why didn't you just send him home?"

Eva was still glaring when Cyril stepped in front of her. "I believe I made a good decision last night—that he stayed with me. He had been through enough and was freezing." Cyril paused for a long moment and then continued while Eva stared at the ground with furrowed eyebrows. "Eva, I think I know why you're so angry, but Datus has never hurt anyone and is not allowed to drive a car, so, in that way, he's not really a danger to others."

Eva, looking a little sheepish, had a more important question on her mind and in a nicer tone she asked, "Will he ... will he be around a lot this summer?"

"No. I usually don't see much of Datus, but he does occasionally borrow things from me." Cyril leaned in toward Eva and shot her a mischievous grin. "However, I often see his stomach sticking out of the water on warm summer days. That Datus! He's a character alright. Loves to float on his back. I don't understand it—he hardly moves his hands and feet, but somehow manages that position for hours. I think that belly of his has helium in it."

Eva forced a smile. Her anger subsided a little when she learned Datus would not be around much. She didn't like the idea of sharing Cyril. She wasn't used to it and she silently wondered if there would be others.

"Can we still go on your walk? Do you think we have enough time?" Eva asked, starting to walk back to the cabin.

"Oh yes. Plenty of time," Cyril replied, following behind her. "I just need a few things inside and we can be on our way."

Chapter 2

Standing for a moment in front of Cyril's unlocked door, Eva smiled at his welcome sign. Made from flattened birch bark nailed to the door, it read in heavy, penciled block letters:

WELCOME TO ALL. MAKE YOURSELF AT HOME. DEPENDING ON THE SEASON, I AM IN ONE OF THREE PLACES:

1. ROWING OR SNOWSHOEING SOMEWHERE ON THE LAKE.

2. HIKING OR SNOWSHOEING ON MY TRAIL.

3. IN SARANAC LAKE FOR THE DAY.

Right next to each number was a round hole, where Cyril placed an acorn which indicated his present location. Reaching for the shelved acorn, Eva smiled back at Cyril while slowly twisting the nut into the second hole.

When they entered the cabin, the first thing Eva noticed was that wonderful aroma that she missed all year long.

"I'm so glad you still make balsam pillows," Eva said, taking in a long, deep breath. She picked one up, squeezed it and brought it immediately to her nose. Eva's chest was rising and falling, repeatedly inhaling the pungent Christmas smell as her half-hidden face and big brown eyes scanned about the room. "It's the best smell in the world! I think it could heal the sick; but don't tell my mom, she'll grind it up into tea and make me drink it when I get a cold. She's always trying these natural remedy things on me when I get sick," Eva said, scowling.

Cyril chuckled. "That pillow is for you. I put the last stitch in it this morning. Actually, if it wasn't for Datus it would be unfinished."

Eva's eyes became smaller.

"What do you mean? How could Datus help you?" she asked quickly.

"He helped by snoring. I was awake most of the night, sewing to the rhythm of Datus. It's much easier to listen to snoring if you're not trying to sleep. But it was so loud at times I couldn't help laughing, and at one point I was worried the stovepipe was going to vibrate right out of the ceiling!"

Cyril smiled wide, but Eva only frowned.

"So you were up all night because of *him*? Aren't you tired?" Eva asked.

"No," Cyril said calmly. "Remember, Eva, I go to bed with the sun. I slept many hours before Datus sang his way onto my porch, and I also napped in the rocking chair earlier while I waited for you."

Eva shrugged her shoulders and pushed Datus out of her

mind. When Cyril turned and walked toward the kitchen, Eva let her eyes wander around the familiar cabin. She loved Cyril's simple home and often drew and doodled pictures of it when she was bored in school. She tried many times to draw what her future home would look like but it always ended up looking just like Cyril's.

Except for the enclosed bathroom, his home was just an open room. Wide, knotty pine boards, glowing with an antique sheen, made up the floor as well as the walls. Long, multi-paned windows spaced four feet apart encircled the entire room. When Eva was little she thought they were glass doors because they were almost as tall as Cyril. The south wall was a simple kitchen with three cupboards and a small countertop containing one deep utility sink. Right next to the sink was a very old, yellowing refrigerator with a large silver handle, and squeezed tightly next to it was a modern upright freezer.

The west side had a long plywood workbench that spanned the length of the wall and extended about three feet wide. A couple of antiquated sewing machines sat on the left end of the bench while balsam pillows in various stages of completion were neatly stacked by size over the rest. The few clothes Cyril owned were hung between the windows on wooden pegs. Freshly washed, multi-colored wool socks seemed to be lying everywhere, drying in neat, flat rows on the bench and draped across the arms and backs of every chair. Along the north wall, facing into the center of the room, was Cyril's double bed. Always neatly made-up, the tall bed was covered with a double-thick red-and-black checkered wool blanket that hung to the floor. Farther down the north wall, and part of the wall itself, was a rough-hewn bunk bed made from cedar logs and twisted yellow birch branches. There were two large, puffy armchairs facing the east wall, each one parked right in front of a huge window looking out to the lake. On a small birch log table that separated the chairs sat a pair of heavily scratched, green binoculars.

The center of the cabin was mostly open, leaving room for a large cast-iron wood stove with heavy chrome trim. Etched in white on the thick glass door was a doe standing in the forest. A silver stovepipe shot straight up through the middle of the pine-covered cathedral ceiling. Propped in front of the stove was a rocking chair that disappeared under multiple layers of blankets. Behind the stove, several feet away, was a small oak table with four wooden chairs tucked under its aprons. Three of the chairs always looked shiny and new, but the one facing the stove, Cyril's, had lost its luster, looking old and out of place.

As Eva admired his unchanged home, she felt her mind and body relax into an unfamiliar calmness. Before she let this feeling completely settle in, she warily glanced around the cabin one more time, looking for any new or modern changes—a phone, a television or a computer. She found none. All was the same. She slowly smiled and the peaceful moment was further enhanced as she listened to Cyril whistle a smooth, beautiful tune. Eva watched him untie his hiking boots, kick his heel deeply back, and carefully lace them up again. Her lazy eyes followed upward when he stood and slipped his long arms through the leather shoulder straps of his backpack, which for Cyril was a large woven pack basket made from black-ash splints. At that very moment, she knew for sure. Goose bumps tingled in her scalp as she excitedly thought, *This is me! This is how I want to be.*

Eva was staring blankly out a lake window, far away in her future, when suddenly her eyes fluttered and her head twitched as Cyril's soft, unhurried voice filled the little room. "Eva, you're very quiet. Not still mad at Datus, are you?"

"Oh, no. I was just thinking how much I like your home," Eva said in a slow, lazy tone. "It's ... it's just perfect. And everything's still the same. I like that the best."

"Well, thank you! I like it too. It's just right for me. We better get going. I was hoping we'd have time to stop by your camp and say hello to your mother."

They left the camp and made their way around a narrow dirt path that skirted the edge of his overflowing wildflowers. Side by side they strode, their gait almost the same, the younger glancing up at the older every few steps. Instead of taking the winding dirt road that led from Cyril's camp to the main road, they chose Eva's path. As they entered the woods, single file, Cyril stepped aside, waved his arm, and Eva skipped right out in front and took the lead. She liked being out front, but more so, she loved knowing Cyril was right behind her.

About halfway up the trail, Eva stopped. Spinning herself around on one heel, she faced Cyril with an expression that resembled both a smirk and a frown.

"Cyril, you'd better get ready for the big hug. Mom's a bit hug crazy lately. I don't know what's wrong with her," Eva said, shaking her head. "Two or three times a day she's got her arms stretched out at me! Once a week would be fine, I guess, but every day?"

Eva, expecting sympathy, looked hopefully at Cyril. But Cyril just stood there wearing his usual serene smile with a patch of sun lighting his white hair and making his eyes bluer than the sky. Eva glumly looked away and turned and walked ahead. After five or six steps, she realized she could no longer hear his footsteps.

"Your mom loves you," Cyril said as Eva turned around. "You might not understand the depth of it until you're older or possibly not until you've become a mother yourself."

Eva looked a little deflated. She shyly turned away and started running her hand over a clump of emerald moss that covered a waist-high boulder.

"Well, you might have forgotten what I told you and I haven't changed my mind," Eva said quietly. "I don't want to be a mother and I don't ever want to get married. I like it here; I think about camp all the time. And ... someday ..."

Eva broke off and turned away, scowling. A handful of green moss dangled from her hand as she started walking ahead, a little faster now.

She hoped Cyril wouldn't say anything. She thought, angrily, *I said too much!* And then she remembered: Out of everyone in her life, Cyril was the only one who just listened. The only one who didn't tell her how she should think or what she should and shouldn't do.

Except for the high-speed thumping of partridge wings and a scolding red squirrel, they continued on in silence until the woods opened brightly onto the thinly paved road that passed right in front of Eva's camp. They were just about to step across the road, when, at the same time, they both stopped and looked to their right. A small red car rumbled down the hill very slowly and passed right in front of them. It all happened in slow motion. The driver, a young woman with auburn hair, was staring out the open window, directly at Eva. Eva couldn't help staring back, and as the car drove farther away the woman's gaze followed Eva until she was nearly turned around in her car seat. Suddenly the car sped up and disappeared around the next bend, leaving a puff of white smoke lingering above the road.

Eva looked searchingly at Cyril and then back at the dissolving fumes that were drifting and melting into the light-green foliage. "I ... think ... I've ... seen her before," Eva said, in a slow-trying-to-remember tone. "I know I have ... at school maybe. It's really weird how she was staring right at me, wasn't it?" Eva turned to look at Cyril.

"It was a bit odd," Cyril admitted. "She's driving and looking as though she's lost something. I've crossed this road twice a day for years and that's the first time I've seen her."

"It's just creepy," Eva said, twitching. "And she seemed to be looking right through me."

They walked across the rock-heaved pavement and kicked through heavy wet clumps of freshly cut grass that surrounded Eva's cabin. Cyril stopped short, sniffing at the air.

"Is that pie I smell?" Cyril asked. "How *does* your mother find time to make a pie on the very first day she arrives with so much to do? And the lawn—it's already mowed!"

"She's amazing. Everyone says so," Eva said on a sighing note. "She has one speed: overdrive. Every room has probably been dusted, swept and sterilized by now."

"CYRIL!" Ann shouted from the porch. "How are you? Oh Cyril, you look wonderful!"

"I'm just fine. Welcome back, Ann! It doesn't seem like a year has passed by already."

"I know! It goes by so quickly," Ann said, flinging the porch door open. She sped down the steps with her youngish blond hair bouncing on her thin back. With three giant strides from her long, skinny legs, she reached out and locked Cyril in a wobbly embrace.

"See, I told you," Eva whispered to Cyril out of the side of her mouth.

Ann glanced down at Eva and then parted from Cyril, but her quick hands grabbed his and held on tight. Turning back to Cyril with a smile, Ann said in her usual hurried, enthusiastic manner, "Thank you so much for looking after the cabin this past year! I hope you didn't have to shovel the snow off the roof too many times and I've noticed the porch steps in the back and front have been repaired. Thank you so much."

"You're very welcome, Ann. No trouble at all. Thankfully it was a mild winter."

A beat of silence lingered while Ann continued her grip on Cyril's hands and stared up at him. Eva looked on curiously, watching Cyril's face become more serious. For a moment she even thought he looked sad.

"And you, Ann? How have you been?" he asked softly.

A summer breeze whisked through the front yard and Ann quickly released Cyril's hands, stepped to the side and straightened her thin back. A fleeting smile replaced her worried eyes as she looked over at Eva. "Oh ... I'm fine, just fine. Now, why don't you two come in and have some pie. I just made it. And how about some coffee. I can whip some up real fast. I know you like coffee with your—"

"Mom!" Eva interrupted impatiently.

"What? What's the matter, Eva?"

"We just saw a woman drive by real slow and she was staring right at me, not at Cyril, but just me. Wasn't she Cyril?"

"Yes, she was definitely looking for someone or something. Very peculiar. She should have stopped. We might have been able to help her."

"I ... I don't know, Eva. Maybe she's just lost. There are lots of old back roads around here, and besides, school's out everywhere. The summer camps will be filling up this week," Ann said, throwing her hands up frantically.

Like a soldier spinning on the spot, Ann marched back toward the cabin, leaving Eva and Cyril looking at each other, bewildered. Halfway across the porch, Ann's blond hair swept a full circle, and she looked back, frowning at the stationary pair. "I think it's cooled off enough now—the pie that is. Well, aren't you two coming in?"

"How about after we get back, Mom? Cyril and I have been

trying to go on his walk for a while now but things keep coming up."

Cyril looked down at Eva and then smiled back at Ann.

"The walk will take a couple of hours and when we get back I would love a slice of pie," Cyril said gently, walking over to Ann. "And of course you're welcome to come on the walk too."

"No. No thanks," Ann said, shaking her head vigorously. "I still have much to do and dinner to get on. Maybe some other time."

She slipped inside the porch and hollered back toward the front yard as she walked into the cabin: "You two be careful and have a good time!"

"We ... will," Cyril said quietly, even though Ann was already inside the camp.

Confused, he looked over at Eva. In agreement with his questioning gaze, Eva's eyebrows and shoulders rose at the same time. Eva then shook her head at the porch door. "Ready to go?"

Cyril gestured toward the trail and off they went. Eva excitedly hiked along, out front as usual. It felt so good to be back on Cyril's walk. She couldn't get enough of the familiar sights, sounds and smells. She even remembered certain trees and boulders that stood out, most of them oddly shaped but very familiar, and suddenly, for the first time, she felt a connection to them as if they were somehow a part of her now. She could hear Cyril whistling, and from time to time whenever she looked back, he always seemed to be reaching out picking raspberries that grew along the trail.

The first part of the hike was a slight uphill grade through a tunnel of bent white birch trees. An ice storm that had taken place several winters ago had permanently molded the young trees into a welcoming archway. After the birches, they walked through a tight, arm-rubbing balsam thicket that opened up to the pole line; a high voltage power line was the last evidence of civilization before entering hundreds of acres of wilderness.

The trail was five miles long and if seen from the air it resembled a piece of pie. It went back at a slight angle for about two miles, turned ninety degrees to the right for one mile and lastly turned right again and ran at an angle straight back to the road just above Eva's camp.

Beyond the pole line, the trail ran through a great pine forest, most of the trees having seen a decade or two of the eighteen hundreds. The smell was intoxicating, and the seasons of falling pine needles had turned that stretch of the walk into a winding carpet of gold. On the right side of the trail was a weather-darkened bench made from a thick slab of pine that Cyril had built many years ago. That bench in the pines was always Eva's first rest stop. She would hand-clear the leaves and pine needles off the top and then sit to one side, waiting for Cyril. While she watched two red squirrels chasing each other, she squished balsam needles between her fingers so she could inhale that wonderful smell all day.

"Eva, you should have seen this area at the end of May. There were pink and red trilliums dotted all throughout the pines—quite beautiful," Cyril remarked. "It was a nice splash of color against the brown matted leaves left over from last fall."

Cyril sat down next to Eva and extended his open palm toward her. It was brimming with plump red raspberries. As they munched on the sweet fruit in silence, Eva wanted to ask a question that had been on her mind over the past year. Her mother didn't have an answer and told her repeatedly, "Just ask Cyril. He'll tell you if he wants to."

While sniffing her balsam impregnated fingers, she tentatively started her big question with a few small ones.

"Cyril, how long have you lived at the cabin and what kind of job did you used to do?"

Cyril was about to pop a raspberry in his mouth, when his hand stopped in midair. He readjusted his position on the bench to better face Eva.

"I ... hmm, let's see now," Cyril said, pondering upward.

His face scrunched up and Eva watched intently as he seemed to be counting in his head.

"Well, for thirty-nine years I was the caretaker for the Whitney Estate at the southern end of the lake. It was a wonderful job, very nice people to work for. The best part was getting to work. I would row the guide boat six or seven months of the year and snowshoe across the ice in the winter. Now, as far as living at the cabin, I've been there forty years. Yes, it will be forty years this August."

"Wow! That's a long time. And has anyone ever lived there with you, or have you always been ... alone?"

"I've always lived there by myself, but I've never been *truly* alone. My dear, Eva, I know it's hard to understand without seeing, but we're never alone. God is here right now, listening to us talk and ...," he said with a jovial slap on his knee, "He's probably enjoying His balsam fragrance just as much as you are."

Eva, a little uncomfortable with his God words, adjusted her baseball hat a little lower and stared at a clump of mint-green ferns swaying in a thin beam of sunlight. She heard what Cyril had said, but there was only one thing that kept repeating over in her mind: "I've always lived there by myself."

Cyril continued eating raspberries, slowly and one at a time. Eva sat hunched forward, quietly plucking balsam needles from a tiny branch and laying them in a neat row on her pant leg.

Cyril offered the last berry to Eva but she shook her head "no." He tossed the last berry in his mouth and calmly said, "You seem very curious today. Anything else on your mind?"

Eva sat straight up and the words just shot out of her mouth: "Have you ever been married?"

Cyril bent over and picked up a small dry twig and started rolling it between his fingers. He did not answer right away and Eva was sorry she had asked, feeling like she had intruded. She was just about to stand up when Cyril said, "Yes, I was married ... once."

When he turned to look in Eva's eyes, she diverted her gaze downward to her green fingertips.

"It was a long time ago. Her name was Eleanor and I loved her very much. When she was twenty-seven, she died during childbirth."

"Oh," Eva said softly.

Cyril paused and took a deep breath.

"The baby was a little girl. The doctor tried very hard to save her too, but she was too small—underdeveloped the doctor said."

Eva's eyes shied away. She could feel a lump growing in her throat and her face was becoming very hot.

"I'm sorry. I shouldn't have—"

"It's okay, Eva. It was a long, long time ago," Cyril said, patting her knee.

Cyril took in another long breath before continuing, "We lived just outside the village of Saranac Lake, in a white house with a nice big wraparound porch; but now, it seems like a lifetime ago."

There was a long moment of silence before Cyril clapped his hands together and said brightly, "We've got many miles to cover. We'd better get our legs moving. By the way, did you see the deer standing on the left, just after the pole line? He was as orange as your hair and his horns were all covered in summer velvet."

Eva didn't reply.

"Eva?" Cyril said, nudging her shoulder.

"Oh yes, I saw him. He's going to be a six-pointer this fall."

"Your eyes are sharp, Eva. A few years ago, you'd have walked right past that deer," Cyril said proudly.

Eva gave him a small one-cheek grin and slowly began walking on ahead. Her pace steadily quickened as confusion and sadness raced through her mind. *I thought he always lived here, by himself, on his own, never needing anyone else. Why didn't he tell me? How can he always be so happy? It's just awful what happened.*

Eva trudged on with her head down, watching the rocks and roots go by until a screeching blue jay brought her back to the woods. When she stopped to get her bearings, she looked up and smiled at a familiar sight. A massive pyramid-shaped boulder lay straight ahead, looming half the height of the surrounding trees. Cyril had dubbed the giant "The Cone Stone" because of its pointed top. A small shelf protruded off the left side and made a perfect seat for one person. It was smooth and speckled with burgundy-colored crystals, and Eva, when she was ten years old, had proudly named it "The Ruby Seat."

Eva stopped and glanced over her shoulder at Cyril, who was pretty far back. She could tell he was happy because his lips were squished into a circle and she could hear faint whistling. As always, Eva quickly and excitedly brushed the leaves and pine needles off the shelf seat just to watch the ruby-colored flecks sparkle and glimmer in the afternoon sun. As she sat down she remembered when she was small Cyril had to lift her up and hold her on the narrow ledge that was too high for her. While she was taking big gulps from her water bottle and wiping the sweat off her forehead, Cyril arrived, rubbing his right flank and breathing deeply.

Eva was not used to seeing him out of breath. He always

hiked along at her speed and never seemed to tire.

"Are you alright, Cyril?" Eva asked. "Do you want to sit down?"

"Oh, yes, I'm fine. Some days ... I do my walk and I have a little trouble breathing ... but on the very next, I'll spring right out of bed and ... almost feel like running the whole five miles," Cyril said, leaning back and chuckling between long breaths.

"Must be the aging thing, Eva," he said, winking. "After all, I'll be eighty in a few short years."

Eva gasped inside. The number sounded very old and didn't register at all with the Cyril she knew. Except for his white hair, she always thought he was forty or fifty years old, and out of all the men Eva had known, including her father, Cyril seemed the youngest, all the others having that hurried, often weary look in their eyes.

While Eva studied Cyril in more detail, the birds started singing and he looked away. Behind them, the sparrows and robins were trying to outdo each other with their rich woodland song. And somewhere, unseen in the distant forest, a woodpecker thumped slow and steady on a hollow tree.

Cyril did not sit and his breathing returned to normal very quickly. But Eva was wondering if they should turn back.

"Eva! We're almost at the back corner. Let's get a leg up!" Cyril said cheerfully.

"Well, if you feel alright. Do you?" Eva asked skeptically.

"I do. I feel excellent! The back line is your favorite part of the walk."

Eva shrugged her shoulders but her eyes were surveying his in a doubtful, motherly way. Cyril just smiled casually and looked off into the woods.

"What have we here?" Cyril asked, walking toward a large beech tree a few paces away. Stopping in front of the tree, he laid a hand on the bark, circled the trunk once and motioned for Eva. The bark was light gray and smooth, but all the way up the tree, spaced about a foot apart, were raised scratch marks that were blackish-brown and healed over. Cyril was pointing up the tree, just as Eva arrived at his side.

"Okay, woodswoman. Can you tell me how all those scratch marks got on this tree?"

"A black bear," Eva said quickly. "They love beechnuts and if they don't fall from the tree fast enough, the bear will climb right up to get them."

Cyril smiled amusingly. "Excellent! Now, tell me Eva, have you been studying? Or have you been hanging around some other old woodsman?"

"You know you taught me most of it. But I do have lots of books at home about trees and animal tracks," she said proudly.

In quiet unison they started down the back line, which was a mile and a half of what Cyril called the "swamp" but to Eva, for as long as she could remember, it was the "Christmas tree walk." Always damp and cool, this quiet, green paradise was a mixture of balsam, pine, hemlock, cedar and spruce trees.

With an inch of soft fir needles underfoot, Eva's long steps landed in silence, and in no time at all, she slowly outdistanced Cyril. Her eyes followed the trail, but her mind drifted away, trying to figure out how many times Cyril had made this very same walk over the past forty years. She began multiplying out loud and settled on fifteen thousand times, give or take a few hundred. Amazed, Eva was musing over the large number when she abruptly stopped and began looking closely at the ground.

"I think I found a path or something right through the middle of all these balsam trees," Eva yelled back to Cyril.

As Cyril approached, Eva stood there with her hands on her hips looking pleased with herself.

"Not much getting by you! Your eyes are sharp, Eva. That trail goes right to the top of West Mountain. I haven't been up there for at least ten or fifteen years. I imagine it's in rough shape, being unused for so long." Cyril bashfully pointed to his knees. "These, they like the flat land now," he admitted with a sad shake of his head. "I don't trust them going down mountains anymore—too wobbly. I do, however, miss the view from the top. Spectacular! You can see all of Whiteface Mountain and most of Union Falls Pond."

Eva reached in the balsam stand and pushed the soft branches apart.

"Pretty thick in there, but the path seems pretty clear," Eva said loudly through the branches. She backed out, brushing the needles off her arms, wearing a smug expression.

"I was wondering when you'd discover that," Cyril said. "Soon you'll know my entire hike better than me."

With his hand resting on Eva's shoulder, she watched curiously as he tipped side to side looking through the forest until a sun beam lit up his face.

"The light is getting low," he said softly. "We'd better keep moving."

As they made for the next back corner, long lanes of sun cut randomly across the darkening woods, igniting the evergreen needles into shimmering specks of gold and silver.

Eva kept looking ahead, craning her neck upward and sideways, searching for the yellow birch tree that grew on top of a huge boulder in the middle of the trail. Resembling rustic artwork, the Rock Tree had thick, black roots running down and gripping the surface of the granite sphere; it always reminded Eva of a giant hand holding a large ball. When Eva passed by, she knew French Brook was not far away, which meant the trail would soon be turning one last time toward camp, just after crossing Cyril's handmade bridge. The brook was as wide as a country lane and the current could easily knock a strong man over. The last leg of the hike ran parallel to French Brook and all the way down to the little red bridge that crossed the road just above Eva's camp.

Just before reaching the brook, Eva looked back and caught fleeting glimpses of Cyril's white hair appearing and disappearing through the sun-streaked timber. Satisfied, she turned quickly, took three stretching leaps and landed with a muffled clunk on the narrow wooden bridge. She sat, threw her hat off to one side, removed her boots and sweaty socks and plunged her hot, tired feet into the rushing cool water. Eva's loud "Ahhhhh" was barely audible over the steady, rhythmic roar that rushed underneath her.

As her happy feet water-skied and bobbed up and down, she thought, *I wonder if this bridge has also been here forty years.* She remembered Cyril telling her how he had built it, and then she dreamily pictured a young Cyril with dark hair chopping down the massive pine tree and felling it straight across to the opposite bank with an earth-vibrating thump; Cyril balancing on it while driving huge steel wedges deep below the bark; and then the log splitting in half to make two flat walking surfaces.

Eva was tying her boots back on when Cyril arrived. She reached up and grabbed the thick braided rope that was suspended alongside the bridge and gave it a good tug. As she steadied her balance, Cyril yelled over the current, "How's the water? Feels great on tired feet, doesn't it?"

Eva nodded with a smile and shouted back, "You gonna do yours?" she asked, pointing at his feet.

"No," Cyril said, clutching the rope and shuffling closer to Eva in order not to shout. "We have two miles left. I think it'll be almost dark by the time we get out. Good thing it's all downhill.

And I'll try to keep up with you this time."

Cyril winked at her and she turned and marched on, her steps keeping time with the tumbling music of the brook and her eyes focused on the worn path with occasional glimpses of the lengthening shadows crisscrossing the trail ahead.

"I wish we had your boat, and then we could float all the way down to the bridge," Eva shouted over her shoulder.

"That would speed things up a bit, but I'm afraid there wouldn't be much left of my old guide boat—too many rocks."

With heads tipped down concentrating on long strides, the last two miles flew by and to Eva's surprise they were crossing the pole line once again.

Darkness was inching down in every corner of the woods, and Eva's mind filled with scary thoughts, as it often did when the sun disappeared. She couldn't help thinking of bears or coy-dogs hidden in the dusky shadows, but as they got closer to the road, she thought of only one thing: fanged, drooling dogs running down the dirty steps of a creepy dark bus or just behind the next dark tree, with her white bony hand extended, the witch. Eva drew her shoulders in close, and shortened her steps to be closer to Cyril. She tried to ease her fears with Cyril's words about Hazel and the simple fact that he was right behind her, only an arm's length away.

Just after the pole line, the woods opened into a golden-rod field, dotted with clumps of clover, which told Eva she was about five minutes away from her warm, brightly lit camp and, most importantly, food, for she was very hungry. As soon as they stepped into the clearing, a deer blew at them with quick loud snorts causing Eva to gasp and stop suddenly. She breathed a sigh of relief when two big white flags floated through the air in silent arcs, disappearing in seconds into darkened hardwoods.

"Now wasn't that a beautiful sight? I've seen that mother-daughter pair in this field on just about every walk this summer," Cyril said, resting his hand on Eva's shoulder.

"They just surprised me," Eva said. "I forgot how loud deer snort. If they were right next to me, they'd probably have blown my hat off."

Cyril chuckled at Eva and they continued on.

Overhead, the eastern half of the sky was deep pink and below, a thin disc of ground fog hovered just above the grass at knee-level. The crickets were chirping at full force and the air was damp and heavy. As they moved smoothly through the swirling mist, Eva kept searching to her right and finally found the small gleaming lights of camp that with each step flickered through the trees. Four tired hiking boots clomped heavily across the little wooden bridge as they approached Eva's glowing camp.

"I hope your mom's not worried. We've never been this late before," Cyril said in a concerned voice.

"I don't think she'll be worried. I'm with *you*, although worrying is her specialty. And I don't see any flares flying up over the camp," Eva said, pointing. "Must be she's okay. She's probably busy boiling something. A germ doesn't stand a chance with her. You're going to stay for dinner, aren't you, Cyril?"

Before Cyril could answer, a screen door creaked open and Ann's voice rang out through the cool half-darkness.

"Well! There you two are. I was getting worried. Is everything alright?"

"Yup, we're okay," Eva said. "The bears weren't hungry tonight, so, here we are!"

"Very funny, Eva," Ann said sternly.

Ann pushed the screen door wide open so they could enter. The camp was warm and inviting but best of all it smelled incredible. She put one hand on Cyril's forearm and with the other tugged and pulled at Eva's pack, trying to help her.

"Mom, I can get it!" Eva scolded.

Ann let go and turned to Cyril, still clutching his arm.

"Now, Cyril, you must stay for dinner," Ann insisted. "It's one of your favorites: beef stew with the little pearl onions, fruit salad, fresh baked wheat bread and you already know about the pie. I won't take no for an answer!"

"I'd love to stay for dinner. Thank you. I'd be crazy to leave a cabin that smelled this good."

Eva and Cyril quickly sat down at the small table that was overflowing with food. Ann spent most of the dinner hour speeding around the tiny kitchen, trying to keep up with the conversation but for the most part not listening to anyone. More than once Eva caught her mother looking at Cyril in a sad, strange way. When Ann clumsily elbowed over a tall glass of milk, Eva looked bashfully at Cyril and shrugged her shoulders and said in a whispering breath to herself, "She's really weird tonight. Weirder than usual."

Cyril and Eva ate doubles of everything, which made Ann very happy, but the long walk and the big meal were taking their toll on the two hikers.

Everyone helped clear the table, but every time Cyril and Eva made one trip to the kitchen, Ann passed them twice. Standing around the table, Cyril tried hard to suppress a yawn but Eva caught a glimpse of him and she couldn't hold back.

"Ann, that was a wonderful dinner. Fit for a king!" Cyril exclaimed. "But as you know, I rise with the sun, so I must be saying good night."

As Cyril shuffled lazily through the tiny living room, Ann was right on his heels, almost bumping into him. She put her hand on Cyril's shoulder while he rummaged around in his pack basket, looking for something. When Cyril stood he had a large silver flashlight in his hand.

"We'll see you tomorrow?" Ann asked, glancing back at Eva. "I mean if you're not too busy. That is, if the weather's nice. Might rain—"

"Mom!" Eva interrupted. "Of course we'll see Cyril tomorrow. We have the whole summer. What's wrong with you tonight? Besides, we have plans to row across the lake and take a closer look at Charlie. He's back, you know. At least we think it's him. We saw him land in a huge pine tree this morning. We're bringing the binoculars to get a closer look and see if that pine tree is his real home."

"Yes. Yes of course," Ann said, looking shyly at the floor and fidgeting with her fingers.

"Yes, Ann, I'll see you tomorrow," Cyril said with a firm nod and a wink.

In a flurry of small talk and many good nights, Cyril shouldered his basket and disappeared into the blackness. As moths fluttered and bounced off the drooping porch light, Ann and Eva stood cramped, side by side in the screen door opening, listening to footsteps but seeing nothing.

"Aren't you going to turn your light on, Cyril?" Eva called out, squinting in the direction of her path. At the same time, Ann and Eva turned to the left as a stream of golden light suddenly appeared coming from the direction of the dirt road that led down to Cyril's home.

Echoing off the trees, over the crickets' song, and under a starlit sky, came Cyril's clear, sturdy voice: "Ah, that's a little better! Good night!"

Two voices rang out loud and clear, one of them much higher in volume than the other: "GOOD NIGHT, CYRIL!"

"Geez, Mom! If you yell a little louder, you could wake up ol' Witch Hazel and her drooling friends," Eva said, chuckling her way back into camp.

"Eva, I won't tell you again. It's 'Hazel' or 'Mrs. Hazel' to you!"

Eva turned away, hiding her smart face. She outstepped her mother and threw herself into an overstuffed armchair. Ann whisked by, cross-armed and frowning. Wearing a triumphant grin, Eva wiggled herself deeper into the comfy chair.

"You know, I think Cyril can see in the dark. I think he told me so when I was little," Eva recalled. "He's not afraid of anything, you know."

Pots and pans were clanging together in the sink and Eva wondered if her mother had heard her.

"Cyril's used to the night woods," Ann said over her shoulder. "He can't see in the dark, at least I don't think so. Anyway, I bet he can see a lot better than us and besides he knows every rock and tree around here."

The running water ceased and the dishes suddenly lay still.

"Eva, I think we'll clean up the kitchen ... in the morning. I'm just too tired tonight."

******

Cyril opened the door to his balsam-bough haven, clicked on the light and in slow motion, took off his pack and boots, brushed his teeth and fell with a few bounces on top of his bed. He was exhausted but he forced himself up again to adjust the windows so he could breathe in the cool mountain air while falling asleep to the soft hoots of an owl that visited most evenings. He also wanted to be ready for the laughing loons at daybreak and the songbirds that kept him company at breakfast. He turned off the light and fell back, once again, onto his thick woolen blanket. Thoughts of the day flew through his tired mind and he couldn't stop thinking of how much Eva had changed from age fourteen to fifteen. *A young woman*, he thought. *Where did that little girl go, the one I used to carry on my shoulders? The one who used to call me 'Cereal'?* An easy smile parted his lips for he was very grateful, yet also a little mystified as to why Eva liked spending so much time with him.

As his head was sinking deeper into the feather pillow, and just before his eyes closed, he recited a small prayer to the ceiling—eleven daily words that had been with him for more than half his life. *"Thank you so much for today. Please keep the nightmare away."* His last thoughts were focused on how thankful he was to have Eva and Ann as friends, but sadly, just before he drifted off to sleep, he realized they were his only true friends.

Chapter 3

The next morning from his bed, Cyril sleepily admired the pearly light pouring through his huge windows from a full moon that hung low in the west. He sat up, checked his watch and then glanced out the darkened east windows. There was a thin band of brightness hovering above Bear Mountain, and Cyril knew that by the time he finished his few morning chores his cabin would be aglow with the first light of the day. The songbirds were hard at work and after a few moments listening to the perfection of his outside symphony, he popped out of bed and was surprised at how good he felt.

He was soon buzzing around the cabin, deep into his routine. Yesterday's clothes were washed and hung about the cabin to dry. He showered while oatmeal gently bubbled on the stove and a small bag of last summer's blueberries thawed on the counter. While he dressed, he downed a brimming mug of orange juice and chomped on a green apple. Every once in a while he would look out the back window, squinting through the predawn light, half-expecting to see Ann hurrying down the dirt road toward his cabin. He often helped her through small worries in the past, but this time Cyril sensed something much bigger troubling her.

He tossed a few necessities into his basket and stuck his head through the porch door to get a better feel for the weather. On the shoulder of Bear Mountain, a sliver of blue sky held the morning sun, but from the west, a thick layer of steel-gray clouds were on the march. He shrugged his shoulders and smiled un- caringly at the likelihood of getting wet. It didn't matter to him— he was always prepared. After hiking thousands of miles in all four seasons, he had experienced just about every one of Mother Nature's tempers.

He shouldered his basket and weaved his way alongside the dew-covered wildflowers. If Ann wasn't up, he intended on tak- ing a short walk just to hear and smell and see the morning. He bypassed Eva's trail and headed up his road, knowing if he was going to run into Ann, that's where he would find her.

As Cyril crested the top of his road he noticed right away his breathing was better than yesterday and he said aloud to himself, "Hmm ... going to be a good day, and my side doesn't hurt as much." He started whistling a favorite tune, but stopped short when he saw Ann sitting on her porch steps with a finger pressed to her lips. She jogged over to Cyril, whispering through long leaps, but Cyril couldn't understand her until she was right next to him.

"Good morning," Ann said, hushing her voice and looking around. "I was wondering if you had a little time to talk with me about ...," and she whispered ever lower, "Eva?" Ann's hands were wringing together in a constant circular motion. Her blond hair was thrown messily into a large bun that teetered on the top of her head, just off to one side.

"Of course, Ann," Cyril said, resting his calm hands over hers. "Nothing serious I hope."

"No, no," she said, shaking her head. "I mean yes, well maybe—"

"Why don't we walk up past the pole line and sit on the bench in the pines," Cyril suggested.

"Okay, that'll be fine. Eva will sleep for another hour or two," Ann said. "I left her a note, saying I went on a walk. We shouldn't be gone too long."

They started up the trail with the woods growing dimmer with each step. By the time they reached the bench, they were walking through swirls of fine mist. Cyril dropped his basket at one end of the bench. He reached in, took out a purple bandana and wiped the wet sheen off the bench top.

"Hope you don't mind getting a little wet, Ann," Cyril said, sitting down.

Ann sat down and then shifted and wiggled on the bench. "No ... it won't bother me," she said, her voice shaky.

When Cyril glanced over, tears were pouring down her face. He put his arm around her rocking body and swayed back and forth with her, saying nothing.

Taking a big sniff, she cleared her throat, wiped her eyes and sat straight up. "I'm so sorry Cyril. I ... I don't even know where to start. So much has happened in the last year. John ... you know John's in prison. It's just been awful. I'm so angry. He was told not to drink and drive so many times and now he's killed someone. That poor family—I think of them and pray for them every day."

Ann's voice started to break and Cyril thought she was going to cry again, but she took a deep breath and continued on.

"I'm trying hard to support John, but he's like a void right now, and if I stopped visiting him I think he'd just curl up in a corner and die. He's so lost and—"

Ann stopped abruptly and then spoke through clenched teeth: "He wants to know why it wasn't him instead, but I have no answers for him. He feels completely worthless. He's so sorry, but now it's too late. He's a good person. Well I guess he is. He hasn't been much of a father to Eva, we all know that, and oh my God, Cyril, they've had some awful battles. If he never drank, he'd be so different. I know he would!"

Ann took long heaving breaths that left her bent over, staring at the ground. Cyril slowly reached out and rested a hand on her back. While the silence stretched on, he just sat there, watching the tiny rain spheres building on the back of his hand. Cyril jumped slightly when Ann suddenly sat bolt upright.

"And then there's Eva!" Ann said, exasperated. "She'll have nothing to do with her father now. She won't visit or write and she keeps everything in. And stubborn! So darn stubborn!! She used to talk to me and cry her problems out when she was small, but now she just pushes every problem away and acts like nothing's happened. She has only a few friends at school, but I don't know if she confides in them. She's not real close with any of them. Oh, Cyril! She's so different!" Ann's voice was becoming loud and shrilly. "Girls her age are chasing boys and hanging out at the mall and shopping for clothes and talking on their cell phones constantly. Eva cares for none of that. She's happy reading about trees and mountains. And now she's reading books about hermits—what's that all about!? Her idea of shopping is a new backpack or a sweatshirt or another stupid baseball hat." Ann threw her bony arms in the air.

Suddenly, Ann stood up and started pacing back and forth over the shiny brown leaves.

"I just think she's missing out on so much. You've never seen her wearing a dress, with her hair down. My God, Cyril! She's absolutely beautiful! You wouldn't even recognize her. We were at a wedding last month and people were looking at her as much as the bride, but no sooner did we get home and she turned right back into a boy with a ponytail. And that hat of hers, it's pushed down so low, half her face is hidden. I don't know what she's hiding from!"

Cyril looked out through the dim woods and watched two gray squirrels playing spiral-chase up a giant maple tree. Except for the distant song of a sparrow and several clucking chipmunks, there was another long stretch of silence. Slapping raindrops began to mix in with the drizzle as Ann kept turning and marching, her blond bun now hanging by her left ear.

"Ann, is there something else? Something more that's bothering you?" Cyril asked carefully.

She all but flung herself back on the bench. Turning away from Cyril she drew a hand over her mouth and started to heave up and down without making a sound. Cyril reached in his basket and draped a heavy wool shirt over her damp shoulders.

Ann reached over and patted Cyril on the knee.

"I'm sorry," she said between sobs. "I shouldn't trouble you with all this. I just don't know what to do."

"It's okay, Ann. I'll try to help anyway I can," he said softly to the back of her head.

The woods brightened slightly and the rain ceased but there were constant fat drips falling from the leaves overhead. Ann righted herself on the bench and grabbed her knees tightly.

"Alright. Now do you remember that woman yesterday, who drove by and stared at Eva?" Ann asked.

"Yes," Cyril said, nodding slowly.

"Well, that was Eva's mother—I mean her *real* mother. NO! I mean her birth mother." Flustered and tongue-tied, Ann pounded her fist on the bench and yelled through the damp woods, "I'M HER REAL MOTHER!"

"Ann, I didn't know, I just—"

Ann interrupted Cyril as her shoulders fell into an exhausted slump.

"Nobody knows, just our immediate family. That's the problem: Eva has no idea," Ann said wearily.

Cyril watched nervously as Ann tried to compose herself.

"That woman yesterday, her name's Mary," Ann began with a deep breath. "And yes, her driving by yesterday was a bit strange, but she really is a wonderful person. She just wants to meet Eva. I kind of promised her. Anyway, at just barely fourteen, Mary got pregnant. Her parents were, of course, devastated. I only met them once, but they seemed so stern and serious. I did learn later that they belonged to some kind of very strict religious order. I've always felt they forced Mary to put Eva up for adoption, but I'll never know for sure. And the father of Eva? No one ever said a word about him. I'm just afraid something awful might have happened."

Ann took a long, shuddering breath and shivered. She stood up and clumsily put Cyril's shirt on before continuing. "Arrangements were made for us to take Eva home from the hospital two days after she was born. When Eva was handed over to me, it was just unbelievable, Cyril! It was love like I'd never known or ever felt. Her dark eyes locked onto mine and stayed. I don't know how to explain it but it felt absolutely perfect—the most perfect thing I'd ever done in my entire life. But my heart ... something didn't feel right. John and I were about to leave when Mary's father stepped forward. He was dressed in a perfect blue suit. He looked so formal, but also angry, no smiles ... neither of them. He was all business when he said, 'We promised Mary she could talk to you before you go but you don't have to. It's not your obligation. All the papers are signed and everything is in order.'

"John and I looked at each other. He nodded for me to go ahead and then reached out and took Eva. I was very nervous and wanted to say no, but before I realized it, I was at Mary's door, knocking and walking into her room."

Shaking her head, Ann said, "Cyril, I can remember everything about that room and every word that was said in it, just like it might have happened minutes ago. You know, Mary could have been Eva's twin today, they looked so much alike ..." Ann took another deep breath. "Mary was sitting straight up, in a white bed, wearing a light-blue hospital gown. Her hair was long and flaming orange and fanned out over the top of her pillows. She was trying to look brave but there was sadness in her eyes that, well, those eyes, they've just never left me. She was so young and I thought to myself, *How could this little girl just have delivered a baby?* I walked over to her bedside and you know, I usually have a million things to say, but my throat was tight and my heart was racing. All I could get out was a weak, 'Hello.' Mary glanced quickly at me with red, puffy eyes and in the tiniest voice, said, 'Hi.' She then stared at her bedsheets and kept fidgeting with them for what felt like forever. I was starting to get really warm when she finally spoke in a shaky little-girl voice. She said, 'I, I just wanted to ask you to take really good care of her. She's so tiny.' And that's all she said, but before I could answer I saw Mary quickly look at the door, and then her face became determined and her voice deepened when she said, 'My parents and that lawyer say no to this but I'd like to meet her someday, maybe when she's my age. I'll be fifteen next month. Will you please let me meet her?'

"I said yes—'Yes of course I will.' Then I told Mary I would take care of her with all my heart till the day I die. I promised her over and over. Mary tried to smile but her lips began to quiver and she turned away. I stood there, frozen, not knowing what to do and then I heard her say a very faint, 'Thank you.' I said 'Thank you, Mary' and I rushed out of the room, but it felt like someone was standing on my chest. It hurt awful, Cyril."

Cyril sat arrow-straight, staring at a huge pine. When he finally blinked, a thin stream slid down from one of his eyes.

"My God, we've been here over an hour," Ann said, looking at her watch.

"I have all day or all week. Let's not worry about the time," Cyril said, patting her hand.

Ann was wringing her hands together and staring at her feet when she suddenly yelled out, "I'M AFRAID!"

Cyril jumped and his wet eyelids fluttered.

"I'm afraid to tell Eva because she's been through so much this year," she continued. "She doesn't need more pain to tuck away and pretend it's not there. How much can one child take? I wish I would have told her when she was little. I always meant to. I should have, but I kept putting it off ... protecting myself."

Cyril cleared his throat, frowned and turned toward Ann.

"Ann" he said calmly. "Protecting yourself from what?"

"What do you mean?" Ann asked quickly. But before he could answer, she pushed off the bench and started pacing again, looking confused and agitated.

"I mean, could there be, might you be *more* afraid of something else?" Cyril asked cautiously.

Stopping mid-stride, her shoulders fell, and she slowly dragged her feet through last year's wet leaves and sat back down.

"I don't want to lose her!" Ann said in a ragged whisper. "I'm so afraid of that; she's all I have now. She's fifteen and so independent and I can't help it but I do pester her a lot, and I worry too much, and when I worry too much, we fight. What if Mary has everything in common with Eva? They look alike, and Mary's so much younger than me. What if they become friends and want to spend a lot of time together? Eva will be off to college soon, what if—?"

Cyril reached out and put a hand on Ann's knee, stopping her in mid-sentence. Ann threw a hand over her mouth and started rocking.

"Ann, I wish I could be of some help to you, in some way."

He swiveled on the bench and slid his rough hands over her soft ones. His eyelids closed placidly and he sat motionless for a long moment. Ann was slouched forward, still very tense and not noticing the long pause until she felt Cyril take a body-lifting, deep breath. With a gentle shake of her hands, he began to speak in a slow, calm voice.

"There is one thing I'm completely sure of Ann. You're a wonderful, caring, and most importantly, a loving mother. All that you've given Eva, even though you don't see it now, will someday be a permanent part of her, and many of her future decisions will be based on the beautiful way you raised her. You have always been and will always be more connected and central to Eva than anyone else on this earth. Eva is strong and resilient and has a good vision for her life and you can take a great deal of credit for all of that, for all that she is. And yes, she's different than most girls but she seems perfectly content with herself. I know she struggles with anger and blame right now, all the while trying to figure out who she is, but I think she has to walk through this and sort it out on her own, in her own time." Cyril gently squeezed her hands and whispered soothingly, "Eva loves you, Ann. You and Eva were always meant to be mother and daughter, *always!*"

Ann slowly turned away from Cyril. Her body stopped shuddering and became very still. Cyril watched her high, tense shoulders slowly begin to fall. Just as he was turning away, Ann suddenly whirled around and flung herself at him, almost knocking him over. She held on for a long time, not wanting to let go.

"Thank you," Ann said wetly into his shoulder. "I wish I could stop worrying so much. I always have. I just don't know how to stop."

After several minutes, Ann collected herself with a deep, calming breath and a few tear-streaked glances toward Cyril. "I think we should go," Ann suggested. "Eva must be up by now."

Cyril nodded in agreement. Ann stood up slowly and gave one last attempt to fix her wet, drooping hair before starting down the trail. When they walked out into the open pole line, Ann stopped and shook the glimmering raindrops off a raspberry bush and started filling her hands with the cool, wet fruit. Cyril followed along, plucking the red berries right into his mouth.

"I have a plastic container in my basket if you want to fill—"

"I'm going to tell her today!" Ann declared, cutting Cyril off. Then shrinking a bit, she added, "I think I'm ready. What do you think, Cyril?"

"Well, for one thing, you should see yourself smiling right now, Ann. It's beautiful. Follow your heart and I bet all will be fine. Eva will of course go through many ups and downs with this news, but do tell her about your conversation with Mary in the hospital room. I think it's very important she knows and understands her birth mother loved her."

Ann tilted her head slightly and peered at Cyril, her eyes narrowing into a questioning gaze. Just then the sun peeked through a small cloud-window and sliced down the pole line, igniting the wet woods with warm golden light.

"Now that's better!" Cyril announced, stretching his arms up toward the sky and looking all around.

When his eyes returned to Ann she was gazing up at him. His arms fell from the air with a relaxed thump against his legs.

"What?" he asked quizzically.

"How do you do it? I mean, how do you always stay ... the same?"

"I don't think I understand," Cyril said with a slight frown.

"You're always so peaceful and content. I've never known you to be any different."

"Peace is within *you*," Cyril said simply. "Surely one of God's greatest gifts, don't you think?"

Ann raised her eyebrows and slowly diverted her attention to her raspberries.

"It's yours for the taking," Cyril said while casually munching on a raspberry. "The Buddha and Jesus and the great Mystics all spoke tirelessly of peace. Yet most people put their gift of peace aside, preferring to bind all their waking thoughts to this world only—repetitive thoughts filled with worry or fear, usually about the past which is gone or the future which has not yet arrived. Our hearts, where peace makes its home, are always open and ready, but sadly, the mind is a thief."

Ann smiled politely, nodded and looked away. Cyril reached in his basket for a container and held it out toward Ann. She slowly dropped her berries inside and snapped the lid shut. At the same time they both turned and started walking back toward camp.

"Ann?" Cyril said, stopping.

"Yes," she said, spinning quickly around.

"I go to town once or twice a week. Do you think John would like a visit from me?"

"Oh yes! He'd love that. He thinks so much of you, Cyril! He'd be so surprised, but the prison is two hours from Saranac

Lake. Are you sure?" Ann asked skeptically.

"It would be my pleasure. I'll just leave very early and I'll be able to get everything done."

"I'm going Thursday, Cyril. You could come with me," Ann said excitedly.

"Well, I thought I should go quietly, without Eva knowing. She's having such a hard time with this and I don't want her to feel, you know, pressured in any way."

"Oh yes. Yes, I see what you mean." But then Ann's eyes brightened. "But maybe you going would show her—"

"I don't think so Ann—"

"Oh, Cyril! She looks up to you so much. It might really help her," Ann said pleadingly

"Ann," Cyril said softly as he took a step closer to her, "I would love to visit John, but I don't think Eva should know, at least not now. It just might force her in a direction she's not ready for."

"I know, I know," Ann said, exasperated. "I just thought ... you're right, and the more I think about it, the more I realize Eva would be, well knowing Eva, very upset with you, and we surely don't want that. Now, do you need directions to the prison? It's medium security. Thank God it's not one of those big scary maximum-security prisons."

"No. I know right where it is. I've been there before. What time are visiting hours?"

"Two o'clock, but you'll need to call ahead."

"Okay. My next trip to town, I'll phone ahead and set up a visit. Shall we?" he said, motioning down the path.

"Thank you, Cyril. That's very nice of you. The phone number is easy to remember. "

"Got it locked in," Cyril said, tapping the side of his head after he keyed in the number.

Ann looked at him a little puzzled, and quickly said, "You know, Cyril, and this has occurred to me before—you would make a wonderful priest."

Cyril shied away, waving his hand and chuckling. "Oh, no, no. Not me. I like many things about many different religions, but I've never felt fully connected to any one in particular. I am, however, very, very thankful, every day in fact, to feel and sense God's oneness with everything."

Ann smiled warmly, checked her wrist watch and turned to continue on. When they approached the cabin, Ann's head began bobbing up and down, looking in all the windows for any sign of Eva. Craning her long neck forward, she peeked around the edge of the camp and looked at the front porch.

"Must still be sleeping," Ann said quietly. She turned and gave Cyril a tight hug. "Thank you again. I do feel better. And somehow, I feel ... lighter," she said hoarsely into his shoulder.

"You're very welcome, Ann."

When she pulled away, Cyril gave her a wide grin before twirling about-face and making for home. Ann watched his white head and brown pack basket striding casually away. She continued her tranquil stare as he whistled his way across the road and vanished under the domed arch of an ancient apple tree. With the branches still moving, she suddenly jumped forward and yelled, "YOUR ..." and then much more quietly, " ... shirt." But it was too late. He was gone.

Chapter 4

When Cyril got back to camp he went on the porch and grabbed the rusted handle of a wooden bucket that was hanging off a long nail. On the walk down to the lake he reached inside for a large yellow sponge that was crusted and stuck to the bottom. He had left his boat upright the last couple of days, and between the lake water and rain it had two or three inches of water standing on the bottom. He wanted to have it clean and dry and all ready to go when Eva arrived.

Walking down the short grade with the bucket swinging and creaking with each step, Cyril admired the stillness all around him. The lake was glass-smooth, mirroring a bright, overcast sky. "Perfect day for rowing," he commented aloud to himself. Then his smile faded as he thought of Eva and Ann talking in their cabin. He didn't know how Eva was going to take the news, but he had a strong feeling she would act like nothing happened.

After giving the boat a good cleaning and resting it upside down on the sawhorses, he looked to the northern end of the lake at a large section of evergreen trees on the opposite shore. He had planned to harvest balsam boughs there this week but he knew Eva was coming, so he stayed close to camp for the rest of the day. He did the same the next day. But on the third day he rose very early and decided to drive into town. When his truck inched its way past Eva's camp in the waning darkness he noticed their car was not there. Not thinking too much of it, he continued on to Saranac Lake. After twelve scenic miles of meandering back roads, Cyril turned left onto Lake Street and entered the little mountain village.

The quiet town was just waking up. He parked and grabbed a few envelopes off the truck seat and spent ten minutes at the small century-old post office. When he exited the brick building, he took a few steps, leaned over a wooden bench and wiped the sun-sparkling dew off one end and sat down. A few feet away, a tall man in paint-stained work clothes talked loudly on a pay phone, his free hand gesturing each descriptive word. When the phone clicked down and the long man loped away, Cyril walked over and called the prison to set up a visit. He then crossed the street and wandered up and down two levels of creaky, heavily-planked wooden floors filling a sparse list at Hamner's Hardware store.

Walking the long way back to his vehicle, his usual long strides began to falter, becoming shorter as he passed a tiny white church with an even smaller graveyard tucked along its side. As he opened the door of his truck, he glanced back at the tall white steeple. A sweeping emptiness passed through his chest and into his throat. He quickly looked away and tossed a small bag onto the passenger seat.

The little red truck, as if it was on autopilot, made its way to one of the two nursing homes that he visited every Friday. Before going in, he grabbed several small balsam pillows and carefully stuffed them under his left arm. He would go from room to room chatting with friends, first about the weather and trivial matters but in no time at all the conversations would step back in time and Cyril would sit, nodding and smiling as he listened to stories he'd heard dozens of times. Vacant, tired eyes that Cyril noticed when he first walked in the room would become brighter and brighter as each precious memory unraveled, often slightly different in the retelling. It seemed to be an elixir for the old people, and Cyril knew it was reciprocal—he needed them as much as they loved seeing him walk through the door.

Every so often, Cyril would find one of the rooms empty or a new face occupying an old chair. With a soft knock on the door frame he would enter, make friends easily, and when it was time to go, a fragrant balsam pillow would be left behind, often tightly clutched between a pair of life-worn hands. Wheelchairs were everywhere, and so were the many hands that reached up and out to Cyril as he walked by. Everyone seemed to know him, and on this day he spent four hours talking, playing checkers, and reintroducing himself to the many residents, who, from week to week, had forgotten him. Just before he pushed the main door open to leave, Josie shuffled over, staring straight ahead. She gently bumped into his left arm and stopped, waiting. As always, she was wearing the same irresistible, yet blank expression. Without a word she leaned in for her weekly hug and then wandered off like it never happened.

Cyril never left the nursing home feeling sad. In fact, it was quite the opposite. Unshakable blind faith steered him through each day, and he felt with his entire being that these beautiful people he had just spent the day with were only a few steps away from their true home, their true selves.

After a quick lunch and a tall coffee at the Blue Moon Café, he stopped at the bank and then drove two hours through the rolling green mountains to visit John. The drive was scenic and relaxing, until he neared the prison.

The "Camp Baker" sign along Route 3 looked inviting, but Cyril knew otherwise. He turned in and parked the truck in the visitor's lot. On his short walk to the entrance gate he eyed the cold, looming concrete walls and the tall metal fence that encircled the entire complex. Above the fence sat rolled barbed wire, its razor sharp spikes glistening in the afternoon sun. A nervous jab twisted in his stomach and suddenly he felt apprehensive. Stopping at the door, he rubbed his stomach and glanced back at his truck before going inside.

He was greeted by a large corrections officer wearing a gray uniform, his massive front held securely by a thick black belt which held rows of dangling keys.

"Afternoon," said the officer in a cheery, deep voice.

"Good afternoon," Cyril said, shutting the door.

Cyril was ID'd and given a key to a locker. He was asked to place his shoes, belt and everything in his pockets in the locker and keep the key in his hand. After going through a metal detector, the officer nodded and gestured him forward. Cyril followed the heavy footfalls and jingling keys down a cement and brick-sided hallway. After passing through many locked gates he was led to the visitor's room where John was sitting on the other side of a long, narrow table. He was slumped forward and his thin face was expressionless. His hair was gray and wispy and his baggy, bright orange prison clothes hung loose and rumpled over his thin frame. Cyril smiled lightly and walked over and offered his hand to John. They shook as Cyril sat down. John twisted in his chair, rubbed his knees and looked down.

"Appreciate it, Cyril. Nice of you to come," John said, looking at his shoes.

"No trouble at all. I'm glad to see you."

John looked up and met Cyril's eyes but only briefly. "Ann tells me you shored up the camp in places—the steps and also the roof."

"Yes, those were easy fixes. Glad to be of help."

"I thank you," John said shyly, looking around the room. "And thank you for being there for both Ann and Eva."

"John, we've known each other since Eva was born. I think of you as family."

John shifted in his seat and began rubbing the back of his hand over his mouth. "How's she doing? Eva?"

"She's not good right now." Cyril inched forward on his seat and excitedly said, "but I really believe time will take care of it. I do. She's young, and if you're truly done drinking—"

"I am done!" John interrupted gruffly.

Cyril sat back and the two men stared at each other until Cyril smiled politely and John frowned.

"I am! And that's that!" John said with a hard slap on his thigh.

An officer ten feet away took a step closer. Cyril glanced at the officer and leaned toward John.

"I know you are and things *will* get better. Just take it one step at a time," Cyril said softly.

"My stupidity has taken someone's life. In my head things will never get better."

"You're right. In your head they won't. But maybe you should look elsewhere."

John ran his fingers through his thin gray hair and looked questioningly at Cyril. He quickly stood up and the wooden chair scratched across the concrete floor. "Thank you for coming, Cyril. I really do appreciate it."

Cyril looked awkwardly around and then rose from his chair. "It was my pleasure."

While they shook hands an officer came over and stood by John. John smiled faintly at Cyril and turned and walked away with the officer at his side.

On his return trip, Cyril was plagued by a deep sadness for John, and equally for the family John had left empty and devastated. His thoughts then shifted to Eva, and how he might help her, followed by Ann with all her worries. He came up with no answers, so he simply released himself of the burden. Cyril called it "closing the door"—on his past and future. Bouncing along slowly on the rough road, he glanced up to find billowing pure white clouds etched on an endless blue canvas. He smiled at the great painting, and then his eyes fell to the sunny July leaves that were waving him onward and showing off every hue of summer's greenery. In a matter of seconds, the tension drained from his body as his thoughts quickly converted to the sights and sounds of the present moment, but mostly to the wonderful silence in between.

Back in Saranac Lake, Cyril made a few more stops and he refueled the truck and picked up groceries for the week ahead. When he drove past Ann and Eva's camp, it was dark and the car was still not there. He had a brief fearful thought of Eva unraveling with the adoption news. *No,* he thought with a firm shake of his head, *that's just not Eva.* When he swung right onto his dirt road he began talking out loud to himself: "And I don't think they'd pack up and go home ... I think they'd have told me or at least left a note."

A floodlight clicked on automatically when Cyril pulled up to his darkened, quiet home. He turned off the truck and rested the keys on his leg, staring at the dashboard, deep in thought. With a quick nod of his head, he made up his mind. He would get up before the sun tomorrow, go on his walk and stop by their cabin on the way back. It wouldn't take Cyril long to figure out if they had closed camp and returned home for the rest of the summer.

The next morning, a Saturday, Cyril woke to his usual music, plus one pileated woodpecker banging noisily on the back side of the camp. It was loud and disruptive, but Cyril didn't mind, figuring the woodpecker was searching for breakfast. He finished his morning routine and scooted down the porch steps. The very first rays of a magnificent sunrise briefly took his vision until he rounded the porch rail and turned sharply to the right. He had every intention of a fast hike up Eva's path, but his feet suddenly skidded to a halt. Mesmerized, he stood there watching his long, thin thirty-foot shadow stretching across the tops of the wildflowers.

Wow! Must have been the rain, he thought, marveling at the flowers that couldn't possibly bloom any brighter or taller. His yard was a dew-speckled, shimmering sea of color and the sun that just peeked over Bear Mountain was igniting them so intensely they didn't look real. He slowly lowered his pack basket and walked into the lush garden, his fingertips gliding over the silky wet petals.

At that very moment, Eva was hurtling down her trail, hoping not to miss Cyril. She broke through the thicket with her eyes fixed on his cabin, and after zigzagging through the birch grove, she jumped with a long stretch over the little stream. Then, all at once, three sounds interrupted the morning stillness: her pack slapped against her back, her feet landed with a thud and Eva screamed so loud she heard her voice twice, as seconds later, it echoed up from the lake. Just a few feet from Eva, off to her left, Cyril's head and shoulders magically popped up just above the wildflowers. He was sitting bolt-upright and looking just as surprised as she was.

"I'm so sorry, Eva!" Cyril repeated over and over as he stood up. "I didn't know you were so close."

The look of shock left Eva's face, but she was bent over with her hands on her knees.

"I didn't ... mean to scream ... sorry. Why ... were you lying ... on the ground in the ... flowers?" she panted.

"I was just leaving to take my walk and stop by your cabin, but I noticed the flowers were at their peak, they're so full and tall ... and the sunlight! It's washing over the top of them at just the right angle. Have you ever lay on your back and looked at a flower when the sun first touches it?"

"Um ... no," Eva said with a confused, yet also concerned look on her face.

"It's just amazing!" Cyril exclaimed. "You have to try it. The flowers are glowing, like the sun is actually in each petal. And the detail! You can see every vein and every pigment of color!"

Eva's heart was still thumping in her ears. She hesitated for a moment, giving Cyril that raised-eyebrow, sideways look, but she knew he was excited so she dropped her pack and walked tentatively into the knee-high flowers.

As soon as the back of her head pressed against the soft black soil, she yelled, "Oh my God, they *are* beautiful! I see what you mean. When the wind moves them they sparkle, just like the lake in the morning."

Eva gazed at the dancing kaleidoscope for several minutes before she, too, magically appeared.

"Mom and I got back last night," Eva said standing up and adjusting her baseball hat. "I found out that I was adopted. Mom said she told you, right?"

"Um, yes ... your mother told me a few days ago," Cyril said evenly.

"She lives in Canton. Her name's Mary, and we sure do look alike! It was a big surprise. I was pretty shocked at first ..." Eva said, looking away, her voice trailing off. "Mom explained everything ... how Mary just wanted to meet me, that's all."

Eva shrugged and added, "She was just too young to keep me. Mom thought I was going to fall apart and get all upset, but that's just her. You know she worries about everything."

Cyril sat on the rim of his pack basket and just smiled back at Eva. He was raising his hand to say something when Eva blurted out, "I'm so glad to be back at camp. It's a beautiful day, isn't it? What have you been up to, Cyril?"

Cyril lowered his hand and crossed his arms. In the few seconds it took him to reply, Eva's thoughts raced to her imprisoned father with its usual mixture of anger and contempt, but now, for the past three days she felt something new—relief. *Now it's really easy to forget about him and the horrible thing he did, because he's not my real father anyway.* Eva suddenly felt free, but this new freedom, somehow, felt very heavy.

"I've been sitting on my porch for three days staring at the birch grove, waiting for a swinging orange ponytail to appear," Cyril said, breaking the silence.

Looking a little sheepish, Eva's face grew red.

"Nooo! I'm just kidding," Cyril said with a big grin. "Although I have missed you. I've actually been quite busy with the firewood and balsam pillows. I also made a trip to town yesterday."

"Oh, sorry. I forgot we had plans to row across the lake. I should have—"

"Nonsense," Cyril said. "Don't be sorry, Eva. You've been very busy the last few days. We can take the boat out anytime. After all, like you said, we have all summer, right?"

"Right!"

Eva smiled and they both nodded in agreement. At the same time, they picked up their backpacks, took a sidewise step to the left and swung their packs over their right shoulders. They looked at each other with the same wide grin and laughed.

Eva backed up a little, putting her hands deep in her jean pockets.

"If you planned on a walk today, I don't want to interrupt—"

"My walk I can do any day," Cyril assured. "Besides I was coming to see you today. How about we pack a lunch and do two things? Do you still like to cut and gather balsam needles?"

"Oh yes! I don't think I'll ever get tired of that. I could do that for hours ... or until my fingers get sore," Eva said, looking at her fingertips.

"A friend who owns land on the other side of the lake has given me permission to harvest balsam boughs," Cyril said, pointing down the lake to the left of where Charlie was last seen. "It's over one hundred acres. We could bring the binoculars and look for Charlie and then, hopefully, bring back three or four pounds of needles. How does that sound to you?"

"Sounds great. Can I row across?" Eva asked. "I bet I can make the whole lake this summer without stopping."

"Sure you can. The lake is smooth and flat today and besides, I hardly ever get to be the passenger. It'll be a nice change."

On that near-perfect July day they lowered their packs into Cyril's Adirondack guide boat. He steadied the narrow craft while Eva adjusted herself in the bow seat. With a firm, balanced push, Cyril vaulted over the stern deck and settled himself onto a rickety caned seat while Eva adjusted her grip over the smooth oar handles. She loved how the eight-foot oars balanced perfectly in her hands, and although awkward at first, she quickly found her old rhythm. Except for a few water drips on the returning oar strokes, the boat moved across the water without a sound.

"Just like riding a bike, isn't it, Eva? You look like you've been rowing all summer. You're doing great!"

They spent the beginning of a beautiful summer day gliding across the smooth lake. Fluffy, snow-white cumulus clouds were reflected all over the silvery-blue surface. With a couple of fingers trailing through the water, Cyril stretched out his long legs, looking very content.

From the boat they found Charlie through the binoculars. The bald eagle was just starting to build what would become a large stick nest, sixty feet up, in the crotch of a huge pine tree. Satisfied that Charlie was staying, Eva turned the boat with a hard pull on the right oar and rowed further down the lake, staying parallel and close to the shoreline.

"I have to admit, Eva, I rather like sitting in the stern seat for once—feels like I'm on some fancy vacation. Are you getting tired?"

"Nope, I'm just fine. This is easy," Eva said, with her head cocked high on her shoulders.

"What a beautiful day. Look at the clouds mirrored on the surface," Cyril said, pointing at the water. "It just can't get any better!"

Eva smiled down at the shimmering water painting and then looked at Cyril's excited face.

"I wish I could be here in the fall when the leaves change color," Eva said. "It's got to be the best season of all! When I finish college, I'm going to spend the entire month of October right here."

"You're right—October is beautiful; so colorful it's almost not real. But my favorite season is winter, especially the beginning of a snowstorm. I don't think there's anything more peaceful than watching big snowflakes sifting down through the evergreens. Takes my breath away. Stops me right in my tracks," Cyril said dreamily.

Eva leaned in deeper on the oars and while staring at her boots, tried to envision what he just described.

Eva suddenly stopped rowing and pointed toward shore with big eyes. Cyril followed her hand and quietly turned to look.

"It's so little," Eva whispered.

Cyril nodded in agreement as they both stared at the black eyes and ears of a tiny bear cub that was eyeing them from behind a sun-bleached log. The log was about two feet off the ground and the bear's little round head kept peeking over the top and quickly disappearing. For the rest of the boat ride, Eva would tell Cyril that it was definitely laughing at them, or at least smiling, but all she would get back from Cyril was a grinning chuckle.

Eva skillfully rowed around a little peninsula, being careful not to hit any outcropping of rocks, most of them hidden just below the surface. She pushed back with the left oar and pulled hard with the right, turning the little boat sharply around the curving shore where they entered a little bay with a small island off to the left.

"We're looking for a yellow-marked trail, and it's supposed to be right opposite that island," Cyril said, trying to point and not wiggle the boat too much.

When the guide boat slid up on a small stretch of sandy shoreline, Eva noticed punch marks everywhere in the sand indicating that whitetail deer had come to the water's edge during the night for a drink. Leaving the boat half on the beach, they walked up and down the waterfront looking for yellow paint on just one tree, but found nothing.

"Well, the owner did say it might be difficult to find. He said the trail was made sometime in the 1970s, so I guess we'll just have to follow our compasses," Cyril advised.

While Cyril reached in his shirt pocket and pulled out an ancient-looking brass compass, Eva plopped her pack down in the sand and slid her hand in a little side pocket. Pulling out a new compass, she held it at arm's-length for Cyril's inspection.

"Nice compass," Cyril said.

"We'd better check them against each other, right?" Eva said, hurrying over to Cyril.

"That's right! You remember."

"A good compass can save your life in the woods and having a spare is even safer," Eva said proudly, mimicking Cyril's deep voice.

Cyril laughed and said, "Well, I guess I don't have to worry about you getting lost."

They stood a few feet apart, holding their compasses flat in the palms of their hands. Eva was satisfied with her reading, but she noticed Cyril kept tapping his compass.

"East is that way," she said, motioning directly into the woods, away from the lake.

"That's correct," Cyril agreed. "That way is definitely east but my compass is reading ... west. This is the first time it's ever failed me."

Cyril threw his compass up in the air and caught it. He then gave it a good shake and checked it again as Eva curiously looked on.

"Guess it's time for a new one," Eva suggested.

"I couldn't agree more," he said, tossing the compass over his shoulder and into his open basket. "I'm glad we have yours, and you're absolutely right, Eva—I should have a reliable spare with me at all times in the woods. On my next go-to-town day, I'll pick up two, just like yours."

"Good," Eva said approvingly. "But I guess you hardly need

one. You know the woods so well, and your hiking trail is so easy to follow."

"Oh no, that's not true," Cyril said with a raised finger. "The woods can change and become very confusing, no matter how well you know them. Snow or an ice storm and especially heavy fog can make the woods appear completely different."

While Eva nodded in agreement, a strong breeze came out of nowhere and lifted her hat. They both turned and watched the wind run up the shoreline. It was over in seconds and none followed. Eva frowned up at Cyril and Cyril looked up at the sky.

"That was odd," Eva remarked, pulling down her hat.

"Yes indeed," agreed Cyril.

They carried the boat over the rough sand and rocks and set it down gently in a high stand of marsh grass. Eva laid her compass flat in her right hand and they entered the shaded forest. The sun had warmed them while in the boat, but the forest was much cooler, causing goose bumps on Eva's arms. After just a few minutes of walking, Eva pointed out to Cyril that the blueberry crop was going to be huge this summer and it wouldn't be long before they were picking a winter's worth of berries.

They walked up a slight grade through an old-growth forest, stopping only once for Cyril to catch his breath. When the terrain leveled off, they hiked due east for thirty or forty minutes before finally coming upon a stand of young balsams that stretched for as far as the eye could see. Scattered throughout the fragile balsam stand were towering pine and hemlock giants, most of which had started growing during the middle and latter half of the last century.

Cyril's basket hit the forest floor with a relieving thud, followed by Eva's much lighter nylon pack.

"How about lunch first and work second?" Cyril asked, stretching and working out the kinks.

"Sounds good to me," Eva replied. "I'm starving!"

By late afternoon, Eva's fingers were red and sore from sliding and shucking the slim balsam needles off their tiny branches. A towering hemlock tree made a good backrest for both of them as they sat side by side with a blue tarp spread out under their knees. While Cyril hummed along and Eva tried to whistle, the miniature leaflike spindles were steadily building up on the vinyl. She felt safe and content just being by his side, but every once in a while she would glance around, looking for a bear cub ... and its much larger mother.

Cyril's humming ceased abruptly and he began looking all around but mostly upward at the sky. Eva looked at him curiously but noticed nothing except a roaring sound coming from the sky. While looking up she suddenly felt the great tree shifting and moving against her back. By the time Cyril was on his feet, sunlight and dark shadows were speeding through the balsam thicket, and almost instantly it became very dark. An icy gloom fell over the forest as the upper turbulence grew louder.

"What is it?" Eva asked nervously as she too jumped to her feet, scattering balsam needles everywhere.

Cyril was spinning around in tight circles, looking straight up at a blackening sky. When Eva looked up, the crowns of the giant trees were bending almost double in one direction.

"A storm ... but the wind ... Eva! We need to get back to shore! Fast! It can be very dangerous if big limbs start snapping off. Quick! Put everything in my basket."

The fury that was only in the treetops moments ago was now down with them. When the blast hit her, Eva thought a giant freezer door had opened as she watched their blue tarp shoot straight up, twisting and whipping through the wild air. She turned stiffly, tucking her chin down to her chest while hard-driving rain pelted her bare arms and slapped noisily off her nylon pack.

Cyril was now shouting orders in a loud, strong voice, but for the first time in Eva's life she saw fear and panic in his eyes. "Get your compass out and put the needle on 'west.' That's right. Now put your compass close to your chest and you lead us straight to the lake. Stay close, right in front me. You watch your compass and I'll watch you!"

Strangely, Eva was not afraid until she heard branches buckling and cracking off to her left, followed by a definite vibration under her feet. A mixture of shiny leaves and twigs were sailing sideways through the air, followed by drenching sheets of frigid rain. When Eva pulled the brim of her hat down to her eyebrows, she noticed what looked like white marbles bouncing and rolling everywhere. The hail crunched with each step and stung much harder than the rain. She felt Cyril's strong hand on her left shoulder. His grip kept changing, and at times was so tight it hurt.

"Big strides, Eva! Take longer steps, you're doing terrif—"

A loud thud replaced Cyril's voice and his hand was yanked off her shoulder.

Eva whirled around to find him lying on his side with a branch next to his head.

"CYRIL!" Eva screamed, but he was already scrambling to get up. "You're bleeding! Look at your arm!" she shrieked.

"I'm okay. The branch hit my basket. We've got to keep moving!" He directed her back into position and yelled through the gales: "You're doing great! Watch your compass and don't stop!"

It was raining and hailing so hard Eva could barely keep her eyes open. After only five minutes of walking they were completely drenched. Eva felt Cyril's right hand clamp down on top of her head. She shivered hard but felt more protected as they marched on, linked tightly together.

"We're going to make it! I KNOW WE ARE!" Eva shouted. She strained her neck to give Cyril a quick look but all she saw was his blood-smeared left hand resting on her wet shoulder.

Cyril didn't respond, but for several minutes Eva thought she heard him mumbling what must have been prayers. There were only three words she distinctly heard: One was "God" and the other two were "Eva" and "please."

Cyril suddenly began shouting into Eva's left ear: "Eva, don't turn around, keep your eyes straight ahead ... now, if something happens to me, you have to promise me you'll keep going, you can't stay in these woods—"

"I'M NOT LEAVING YOU HERE!" Eva shouted back. "And besides I told you we're going to make it—"

"BACK UP!" Cyril yelled as he grabbed under her arms and dragged her backward on her heels. A poplar tree as thick as Cyril's leg crashed in front of them. They had to weave through its tall branches, bending and pulling them apart to get on the other side of the fallen wood. Eva went to take off but Cyril quickly grabbed her arm and yanked her to a stop. He was panting and his wide eyes frightened her.

"Eva, listen to me. It's very ... important! You have ... to get out of these woods as fast as you can. I've never ... seen a storm like this!" He nudged her forward to keep walking. Eva started crying when his grip tightened on her shoulder and his voice became stern and deep. "You can send help for me later. This is an order you must follow! You need to get to the boat fast, turn it over and stay under it until the storm passes. DO NOT come back in the woods looking for me. Row back and get help. Do you understand? I need you to hear you say yes!"

Eva turned and said a very faint "yes" but she knew she was lying, not knowing what she'd really do if something happened to Cyril.

For another half-hour they trekked on relentlessly through the tearing wind and rioting timber, plastered with wet leaves, twigs and bark. Eva's teeth were chattering noisily and her body was shaking. Her cotton clothes were soaked through to the skin and she felt as though she had just fallen through a frozen lake. She knew she'd never felt this cold, and as she trembled, she could not stop thinking of a steaming bathtub, full of hot water that she could just fall into.

"THAT ROCK! OVER THERE!" Cyril yelled, directing his right arm straight out, nearly hitting Eva's ear. "I remember it. We're not far from the lake ... YES! I can see little bits of the water through the trees."

Cyril felt Eva's fast walking turn into a stiff-legged jog and he kept right up with her, holding on tight. They bounded down the sloping grade with eyes fixed on the gray light of the lake. When they broke through the bushes and their feet hit the sand they were hammered even harder by driving hail and numbing rain, forcing them to turn away and face the woods again. The lake was wild and white-capped, but to Eva's surprise the incoming mud-brown water was warm and soothing. It filled her boots and quickly swelled up around her legs, saturating her blue jeans all the while making her feet sink deeper into the sand.

"WE'RE WAY OFF!" Cyril shouted, gasping for air. "I didn't even see the island; did you? Eva? EVA!"

Eva was hunched over and slowly backing into the water, its warm waves slamming against her back.

"EVA! NOOO! I KNOW IT'S WARM, BUT YOU CAN'T GO IN. IT WILL MAKE YOU EVEN COLDER! WE HAVE TO FIND SHELTER!"

Eva stopped but didn't move. Cyril waded backward, glancing every few feet over his shoulder. As he got closer he reached out his hand.

"EVA! TAKE MY HAND!" he ordered.

Her arms were folded in tight. She was bent over and shaking. She didn't move, so Cyril pulled her rigid arms apart and took her by the wrist. He bent over, resting his forehead on hers and said, as calmly as he could, "I know the water feels good, but we have to stay together. We have to find the boat."

Steering her behind him, Cyril told her to grab one of his basket straps.

"Hide your face behind my pack," he shouted. "Now, hold on tight and follow me. I think the boat is down the lake, to our left. I just hope it's still there—"

Hunched up, away from the wind, Cyril started sloshing along the beach while ice pellets pummeled his left side and waves crashed at his knees. Eva scooted around to his right side and immediately she felt his arm clasp around her and draw her in close. She reached up with her free hand and locked onto his elbow.

"I can help look! And I'm getting hit less on this side," Eva shouted, her quivering voice muffled against his arm.

They had only trudged a few minutes when Cyril stopped and pointed at a huge, blackish-gray something, hidden just beyond the wooded shoreline.

"EVA! LOOK!" Cyril shouted.

But to Eva it just resembled more whipping and bending trees surrounded by dark shadows.

"Quick, go this way!" he shouted. Cyril turned and escorted Eva along, almost dragging her toward the wild woods.

"What about the boat? Why are we going back to the woods?" Eva mumbled.

"This will be safer," he said. "I think it's a massive rock and we can hide behind it. If any trees or branches break, the wind will carry them away from us, further into the woods."

With their hands locked together, they squeezed sideways through narrow rows of whipping black alder and birch trees. After four or five quick steps they were standing behind a wall of rock the size of a small garage. The top of the great boulder sloped forward, giving them a slight roof. There was instant relief, but the wind, hail and rain roared past the sides of the rock and ricocheted over their heads.

Eva huddled closer to Cyril as he wiggled and twisted, trying to pry his rain-sodden basket off his back.

"Eva, I think we're safe from the storm but we've got to get you warm. I have dry matches but everything is saturated and the wind ... I think it would be near impossible to even try."

Cyril's basket hit the ground with a wet crunch and so did he. He was kneeling and throwing everything out, trying to get to the bottom. Eva watched thin, watery streams of blood running down his left hand and dripping off all of his fingertips.

"Small cut. I'll fix that in a minute," he said, wiping his hand on his shirt.

"I'mmm soooo cooold," Eva said rigidly.

"I know and we're going to take care of that," Cyril said calmly as he tied a bandana tightly around the gash in his forearm.

"The storm can't hurt us here and I believe it's going to pass very soon. Then, hopefully, the sun will come out and the air will get warmer again. But right now we have to do everything we can to get *you* warm, okay?" Cyril said, with a reassuring smile.

Eva said nothing and just stared blankly at the ground, shaking and wobbling back and forth.

"EVA!" shouted Cyril, his smile vanishing.

Her defeated brown eyes slowly looked up between shakes and caught Cyril's serious blue ones. She reluctantly gave him a trembling nod.

He frantically tore open a scruffy plastic bag and Eva watched something blue fall out. At first Eva thought it was a blanket until Cyril picked it up and held it by the shoulders. When he shook the large sweater a red wool hat flew up and landed on the glossy brown leaves.

"Oh, good!" Cyril said. "I forgot that was in there. That'll help too.

"I'm going to turn around, Eva," Cyril continued. "You need to take that cotton shirt off and put this sweater on and this hat. It's going to be a little itchy but I know this will help. It's wool, about an inch thick and will keep you warm even if it gets wet. I'm pretty sure this sweater saved my life when I fell through the ice—"

He stepped forward, but before handing her the sweater he wrapped his arms tightly around her. Eva's body instantly stopped shaking. She felt him squeeze tighter and she didn't want him to stop.

"Don't worry. We're going to get you warm and we're going to get back to camp, I promise you," Cyril said in his usual calm voice. He pulled away and handed her the sweater and hat. "Now quickly, change into this."

When he turned around to let her change he yelled over his shoulder, "Eva, did you happen to bring a phone with you?"

"No. It's at camp, and I forgot to tell Mom where I was going. She's going to be so mad."

"She'll be fine when she sees you," Cyril said. "And besides, she knows about where we are. I left a note on my kitchen table explaining where we were going today."

Cyril made her eat and drink the last of the food and water. Eva watched, tight-armed and still shaking, as he spread her empty pack on the ground at the base of the rock and sat down. He patted the nylon, indicating for her to sit right next to him. With his arms outstretched to catch her, she slid in firmly against his side, snuggling in close and wedging herself under his left arm. Cyril anchored his strong arms around her and locked his hands together. It felt good to Eva and the tighter he squeezed the warmer she felt.

"I've never seen a storm this powerful in all the years that I've lived here. We're very fortunate to be sitting behind this rock ... very fortunate indeed," he said, wiggling and shifting to get more comfortable. "Do you feel any warmer, Eva? You seem to have a few breaks between shudders."

"I don't know, but I'm so tired I just want ... to close my eyes."

"You rest, and maybe when your eyes open, this awful storm will have passed," Cyril said in a lazy, exhausted tone.

Eva freed her mouth from his warm arm.

"Are you tired too?" she asked.

"Yes I am, but I'll stay awake. You rest now."

******

Cyril felt a strange numbness throughout his entire body, making the hard rock feel almost comfortable. He leaned back trying to figure out why Eva was approaching hypothermia and he was neither warm nor cold. He thought it might be the heavy wool shirt he had on, but he quickly reasoned it must have been adrenaline and frayed nerves that kept him from freezing. With his head supported in a smooth crevice, he hypnotically watched another wave of pearl-sized hail stones, hopping and skittering in all directions, when he suddenly realized he'd forgotten what it felt like to love and worry so intensely about another. He glanced down at Eva's red-capped head and knew at that very moment that he loved her as if she were his own.

His face suddenly tightened as past memories crept in, and

he tried hard to push them away. He pulled Eva tighter into his side, forcing his mind to think only in the present. *We need to keep warm. We need to find the boat. The sun will be out soon and everything will be better.* Cyril went on and on, but his eyelids were beginning to droop, and he had to keep stretching and forcing them upward to stay awake.

While he struggled to keep vigil, it dawned on him that Eva had not moved or shivered for several minutes. Holding his breath and leaning closer, he could feel her little body rising and falling in peaceful sleep. He reclined his head back and whispered, *Thank you.* He then closed his eyes and envisioned his prayer speeding through the wind-whipped treetops, past the pelting rain, beyond the black clouds, and into the light of God's opening hands. As his face relaxed, he tipped his head down so his chin touched her hat. In a matter of seconds, a familiar calmness settled in and, as the tension sifted out of his body, he could feel a strange, unexplainable warming sensation passing from Eva into him. His breathing slowed, his body loosened, and his eyes were becoming heavier and heavier ... and soon the howling tumult melted away. When his eyelids finally slid shut, his last vision was that of bending and clashing trees against the back of his darkening eyelids, and almost immediately he began to dream.

He was standing on the topmost of three oak steps, on an altar in what looked like a church. His left hand was resting on a cool white-marble railing and when he glanced down he saw that his hand was very young looking. There were no scars. He looked at his other hand and it was the same. He felt excited, but at the same time very nervous. *Something important is happening here*, he thought. The distant walls of the church were hazy, but right in front of him, clearly, was a tall wooden table that was draped with silky purple cloth, and on its smooth surface stood three glistening gold cups and a large open book with thick red binding. Stationed behind the table was a short, round priest with a wonderful smile. His arms were tucked in his opposite sleeves and resting comfortably upon his protruding stomach. And the music—an organ, it sounded so familiar.

Suddenly he felt a small tug on the sleeve of his suit coat and when he turned around his heart jumped with excitement. He was looking at the grinning, youthful face of one of his dearest friends. *What's George doing here?* he thought, *and all dressed up in a suit, like me.* Then he remembered he was George's best man at his wedding. But then confusion and sadness crept in as he also remembered that George had died years ago—but he was here now and he was so real. He couldn't take his eyes off George and he felt a great contentment just being next to him. He wanted to reach out and wrap his arms around him, but he couldn't move. George winked at him and then nodded his head to the left. When Cyril turned around, a church full of people dressed in fancy clothes were looking up at him. They seemed far away and he couldn't make out their faces.

George raised his eyebrows and gestured for him to look up the aisle. The organ began to play and he couldn't believe his eyes. Happiness filled him to overflowing as he watched his beautiful Eleanor marching slowly toward him, her light-brown hair resting on the shoulders of a long white gown. *This is my wedding*, he thought, and George winked at him again. When he looked back at Eleanor, she seemed to be slowing down. He leaned forward, wanting to run to her, but he just teetered and swayed in shoes that wouldn't move. He looked at George for help, but he was backing up and becoming blurry. Panic-stricken, Cyril opened his mouth to yell her name, but nothing came out. She stopped and he felt frantic as she just stood there with the warmest, most beautiful smile he had ever seen. When she raised her hand out toward Cyril, the church began to dim and he felt many hands pulling him backward into increasing darkness. His arms were out straight and he was silently screaming her name over and over, reaching and straining to break free. A huge door slammed shut and the church became a distant, whirling black mass.

He was still reaching and yelling, but he began to notice an increasing calmness overtake him as he traveled into this warm, enveloping darkness until his feet hit with a clunk and he was suddenly standing on a wide, sloping porch that seemed to wrap completely around a little white house. He turned around and faced the door. It looked familiar, and suddenly he felt a rush of excitement. The bottom half was made of beautifully varnished wood, while the top half had two long panes of beveled glass. Just below the panes of glass was a brass knocker with writing on top. It was a cool summer night but as he stepped closer to read the inscription he could feel heat coming from the door. Engraved on the brass plate were the words *BANKSTROM, 12 ELDERWOOD STREET*. Smoke began to curl out of the door cracks, and he suddenly realized he had to get through this door. When he reached for the doorknob his heart starting pounding furiously—the doorknob and his hands were covered with blood. As soon as he lunged forward he felt the same strong hands pulling him back, and he yelled as loud as he could, but this time the words rang out through the quiet woods.

"LET ME GO-O-O-O-O!!!"

******

Eva screeched and scrambled away from Cyril, creeping backward on her hands and heels, glaring at him in confusion. When she stopped, a lone sunbeam made her squint and she moved around until she could see him more clearly. He was bent forward and wide-eyed. His chest was heaving like he had just run up a mountain. When his huge eyes found Eva, she saw his face relax, but only for a moment.

"What's the matter? Are you alright?" Cyril asked.

Still frightened, Eva lowered her hand and gaped at Cyril.

"You screamed something ... really, really loud," Eva said quietly.

"I'm so sorry I scared you," Cyril said heavily. "I was just having a dream ... a bad—EVA!" Cyril shouted, and she jumped again. "The sun's out. There's no wind. It's over!"

Cyril stiffly got to his feet and grabbed Eva's hand. They skirted around the great boulder and ducked through the alders and didn't stop until their feet hit the wet sand on the silent, sunlit beach. Immediately their hands flew to their eyebrows, shielding away the intense, incoming brightness. When they turned to face each other they were both wearing squinting smiles.

"AAAAAH!" Eva rejoiced. "The sun feels so good and everything's so quiet now. But look at the water." Eva tried to point, but her hands were lost in the long blue sleeves of Cyril's sweater.

The lake was flat and still, but the water was mud-brown and littered with floating sticks and leaves. Large domes of bubbly white foam were washed up on shore and bobbing like little boats all over the lake.

"I'm not cold anymore," Eva marveled. "It must've been your sweater, and look, there's steam coming out of it!"

When Eva looked up, Cyril's face was sad and his lower lip seemed to quiver. He replaced it with a quick smile and pulled her in close for a tight side-hug.

"You were worried, weren't you?" Eva asked quietly.

He squeezed her tighter and then released her. "Yes I was. But not for me."

Confused and frowning, Eva turned away from Cyril to let the warm sun absorb into the back of her dark sweater.

"Do you hear that, Cyril?" Eva asked, spinning around.

"What?"

"A boat. I hear a motorboat way up the lake, on the other side of the peninsula ... I think. Can you hear it now?" she asked again, watching Cyril's face intently.

Cyril leaned an ear to the lake and took a few steps forward.

"I think I hear something but I can't tell. Does it really sound like a boat?"

"Oh yes, it sounds just like the buzzing of a motorboat," Eva assured. "Maybe someone's out looking for us! I wouldn't be surprised if Mom called out the National Guard."

Eva giggled and looked up at the sky.

"I don't see any now, but I imagine the helicopters will be arriving soon."

Cyril looked down at her, laughing and shaking his head.

"Well, one thing's for sure," he said, pointing down the beach to the right, "the guide boat's this way. Why don't I go find it while you wait here? If the motorboat comes close enough, try to wave them over. We might need help. I don't know what kind of shape our boat is in."

Eva retrieved their packs from behind the rock and put everything in the sand, close to the water. She tried to sit on Cyril's basket while watching for the boat, but it buckled, causing her to topple off and land in the wet sand. She stood up quickly, dusting the sand off her pants, when she noticed the sound of the motorboat was getting louder. The sun was just above the trees on the opposite side of the lake, making it difficult for her to see the peninsula. Just when she cupped both hands around her eyes, a little white boat made its way around the bend. It was so far away Eva couldn't tell how many people were in it. It was moving very slowly, but she was happy to see it was following the shoreline and she was hoping it was her mom or someone out looking for them.

"I found the boat!" Cyril yelled.

Eva whirled to her right with her hands circling her eyes like she was holding binoculars. Cyril was walking toward her, knee deep in the lake, hand-guiding the boat along by its bow.

"I sure hope someone's looking for us," Cyril said, holding a piece of oar in his hand. "We're definitely going to need a ride back. One oar is broken and the gunwale is cracked in two places."

"There's a boat!" Eva said suddenly. "Someone's coming."

Cyril stopped short and the rowboat bumped into his leg. He shielded his eyes in the direction of the motorboat and then back to Eva.

"That little white boat," Eva said pointing, "was staying close to shore but it just turned out into the lake. It's still coming in our direction but it's pretty far away. I think there are two people in it and one of them keeps standing up and sitting back down."

"When they get a little closer, Eva, wave your red hat in the air," Cyril suggested.

Right away, Eva started swinging her hat in a circular motion over her head and almost instantly she could hear the motorboat speed up.

"OVER HERE! OVER HERE!" Eva shouted, her arms flailing in the air.

Cyril swiftly slid the boat up on the beach and walked over to join Eva, waving. Eva was about to yell again when the person in the front of the boat suddenly stood up and began thrashing his arms around like a windmill. Eva then heard loud voices but it mostly sounded like a man yelling, at what now looked like … a tall, thin woman.

"Oh my God, Cyril. That's ... my mom. But who's she with?"

"I think you're right. It does look like your mom and I'm pretty sure that's ...," Cyril paused, squinting, "Datus driving. She'd better sit back down or she's going to end up in the water. Datus can't turn that little boat toward us while she's standing up."

"Datus!" Eva said, frowning. "She doesn't even know him! What if he's drunk, Cyril? He's not supposed to be driving ... anything ... is he?"

"He has no driver's license, but I'm not sure about operating a boat. From what I know of Datus, he does his drinking in the evening. I've yet to see him drunk during the day, or at least not until dinnertime."

Eva folded her arms and looked away, shaking her head.

"Eva," Cyril said calmly, "your mom went to Datus for help and he's helping her and us. He could have said no."

"I know," Eva mumbled, still looking away from Cyril.

After much hand waving and shouting from Datus, Ann finally sat down. The little white boat veered to the right and was now coming straight at them.

Ann was yelling something but Eva and Cyril just looked at each other in confusion. When Datus cut the engine to let the small craft glide into shore, Ann's voice rang loud and clear.

"EVA! CYRIL! ARE YOU ALRIGHT?!"

"Yes, we're alright," they said at the same time, smiling at each other.

"OH MY GOD," Ann bellowed. "WHAT A STORM. I'VE BEEN SO—"

"MOM!!" Eva yelled over her. "You don't have to shout. We're right here in front of you!"

When the boat slid up onto the sand, Cyril reached out and steadied it while Ann vaulted over the side and locked Eva in a tight hug. Cyril smiled as he watched Ann blinking away the tears.

"Wasn't it a wicked storm?" Eva said, pushing out of her mother's tight embrace. "A tree crashed on Cyril and another one almost hit me. And the rain and hail! I thought I was going to freeze to death, but then Cyril found this huge boulder and we hid behind it."

Eva looked at Cyril, giving him a proud grin and Ann walked over and hugged him too.

"I'm sorry, Ann. I didn't know a big storm was coming. I wouldn't have—"

"Nonsense! I didn't know about the storm either. Thank you so much for taking care of Eva," Ann said in a relieved, shaky voice.

Cyril gave her an acknowledging squeeze and slowly pulled away.

"How are the camps?" Cyril asked. "Any damage?"

"None that I could see," Ann replied. "Although there are trees down everywhere and the power is out."

"Well, the good news is, all those problems are fixable," Cyril said, turning toward Datus. "Datus! Thank you. Thank you very much!"

"Weren't nothin', sort of," Datus said, frowning at Ann.

Datus was sitting in the back of the boat, wearing what was once a white T-shirt that didn't quite cover his bulging stomach. There was a bent cigarette sticking out of his sharp black whiskers, and his thick hair was tossed in six different directions.

"It's good ta see ya both upright! Worried, I was. Hellava storm, Cyril! Hellava storm!" Datus mumbled from the cigarette-free corner of his mouth. "Now let's git that rowboat of yers laced up ta mine and git movin'! It'll be gittin' dark in two shakes of a rattlesnake's tail."

Ann and Eva looked at each other, exchanging the same blank expression and then began loading the backpacks into the aluminum boat while Datus and Cyril walked over to retrieve the guide boat. Halfway to the boat, Datus smacked his forehead with the flat of his hand as he glanced back over his shoulder at Ann.

"Good God, Cyril!" Datus said in a gruff whisper. "That woman should be on nerve pills or some kind of medication. I almost dragged her back to camp just to throw some whisky down her throat, calm her down a bit, ya know what I mean?"

Cyril smiled and walked along, but said nothing.

Datus loped at Cyril's side with his hands held out pleadingly. "And worse yet! That chatterin' broom handle would not sit down. She almost upended the boat three times. But I told her so. I says, 'You fall in that lake and I ain't stoppin', no-sirree, but I'll pick ya up on the way back.' That sat her down right quick! But then she spotted you two and she sprung up again! I had all I could do not to yank that motor just to teach her a lesson. Waters warm enough, ain't it?"

"Datus, she was very worried," Cyril said in a hushed voice. "I'm sure you can understand, but you did a great job getting here, under *all* the circumstances ... thank you."

"Yeah, well, that's all fine and everthin' but my dog, Chester, he's dummer 'n dirt and half-dead and *he* lissins better than *her*."

Datus scowled and ran the back of his hairy hand over his stubbly chin while Cyril gave him a reprimanding look, accompanied by a slight grin.

"Yeah ... yeah, I know," Datus conceded. "She was worried alright. An' I guess I can give her one good credit. She's got cat-like balance. She'd do well shinglin' a roof." And in a lower voice, he added, "Dang good place for her too."

Cyril chuckled lightly and patted him on the back while Datus took a long draw on his shrinking cigarette.

The glinting sun was half-hidden by the tallest trees on the other side of the lake, making the evening air noticeably cooler and causing Eva once again to start shivering in her wet clothes. Ann immediately wrapped her up with one of the two large blankets she had brought from camp. She helped Eva climb into the boat and then pushed it out into about a foot of water. She then steadied the bow with both hands while Cyril and Datus finished tying the two boats together.

"I'll hold her an' you get in first," Datus said tonelessly to Ann as he raised a hand to flick his cigarette into the water.

"You're not going to throw that in the lake, are you?" Ann asked quickly.

Datus's head recoiled back in disgust. "Whudaya spect me ta do with it?" he asked with his arm frozen in midair.

Ann stepped into the boat and quickly grabbed some crumpled up paper.

"Here, wrap it in this," Ann suggested. "And I'll throw it out when we get back to camp."

Datus gave Ann a nasty look as he doused his cigarette out in the lake and slowly handed it over. Wearing the same expression, he glanced at Cyril but Cyril was occupied with other matters.

"ALRIGHT! I'm thirstier than a dead man in the desert. Ever'one in the boat!" Datus ordered, glancing at the back of Ann's head with a cross-eyed glare. "CYRIL! You drive. You know the whole of this lake better than any of us!"

"Aye-aye, Captain Datus!" Cyril announced, winking at Eva, whose brown eyes and freckled nose were peeking out from the orange folds of a thick fleece blanket.

From opposite sides, and at the same time, the two men

hauled themselves into the small craft, splattering water every-where. Ann and Eva sat cozily together in the bow seat while Datus plopped down in the middle seat, putting his back to both of them. He automatically reached for another cigarette, then scoffed and stuffed them back in his chest pocket. Cyril took up the stern seat, facing forward toward everyone. He was about to start the motor when Ann quietly stood up, bent full over at the hips, and began rummaging through a bag on the floor of the boat. When she reappeared she had another blanket in her hand.

"Now, Cyril, once we get going, that cold air is going to freeze you in those wet clothes so you must take this," Ann said, hold-ing the blanket up high. She then eyed the back of Datus's head, and boldly added, "Now that's that and when the engine starts, I promise I won't stand up anymore."

As the blanket skimmed the top of Datus's wild hair the boat jiggled and tipped to the left causing Datus to quickly grab the gunwale. His jaw clenched and his left eye began to twitch. Turning halfway around, he fixed his glare just over the top of Ann's head.

"In a boat, 'specially a small one," Datus informed in a slowly rising voice, "yer supposed to *hand* things back an' forth. It's jus' proper boat eddicate. Fer example, if there were a cooler up front, one of you could *pass* me a couple of beers right now, *all without standing up!* An' then I'd *pass* one to Cyril, see, but he don't drink, so's I'd end up with two—anyway, ya don't stand up, UNDERSTAND?!"

"I'm really sorry, Mr. Datus," Ann said sincerely. "I know I haven't been a good passenger ... Eva, quit giggling! ... But I am *so very* thankful for all your help."

Eva was trying to find Cyril's eyes but he was unfolding his blanket and seemed to be holding it in front of his face a long time. When the blanket finally came down, Eva caught his eye and they both started laughing. Cyril cleared his throat and with great difficulty he straightened up his face and looked straight at Datus. "Datus, did you have any damage at your camp?"

"Naw, the camp's fine, but that little shed I jus' finish build-in'—the dang roof went flyin' through the air like a Frisbee. Should of used screws instead of nails. Landed right in ol' Floss's flower garden, just planted," he said with an impish chuckle. "An' we'll be usin' lanterns tonight. Power's out."

Datus nervously patted his shirt pocket, where his cigarettes were kept. He then looked at Cyril with a tightening face and threw his arms in the air.

" 'Parently we're not movin'! Well! Git 'er goin', Cyril, an' use full speed. The sky's starting to git that purple look to it."

With one pull of the rope the motor kicked to life, interrupt-ing the stillness and their echoing voices. Cyril gradually slid the throttle lever to number ten and, as the bow rose up, they left a puff of white smoke hanging in the clear mountain air.

Chapter 5

Cyril woke the next morning with aching knees and hips, but his right side was giving him the most trouble. He felt exhausted and lay in bed for an extra hour. When the sun shafts slid down the west wall and finally touched the floor, he begrudgingly got up and started slowly moving about the cabin. Doubting he had electricity, he flicked on the closest light switch. To his surprise, it popped on. He then ran the hot water in the kitchen and after a minute, steam was swirling out of the sink. A long hot shower did his aches and pains a world of good, and after a hearty breakfast he was feeling somewhat better.

He had someone on his mind that he wanted to check on, so he laced on his spare boots and checked the weather through one of the lake windows. Before tossing his axe and handsaw into his pack basket, he performed a quick makeshift repair on the fractured rim of his pack. Thumping down his porch steps in the shade, Cyril gazed across the lake at a single fluffy cloud that obscured the sun. The rest of the sky was deep blue. He stood for a moment, hoping yesterday might have been a bad dream as his eyes roamed across the smooth, motionless lake and then up the shoreline where the leaves hung in perfect stillness. But just one look around, mostly to the right toward the Datus camp, told Cyril that a powerful storm had definitely passed through. Some areas were untouched but in certain places it looked as though a giant had walked through, bending and breaking everything in its path.

He took a deep breath, sighing heavily and said out loud, shaking his head, "Could have been much worse, but there sure is a lot of work to be done. I know what I'll be doing for several weeks."

Cyril decided to leave the basket by the porch with the saw in it. He grabbed his double bit axe, flipped it up onto his shoulder and headed straight for Eva's path. The first part of the trail was mostly open and easy walking, but as Cyril neared the halfway point he was doing a lot more chopping and throwing branches. The work was exhausting and the aches he had earned yesterday didn't help matters. Plopping down on a leaf-covered spruce stump, he wiped his forehead and tried to catch his breath. *For the rest of the cleanup,* he told himself, *the chainsaw will be coming along.*

When his breathing slowed he looked at an opening in the hardwoods off the left and decided it would be a good route to follow. With a one-arm swing, the axe sunk deeply into the rotted stump. Cyril let go of the handle and walked away in the direction of Hazel's bus. About fifteen feet away, he stopped and stared at the gloomy, greasy windows.

"Hello ... Hazel?" Cyril called out pleasantly.

Wild barking erupted from inside the bus. The dogs were

jumping and scrambling from seat to seat. They sounded vicious, and Cyril was hoping she would not let them out. He could see the hounds leaping and slamming into each other, but he couldn't see any sign of Hazel. He thought he might yell louder, and just as he took one step closer a flash of light shimmered off the side of the bus. A window pane slid up about two inches and the only thing Cyril could see of Hazel were two big teeth surrounded by matted black hair. Her face quickly disappeared and was replaced by four fingers that were turning white as they strained to get the window up a little higher. The barking was so loud that Cyril knew if he was to speak she wouldn't be able to hear a word he said. Her hand jerked away from the three-inch opening and she shouted at the top of her lungs, surprising Cyril and making him take several steps backward.

"SHUT UP! ALL OF YOU! NOW LAY DOWN!"

Instantly, the barking ceased. Cyril squinted at the window and suddenly the hand returned.

"Hazel, my name is Cyril Bankstrom. I live down by the lake. I just stopped by to make sure—"

"YOU have no business here! You stay away from here! I know all about you! GET, or I'll be fixing to let the dogs out!"

The window slammed shut with a final tight snap. Cyril backed away, shaken and confused. He turned and headed for home, his steps lengthening as the dogs started another round of savage yelping. He grabbed his axe handle, giving it a swift yank, and rested it over his shoulder. Nearing the cabin, his pace slowed and his body began to slump as an old, familiar sadness relentlessly pressed in.

******

The remaining two weeks of July went by in a blur. The three camps kept taking turns helping each other get cleaned out from the storm. Eva was often amazed at how hard Datus could work during the day, and also how friendly he was. But by late afternoon he would become irritable and short tempered, reminding Eva of her father. She silently tolerated Datus during his good moods simply because she had to, but by the end of the day her anger would swell and she couldn't stand to look at him or be around him.

After the camps were cleaned up, Eva and Cyril worked on her path, during which time he taught her how to use an axe and a chainsaw safely. For Eva, it felt great to be free from everyone and once again have Cyril to herself. He was a constant, happy reminder of how she would live one day. She often felt foolish, but she couldn't stop herself from wishing and daydreaming that everything at camp would always stay the same—that Cyril would never get old and always be there for her.

On an autumn-cool August morning, Cyril and Eva were finishing the cleanup on her path when Eva noticed the branch that formed the archway had snapped off and was now lying in the middle of the trail. Over the idling noise of the chainsaw Eva looked at Cyril and shrugged her shoulders with a sad look. Cyril glanced down at the tree and while shaking his head, he returned her sad expression.

Eva revved the little saw and began slicing the gnarled apple tree into logs, three or four feet in length, while Cyril tossed and pushed them aside. When Eva came to the part that formed the arch she carefully cut off the curved branch and set it aside. She then turned the saw off, picked up the arched branch that was about seven feet , and smiled at Cyril.

"Do you think we can somehow wedge this in the crotch of that double pine tree by the road?" Eva asked, hopefully.

"I don't see why not. A little rope and a few long screws ought to do the trick. Sure, we can fix it," Cyril assured, walking over to examine the pine tree. "Tomorrow we'll take care of that and your archway will be back in place."

******

At first light the next morning, Cyril was headed down to the water's edge carrying a towel, binoculars and a heavy wool sweater. After drying off his Adirondack chair, he slipped the sweater on and settled back deeply into the curved seat.

"Hmm ... incredible!" he said quietly, just before taking a deep, refreshing breath. Wearing a serene grin, he took in every detail of the new morning: Rags of golden fog drifted about the peaks as the first fingers of light inched their way down the three shoulders of Whiteface Mountain. Loons laughed their haunting, echoing cackle from a distant bay. A beaver vanished and reappeared through curtains of shifting mist as it cruised by with a birch branch held sideways in its mouth. The sharp whistling sound of mallard wings told Cyril that the ducks were happy to feel the warm sun. And high above the cool, foggy shadows, he glassed a red-tailed hawk, gliding motionless in the warm thermals.

Cyril never tired of his morning show, feeling it was all new and different each day. Although he sat alone, he always felt he was viewing it with lots of company.

Turning his head to one side, he leaned forward slightly to better hear a distant sound out on the foggy lake. It was an intermittent creaking and it was straight out in front of him. He knew that sound. Someone was rowing. Just as Cyril pulled himself up out of the chair, the bow of a boat suddenly emerged, coming out of the thin mist like a wooden ghost. He noticed right away that it looked a lot like his boat, except that it was newly varnished and shimmering like crystal.

A small figure resembling a man was perched in the center seat. As he pulled on the oars slowly and rhythmically, he would occasionally check over one of his shoulders, glancing toward shore. Cyril could now hear the familiar sounds of oar blades dipping in and out of the water and, on the return stroke, the definite squeak of metal pins swiveling in their sockets. As the boat got closer, the oarsman gave a hard pull-stroke with his right arm and pushed in reverse with his left. The little boat turned immediately and Cyril could now plainly see that a young man was sitting in the boat. The oars were bobbing freely in the water as he sat hunched forward, looking in Cyril's direction.

"Good morning!" Cyril said in a welcoming tone.

"Good morning," answered a young voice.

"That's a beautiful boat you have there," Cyril commented.

"Thank you, it's my dad's ... but I'm working on building one myself. I rowed by last evening and noticed the guide boat over there," the young man said, pointing off to the left. "Is that yours?"

"Yes, it's mine. Quite old though ... maybe fifty or sixty years."

"Really?! Is there any record of who built it?"

"No idea," Cyril said. "There's no identifying tag. I guess it's a mystery boat. Do you know much about older guide boats?"

"Oh yes! I mean I know some. I've been researching the old builders for the last two years. I've been to the Adirondack Museum so many times they're getting tired of me. And my dad learned how to build them from one of the last master builders in Long Lake," he said in one continuous breath.

"Well then, would you be interested in looking at mine? Maybe you could identify it."

"I sure would!"

The young man wasted no time scrambling out of the tippy

boat. Landing in ankle-deep water, he pulled his boat far up on the sandy shore. He glanced up at Cyril's cabin for a moment and then looked Cyril right in the eye and held out his hand.

"My name's Jared Cole. It's nice to meet you, especially a fellow guide boat owner."

"It's very nice to meet you, Jared. My name's Cyril Bankstrom."

Jared was in such a hurry to look at Cyril's boat that their handshake turned into a walking stretch. On the few short steps over, Jared once again looked up toward Cyril's camp and then quickly focused on the wooden craft lying upside down on two weather-beaten sawhorses.

"Well, it definitely has the sweep of the builders of the Fulton Chain of Lakes region," Jared said, pointing. He then slid his hand down the side, counting out loud. "Eight planks per side, that's another indication of it coming out of a Southern Adirondack shop. Can we turn it over?"

"Certainly," Cyril said, walking to the other end of the boat. "On three. Ready. One, two, three."

When the fifty-five pound boat flipped upright, Jared walked to the middle of the sixteen footer and began running his hands over the rounded, smooth ribs.

"Wow! I just love these old boats. It sure is a beauty!" Jared said with a look of amazement. "It looks like a Grant or Parsons. Have you ever taken the yoke cleats off?"

"No, I've always just varnished around them," Cyril admitted. "But I probably should've taken them off."

"Parsons and Grant would always stamp their name and the year they built it on the underside of the cleat. If these are the original yoke cleats then we might be able to solve your mystery," Jared said excitedly.

"Well, it looks like an antique, that's for sure," Cyril said.

"Oh! Did you happen to notice the cracked gunwale on the other side? It was damaged by that huge storm we had several weeks ago."

Jared quickly rounded to the other side and leaned in close to access the damage like a doctor examining a patient.

"Broken in two places. Hmm. You're going to need a new gunwale to keep it traditional but a quick fix would be to make a long scarph and splice in a piece of cherry with epoxy. That should get you through the rest of the summer, I would think," Jared surmised.

"I was planning on taking it to Robbie Frenette's guide boat shop in Tupper Lake for repair; but if you're interested, would you like the job, Jared?"

"Really?! I could do it. No problem, I help my father in the shop all the time."

Cyril smiled. "Well, that settles it then."

But Jared was looking past him in the direction of the cabin again. Cyril was about to turn around when Jared said, "Someone's sitting on your porch steps, and he's been there since I arrived."

Cyril turned and looked up toward the camp.

"Eva!" Cyril shouted, waving his arm. "Good morning! Come down and meet Jared. He knows all about guide boats."

"Oh ... she's a girl," Jared said under his breathe. "You won't tell her, will you?"

Cyril chuckled. "No, no, your secret's safe with me."

Begrudgingly, Eva forced herself off the steps and slowly made her way down the hill. She wondered who this Jared person was and was hoping if she sat long enough he would just go away. She had plans with Cyril today and wasn't expecting any distractions. As she got closer she sighed heavily and mumbled to herself, "Oh great, he looks about my age." Eva always had a hard time connecting with people, especially people her age. At school, boys often made fun of her, but mostly they just avoided her or laughed behind her back. The label placed on Eva as being *different* began in middle school and the cloud followed her into high school.

She was relieved to see that Cyril and Jared were engrossed in the boat and not looking at her when she arrived. She stopped and stood about ten feet away as Jared was talking nonstop while pointing at different areas of the boat.

"Eva, I believe we've found someone to fix our boat!" Cyril said with a ring of excitement in his voice. "This is Jared Cole. Jared, this is Eva Robinson, a very dear friend of mine."

Eva could feel her face getting warm. Her eyes found the ground and she was just about to walk forward when Jared hustled right over, grabbed her hand and vigorously shook it.

"Hi, nice to meet you. Hey! Your hands are all callused. Does that mean you like to row?" Jared asked with a gleam in his eyes.

"Um, nice to meet you too," Eva said quietly. "Yes ... I row, but I haven't lately."

She felt her face go from warm to very hot as she wrung her hands together, wishing she could hide them. She then looked over at Cyril.

"We've been working in the woods with an axe and chainsaw. That's why my hands are like this," she said shyly.

"You're allowed to use a chainsaw?" Jared asked. "My dad won't let me go near one, not until I'm seventeen. He watches me like a hawk, thinks I'm going to break or something. He does let me use the boat tools, but he has to demonstrate about a gazillion times before I can touch them."

"Your dad sounds a lot like my mom," Eva said, turning and smiling at Cyril.

"Worrywart too, huh?" Jared said nonchalantly. "My mom's

the calm one, thank God for that! It took my mom a whole year to talk my dad into letting me get my driver's license when I turned sixteen. He was going to have me wait till I was eighteen! Can you believe it?"

Eva grinned and shook her head in disbelief. When she slipped her hands inside the pockets of her hooded sweatshirt, she embarrassingly noticed that she and Jared were dressed alike in blue jeans, hooded sweatshirts and baseball hats.

Jared walked back over to the boat and continued his examination. His hands were sliding over each plank and he was bent in half with his face so close to the wood that Eva thought he was trying to listen to it. She walked over and rested her arm on the stern deck.

"An oar broke too. Do you think that can be fixed also?" Eva asked in a surer voice.

Jared's head popped out of the boat. "No band-aiding that one," he said. "If you try splicing and gluing an oar it might last a day or two. Rowing would snap it apart pretty quick."

He returned to the boat inspection until music started playing in his pocket. Eva watched him frown before pulling out the phone. He studied the front of it for a second and then looked at Eva, shaking his head with upturned eyes.

"My father—what a wonderful surprise! Excuse me a minute," Jared said.

He turned and walked into the low sun, casting a long, slender shadow on the golden sand. In a daze, Eva's eyes followed him until she remembered Cyril was behind her. When she shyly looked at Cyril, he averted his eyes, lifted the oar and cleared his throat.

"We won't need a new oar, Eva. I have a spare up in the ceiling rafters at camp," Cyril said, studying the oar.

Eva gave another quick glance at Jared and said, "Oh …

that's good."

Jared was talking and pacing back and forth when suddenly Eva heard the familiar snap of a closing cell phone. She peeked over her shoulder and saw that he was coming back, taking hurried strides and wearing a slight frown.

"Well, I need to get going. I kind of forgot I was supposed to watch my little sister this morning. My parents are going into town today, and Wendy ...," Jared paused and grimaced, shaking his head. "She's five and, well, mostly, she's a problem. She gets into all my mom's clothes and makeup—a real nuisance right now. My mom says it's just a phase but she's driving us all crazy. Oh, Mr. Bankstrom, I talked to my father about your guide boat, and he said he'd like to see it too." And then, kicking the sand, and looking a little depleted, Jared added, "But I think he just wants to make sure I can handle the job."

"I'm sure you'll do a great repair job, Jared. I have full confidence in you. And please call me Cyril."

"Okay, Cyril! Thank you," Jared said with a smile snapping back into his cheeks.

"I'd like to get started today," Jared continued, now in a businesslike voice. "That is, if I can get away from the little pest ... I mean Wendy. I just need to throw all my tools in a bucket. Let's see, I'll need to make a list. Don't want to forget anything."

Jared was still talking while he slid his boat out into the lake. He gracefully settled into the middle seat, turned and glanced at Cyril and then looked directly at Eva.

"It was nice to meet you both. I'll be back later today or early tomorrow," he said while making the water swirl with his left oar blade.

"Bye. it was nice to meet you too," Eva said.

"Goodbye, Jared. We'll see you soon and thank you very much," Cyril said, waving.

The boat was slipping away rapidly when Jared swiftly grabbed both oar handles with his right hand, and with his other waved back at Cyril and Eva.

It took Jared only five good pulls on the long whippy maple oars and he disappeared silently around the point.

"Well, that's good. Now you have a repairman for the boat," Eva said matter-of-factly.

"Yes, we're fortunate," Cyril agreed. "Seems like a very nice young man and so knowledgeable and excited about guide boats. It's nice to see in this day of plastic boats. Why, for every wooden boat I see nowadays, I'll see twenty plastic boats of every color."

Eva didn't flinch as Cyril talked. She was staring at the sand and hadn't heard a word he said. She couldn't believe she actually met someone who liked guide boats, and, as it seemed, the mountains. And more than once she astonishingly repeated aloud to herself, "And he's so easy to talk to."

When a loon cackled and brought Eva to the present moment, she looked up to find Cyril grinning at her with his arms crossed.

"So, did you still want to fix the archway today?" Eva said quickly.

"Certainly. And maybe we can start the cleanup on my trail. I'm so glad to hear after your hike last week that very few trees were down. I can't imagine trying to clean out five miles of trails. But before we head out, how about we start off with a big stack of blueberry pancakes first?" Cyril suggested as they walked up the small incline to the cabin.

"That sounds really good," Eva agreed. "As long as I get to cook this time. You know, I'm finally starting to like cooking, but you can't let my mother know. She'll want to have this mother-daughter baking time together and we already tried that and it didn't work out—at all."

"Okay, I won't say a thing. And I'll gladly stay out of the kitchen. It'll give me time to give the chainsaw a good sharpening. Now, you know where everything is, right?"

"Yup, I do," Eva said with an affirmative nod.

Eva stopped short on the first porch step and Cyril almost bumped into her.

"Cyril, I've never seen Jared on the lake before. Have you?"

"No. This is his first time here. He told me he'll be staying for about two weeks. His family rented a camp on Stickney Point. He said if his mom likes it, they might even stay until school starts, which I think he said is in three weeks."

Eva really liked the idea that Jared might be here for the rest of summer vacation. She dreaded the thought of summer ending and going back to school, but quickly reminded herself that if she kept working hard she would graduate early and be off to forestry school at Paul Smith's College at the age of seventeen.

Eva buzzed around the kitchen with a newfound energy that she couldn't quite understand. In no time the little cabin took on the fresh aroma of warm pancakes. When she heard his heavy boots coming up the stairs, Eva called out in a singing voice that stopped him right in his tracks. "Fresh blueberry pancakes! Come and get it! Don't be late or Mr. Bear might take your plate!"

Cyril entered cautiously and wide-eyed, looked at Eva and then over to his little table.

"You have a very nice singing voice, Eva! And judging by the smell and look of those golden flapjacks, you're a very fine cook also."

With her arms behind her back, Eva smiled broadly as she too admired the two large stacks of perfect pancakes.

Chapter 6

Fixing the archway was an easy enough chore. Cyril used rope and a screw gun to anchor the limb into the crotch of a pine tree. When they finished, they crossed the road to see how it looked. It wasn't the same as the twisted apple tree, but it did the job, making the entrance to Eva's trail visible and easier to find once again. While they stood in Eva's front yard admiring their work, Cyril slipped off his pack and walked over to sit on Eva's porch steps. When Eva turned around he was holding his right side and looking tired.

"You alright, Cyril?" Eva asked, coming to sit beside him.

"Oh yes. Just need a little sit-break, that's all."

Cyril started his usual whistling but Eva noticed right away it wasn't his usual smooth tone.

"I see the car's gone. Has your mom gone to town?" Cyril asked.

Eva grimaced and stood up quickly.

"Um, no, well sort of. She's gone to see … my dad. She goes once a week, sometimes twice," Eva said heavily.

"Oh, I see," Cyril said. "Will she be gone long?"

"No, she's usually back around three or four. Did you want to head up your trail and start cleaning things out now?" Eva asked, changing the subject. "I didn't take a count on my last walk, but I know there're not many trees to cut. I wonder why the storm didn't affect that area very much."

"I think the most powerful winds hit only certain areas for some odd reason," Cyril said, shrugging his shoulders.

Eva quickly started out and in no time was way ahead of Cyril. She slowed and checked for him often but by the time she reached the balsam and pine forest where the bench was, Cyril was no longer behind her. *He said he was fine*, she reminded herself as she sat down on the bench. Before she let herself get too worried, she spied his white head slowly coming up the trail and then he stopped and turned around.

"Cyril," she called out, jogging toward him.

He turned around and smiled weakly at her. He was rising up and down with each fast breath.

"You're not alright," Eva scolded, taking the chainsaw out of his hands. "You've been working too hard lately. That must be it, right?"

Cyril only smiled as Eva helped him over to the bench. He sat down heavily and put his hands on his knees.

For a moment, Eva stood with her hands on her hips nervously watching him before she too sat down.

"That's it, right? You're not used to all this work. It's because of the storm, isn't it?" Eva asked, trying to convince herself that Cyril wasn't getting old.

As Eva skeptically watched him, she was relieved to see his

breathing return to normal along with the sparkle in his blue eyes.

"You're absolutely right, Eva. I've been working much too hard lately. That must be it. I guess I need more rest and I probably shouldn't push myself such long hours."

"That's right," Eva enthusiastically agreed. "Now, I'll carry the saw and we'll take our time back to camp where you can rest and from now on we'll only do little sections at a time, okay?"

Cyril smiled sheepishly and nodded.

The long walk back to camp was slow with many rest breaks. Eva kept switching the heavy chainsaw from one hand to the other. She had plenty of time to convince herself that Cyril was really okay and that he would be his old self in no time. *It's just because of that stupid storm,* Eva kept repeating over and over in her mind. But by the time they reached Cyril's home, Eva was worried again, remembering how much younger and stronger he was last summer.

As Cyril trudged up the porch steps, Eva's thoughts switched to Jared and she wondered if he would return today. She turned and scanned out over the breezy lake, looking north and south, but there was nothing moving on the lake except small rolling waves that were sparkling in the late morning sun.

"Would you like to come in, Eva?" Cyril offered, turning to face her from the top step.

"No thank you. I'm kind of tired too. I think I'll go down to the beach for a while and sit in your chair, if that's okay."

"Of course. And why don't you take the binoculars with you? You might spot Charlie or a deer feeding on the other side of the lake."

"Thanks. I'll come in and get them so you don't have to go back and forth. And as I learned from that awful storm, someone should know where you are when you go in the woods, so if

I'm not here when you wake up, I'll be doing a little more work on your path later. I know I can't use the chainsaw alone but I have a good handsaw."

"Eva, if you do any cutting—"

"I know, I know—take my time and work slow," Eva said, smiling. "Well, I hope you feel better after your rest."

"Thank you. I'm sure I will. Right now I feel like I could sleep for a week."

"Bye," Eva said, jumping off the porch steps.

"Goodbye, Eva."

As Eva long-stepped down the bluff, her eyes scanned up and down the lake searching for a shiny guide boat. When she reached Cyril's chair in the sand she slid in and lost herself in the reflected panorama. Adjusting her hat lower to shield out the sun, she raised the binoculars to her eyes every few seconds, trying to make herself look busy in case Jared came back. She sat for almost two hours. She dozed off for twenty minutes and then spent most of an hour glassing a beaver further up the lake chewing endlessly at the base of a large poplar tree. Her stomach was growling, so reluctantly she decided to go back to camp for lunch and then work on Cyril's trail for a couple of hours.

She shuffled along, making her way up the small grade to Cyril's porch, glancing back at the lake from time to time. Tentatively resting one foot on the first porch step, she grabbed the metal handrail and leaned in toward the camp, listening for any sound that would indicate Cyril was up and about. After a minute of silence, she slowly stepped down and slouched away toward the small stand of birch trees. Again, she thought of Cyril and couldn't help worrying, and then her thoughts drifted to Jared. She kept plodding along and thinking, her mind racing as usual. *Where does he live? He seems really nice. What grade is he in? Does he have a girlfriend? He likes camp and guide boats, like me. I wonder if he's going to college?* And then she dreamily thought, *Maybe he'll go to my college.*

Eva snapped out of her trance and whirled around when she heard a little voice down by the lake, but the only word she could make out was, "lipstick." Then, a reprimanding, deeper voice echoed from the lake, "Wendy! You don't own lipstick. That has to be Mom's."

Eva started to run back, but as soon as she got to the wild-flowers she abruptly composed herself and began walking casually down the hill. When she reached the shore, Jared was lifting Wendy out of the boat.

"Hi, Eva. I decided to come back today. I just *had* to find out who the builder of this boat is," Jared said. "I just hope something's written under the cleats."

Wading alongside the boat in shallow water, Jared reached in and lifted Wendy out of her seat and plopped her down in the sand. "Oh, Eva, this is Wendy, my little sister. And Wendy, this is Eva."

"Hi, Wendy. It's very nice to meet you," Eva said, stepping forward.

But Wendy said nothing and inched around the back of her big brother's leg. Her half-hidden face stared back at Eva from behind Jared's thigh, and from what Eva could see she didn't look very happy.

"She's always like this at first," Jared said, shaking his head. "In about two minutes you'll know what she sounds like, believe me." And then Jared said in a not-so-low voice, "Nonstop chatterbox."

Eva grinned and looked down at Wendy. Hanging down below her bright-red life jacket was a pink dress that just covered her knees. Frilly white and pink socks were sticking out of shiny black shoes. Black too, was her hair, wavy and long, and her eyes were bright blue. Eva thought she was the cutest little girl she had ever seen.

Eva glanced at Jared and then back to Wendy. "It's very easy to see you two are brother and sister. You look so much alike," Eva said without thinking.

"Hear it all the time, don't we squirt?" Jared said, nudging Wendy away from his leg.

Wendy looked at Eva shyly, then walked around to the front of Jared and put her hands on her hips.

"I'm a girl! Girls don't look like boys and I'm gonna tell Mom you called me a chatterbox!" Wendy cried.

"Hmm, sweet isn't she?" Jared said with a tight smile and glaring eyes.

"Yes! She is sweet," Eva said defensively. "And I'm sorry, Wendy. You're right, girls don't look like boys, and that's a really pretty dress you have on."

"Well, anyway," Jared said impatiently, "I brought some sand toys for you, Wendy, so why don't you go play for a while?"

"I bring my baby. She's in my pack-pack and she's probably hungry," Wendy said in her developing English. "Yes, she's crying. I can hear her. You left her in the boat, Jared! Can you get her?"

"How about you first ask me nicely, Wendy, and remember that word you always seem to forget? It begins with the letter 'P'."

Wendy frowned at Eva before kicking Jared's foot. "Jared!" she snarled through clenched teeth.

Jared folded his arms and started humming while Wendy stubbornly stared at the sand with an occasional half-glare toward Eva. The silence lingered on for a long minute. Eva thought Jared was being too strict and was just beginning to feel bad for Wendy when he cleared his throat and looked down at her.

"Pleeease," Wendy said, tugging on Jared's pant leg.

Jared stopped humming, waded over to the far end of the boat and retrieved a small pink backpack that had doll legs sticking out of the top. He handed it to Wendy, but held on tight.

"Thank you," Wendy said. She scowled, pulling the pack sharply from her brother's hands and ran off.

"Well, that was fun!" Jared said sarcastically. "And lucky me gets to spend most of the day with her. Now, I'd like to get those yoke cleats off and hopefully there's a name and date stamped on the underside. Eva, do you know if Cyril's home?" Jared looked toward the cabin. "He'll be interested if I find something."

"Yes, but I'm pretty sure he's sleeping. We tried to do some work on the trails today, but I think he's been working too hard lately," Eva said, also looking toward the cabin. "He's usually always so strong."

"Well, after his nap we might have some very interesting information for him," Jared said with a quick nod. He grabbed a bucket that was toppling over with tools from the center of his boat and slogged through the soft sand over to Cyril's boat.

"Could you please help me turn it over, Eva? I have to work kind of fast," Jared said, hand-motioning toward Wendy with rolling eyes. "She'll be bugging me soon enough and I'll probably have to take her home."

"I can try to keep her occupied while you work," Eva offered, grabbing her end of the boat. "I don't mind."

Jared and Eva were both bent over, each clasping an end of the boat, staring at each other. Jared shook his head and chuckled at Eva.

"We'll flip it to the left, okay?" he said, smirking and laughing. "On three ... ready?" The wooden antique spun around and landed with a soft thud on the sawhorses.

"What's so funny?" Eva asked.

"She's a handful! If you're not used to her she could make you crazy," Jared warned, his eyes bulging, wearing a goofy expression. "But hey, if you want to give it a shot, I'd really appreciate it and that would give me more time to work."

"She can't be that bad. I have cousins—I know how to handle kids," Eva informed him.

"Be my guest," Jared said, gesturing toward Wendy with a slow one-arm sweep and an ear-to-ear grin.

"No problem," Eva said smugly.

Eva confidently walked away in the direction of Wendy with her head aloft and wearing a rather pleased look.

"Thank you, Eva! It shouldn't take me too long."

Wendy was perched on a weathered piece of driftwood, rocking gently back and forth. As Eva approached all she could see of little Wendy was her long black hair and the bottom of her puffy red life jacket.

There were foamy waves lapping noisily at the shore, but Eva could hear over them and as she got closer she realized Wendy was talking to herself in a hushed voice.

"Hi, Wendy! Is your baby better now?" Eva asked cheerfully. "I don't hear her crying anymore."

Wendy turned around quickly, pulling her life jacket closed. Eva planted herself down, cross-legged in the warm sand, right in front of Wendy.

"I know when I'm hungry I feel like crying too," Eva sympathized. "And right now I'm hungry because I haven't had any lunch yet. Have you, Wendy? I bet you're big enough to make your own lunch, aren't you?"

"I make peanut butter and jelly all by myself, but Jared made me mac 'n cheese today, 'cause that's all he knows how to make and Mom makes it better. Jared doesn't use the measure cups like Mom does. He just pours everything in. You want to hold my baby? I think she's done eating now," Wendy said breathlessly.

When Wendy opened her life jacket and brought her doll out, Eva's chin began to dance as she fought hard to keep a straight face, but she couldn't stop her belly from vibrating. Wendy handed her the doll and took off her life jacket.

"Her name's Katie and she only likes real food. That's why I have my boobs on," Wendy said casually.

Eva looked away and took a deep breath. "Oh, she's a beautiful baby, and she looks so much like you," Eva said in a jumpy voice. "Of course you're much older. It's a lot of work being a mom, isn't it?"

Wendy let out an exhausted breath. "Oh yes, phew! I only get a rest when she sleeps you know. Oops! I forgot to burp her! You can do it if you want but you have to hold her like this."

While Wendy demonstrated, Eva's eyes roamed over to Jared. He had tipped the boat up on its side and all she could see were his blue-jean legs.

"Now you try it, Eva, but don't pat her back too hard or she'll spit up all over you. Yuk. I hate when that happens!"

"WENDY!! YOU'RE NOT SUPPOSED TO HAVE MOM'S BRA ON!" Jared roared from under the boat. "I told you to take it off before we left!"

"How else Katie's s'posed to eat? She's only a baby, you know … geez!"

Eva turned away and looked out over the lake. She just couldn't hold it in any longer. She tried to pretend she was coughing but her eyes were watering with laughter.

Jared growled. "Yeah, she's real funny. You ought to spend all day with her!"

Eva composed herself and turned around to find Wendy singing to her doll and rocking it.

"Jared made her cry *again*," Wendy said heavily. "He does it all the time, you know, but she'll be okay in a minute."

"IT'S A PARSONS!" Jared announced, as if a newborn baby had just arrived. "R-RILEY! Built in 1904. I'll be damned!"

Wendy gaped open-mouthed at Eva with huge blue eyes, and then promptly turned to her doll and said in a hushed, motherly voice, "Is that a bad word, Katie? I think so! That's two times today!"

Wendy craned her neck up toward the sky. "I'M TELLING MOM YOU DID TWO BAD SWEAR WORDS!"

Jared ignored her as he twirled the yoke cleat in his hand, wearing an ear-to ear smile directed right at Eva.

"Wait till Cyril finds out," Jared said excitedly. "His boat's over a hundred years old!"

"Wendy, do you want to walk over with me and see what Jared's all excited about?" Eva asked, getting up and brushing the sand off her jeans.

Wendy reached in her pack and pulled out a yellow fleece blanket. "No, but you can go. I'm needing to get Katie to sleep anyway."

Eva walked off in the direction of Jared. The sun was high and warm but the air was cool and there was a steady, refreshing breeze coming from the south. Halfway to Jared, Eva glanced up toward Cyril's cabin, searching for any kind of movement. Everything was still except for the swaying wildflowers.

Jared was leaning against the gunwale looking at the yoke cleats with a puzzled expression.

"I guess I'll leave the cleats off for now," he said. "Cyril will want to see this with his own eyes. You know, Eva, this boat really needs other work. Does it leak when you first put it in the water?"

"Every time, but we just dump it out. After it's in for a day or two, it leaks a lot less. Cyril calls it 'tightening up,'" Eva said as she too leaned on a gunwale, opposite Jared.

"Hmm ... what this boat really needs, at some point, is a thorough restoration and the sooner the better," Jared said.

"I know Cyril's mentioned something this past summer about it needing a good overhaul," Eva said with her eyes glued on Jared's. But Jared's eyes were busy, wandering from one end of the boat to the other.

"Have you started building your boat?" Eva asked. "I imagine it's going to take a long time to make."

That question brought Jared's attention front and center, right to Eva.

"I have," Jared said proudly. "The bottom board and the stems are cut out—"

Jared suddenly leaned to Eva's right and looked over her shoulder.

"WENDY!" he yelled. "Where'd she go?! She was just there."

As Jared sprinted around the end of the boat, Eva whirled around just in time to see Wendy's little head pop up from behind the piece of driftwood that she was sitting on just seconds ago. Jared's leaps turned into a relieved walk as he took a deep breath and shook his head.

"What are you doing, Wendy?!" Jared scolded.

Wendy was sitting upright with a finger pressed tightly over her lips, wearing a deep frown.

"Katie's not wanting to take her nap, so I has to lay with her," Wendy said sternly, trying hard to whisper.

Jared took an exasperated breath and shook his head. "Alright ... but Wendy, you stay there. And don't leave that log unless you tell me, okay?"

Wendy reclined backward without answering her brother. Eva felt a smile growing on her face as she watched Wendy's head completely disappear from sight. Jared walked back, shaking his head with his hands waving through the air. At that exact moment she liked Jared even more. She saw that Jared complained about Wendy and seemed to have little patience with her, but Eva could plainly see that he cared deeply for her.

"You want a little sister, Eva ... free?" Jared asked with a hopeful smile.

"She's not that bad. I think your mom's right: It's probably just a stage she's going through."

"Yeah, I know, but she wears me out and she's not a good listener at all. And she's sneaky! Do you know she had that stuffed bra on all day? I finally got her to take it off just before we came. I turn my back for one second and she somehow got it back on, and then she grabbed the life jacket, knowing she could hide it. My parents are going to have to watch her closely when she gets older. She's tricky ... and smart!"

With an agreeing smile, Eva nodded her head while Jared pulled his phone out to check the time.

"Three-thirty," Jared said irritably. "We probably should get going. My dad's a little nervous about Wendy being in the boat, even though she has a life jacket on." Then Jared ordered, "Wendy! Get your things together. It's time to go."

"Eva, do you mind watching Wendy for just one more minute? I'd like to run these yoke cleats up to Cyril's house and put them on the porch. I wish I could see his face when he finds them. Hey, maybe I should leave a note for him to call me when he finds the cleats," Jared said as an afterthought.

"He can't," Eva said, shrugging. "He doesn't have a phone or anything electronic, not even a TV. He lives pretty simply."

"Wow!" exclaimed Jared, peering up at the cabin and then back to Eva.

"Do you stay with him during the summer?"

"No, I stay with my mom. We have a camp up on the main road," Eva said, pointing off to the left and past Cyril's camp. "You see that small stand of birch trees over there?"

"Yeah," Jared said, squinting.

"That's where my trail starts. Cyril and I made it when I was seven. It leads right up to the main road, and my camp's just on the other side."

"Are you staying for the rest of—?" Jared's phone started to ring, stopping him in mid-sentence. "Stupid phone. I'd like to throw it in the lake! Hmm, I wonder who it could be," he said sarcastically.

He walked over toward Wendy, and Eva could hear him answering an array of parental questions before ending with a glum goodbye. Since Wendy hadn't listened to him earlier, he impatiently helped her pack up her things.

Eva was thinking about a lot of things at the moment but mostly she was secretly relieved that Jared only seemed to get phone calls from his parents. She walked over with a spring in her step and knelt down in the sand at eye level to Wendy.

"You're a really good mom, Wendy! And the next time you come ..." Eva paused because Jared was shaking his head "no." She frowned at him and looked right back at Wendy. "Maybe we could take Katie for a walk in my stroller. I have one on my porch, where I live right now. It was mine when I was five years old."

"I'm five! But I'll be this many on ..."

Wendy frowned. She was holding six fingers up, and at the same time looking at her big brother for help.

"September tenth," Jared said abruptly. "Wendy, we better get you in the boat. Dad probably has the binoculars out, looking for us right now."

He lifted her into the boat and gently put her pack on her lap. He then sloshed back through the water toward Eva.

"Thanks, Eva. I'm glad you were here." And then in a hushed voice, Jared said, "But I won't be bringing *her* again ... no way. I have to work on the boat."

"That's okay. But if you have to bring her, I don't mind watching her. Really, she's no trouble at all."

Jared raised his eyebrows. "No trouble at all, right, yeaaaah. Well anyway, thanks for the nice offer."

"I have to go right by Cyril's so I can put those cleats on his porch for you," Eva offered.

"Thanks. That would be great. Hey, Eva! Do you have a phone that Cyril could use? Oh, that doesn't matter anyway because I'll be over first thing tomorrow to get started on the repair and I can talk to him then."

"I do have a phone, but it's at camp. It's charging right now."

"Are we going now? You've been talking forever, Jared!" Wendy said, wiggling in her seat and trying to stand up.

"Yes, Princess Wendy, we're going right now. But sit back down so I can push the boat out."

Jared handed the yoke cleats to Eva. "I'll see you tomorrow, I mean—that's if you're at Cyril's tomorrow," he said awkwardly.

"I'll probably be here," Eva said. "I usually spend most of the day with Cyril."

Jared lifted his tool bucket out of the sand and gently put it down in the center of the boat. He pushed the boat out and carefully lowered himself into his seat.

"Oh! I almost forgot. My dad said it's okay for you and Cyril to use this boat while I'm working on Cyril's. I think I'll only need a few days to fix it anyway, so you won't be without a boat too long," Jared yelled.

"Thank you, and I'll let Cyril know. Bye, Wendy, it was nice to meet you ... and Katie too," Eva yelled back.

Wendy's little arm rose out from her ballooning red life jacket and whirled in the air. Jared stopped rowing and held both oars in one hand while waving back at Eva, exactly like he had done earlier in the day.

Eva turned slowly and started up toward Cyril's cabin. She didn't realize a wide smile was etched on her face until she bumped into the porch railing. Suddenly remembering Cyril, her smile fell as she quietly walked up on the porch and peeked through the window. He was still in bed, curled up on his side, the back of his white head showing brightly in the dim room. She stood the yoke cleats against the door casing and glanced one more time before lightly heading down the stairs. When her foot hit the bottom rung, her thoughts crossed to her mother who was sure to be back by now, and Eva's good mood suddenly faded into anger.

Every time her mother returned from visiting her father, Eva had to listen while her mother talked endlessly about how sad he was and how she wished Eva would visit or write him. Eva always felt bad, but in no time she would speedily remind herself the of same thing she always repeated to herself: *He was hardly ever around, he's mean, and he didn't care if I was home or gone, and now he's killed someone with his stupid drinking.* She further convinced herself by adding, *And besides, he's not my real father anyway.* Eva cleared her determined, guilt-ridden mind almost instantly. She could rearrange and adjust incoming thoughts so fast; it was as though they were never there.

Before heading back to camp she looked out over the water and thought of Jared. She then thought of college, knowing very soon she would finally be completely away from all her problems. Her spirits lifted and she marched right up her trail and into her camp and gave her mom a jovial hello. While her mom rambled on about her father, Eva sat patiently, wearing a blank expression. She pretended to listen but her mind crisscrossed between Jared, college, camp, and then back to Jared.

Chapter 7

Eva woke very early the next morning, thoughts of yesterday replaying. She tossed and turned in the half-darkness, wrapping her pillow tightly around her head, trying to block out the bird's singing, which she thought sounded extra loud and annoying this morning.

She knew Cyril would be up and she wanted to see how he was feeling, so she forced herself out of bed and headed straight for the kitchen for a bowl of cereal. After her shower she found herself fussing with her hair in front of the mirror, something she rarely did and wasn't very good at. Her hair was thick and hung down to her lower back. She brushed it off to the left and then turned her head side-to-side as her eyes stayed in one place, glued to the mirror. She then flipped it over to the right and did the same thing. Frowning slightly, she bent over and with a big upright "swoosh," her flaming hair flew behind her. She parted it down the middle and then gave the mirror another thorough evaluation. Sighing with shrinking shoulders, she stared blankly ahead trying to envision how French braids would look on her. Eva liked the idea, but she didn't know how to do it. Her mother knew, but Eva wasn't about to ask. She knew all too well the many questions she would have to answer.

Tight-faced, her brown eyes roamed from her freckles to her bright orange hair, and, as usual, she didn't like what she saw. When she was ten she tried to scrub her freckles off with a cleaning pad, and she always wished her hair was any other color except red.

Leaning in closer to the mirror with wrinkled eyebrows, she whispered out loud, "This isn't you." And then, frustrated, she quickly braided up her standard ponytail and grabbed her baseball hat off the edge of the sink. With skilled hands, Eva looped her hair through the hole in the back of her hat and pulled and twisted the brim down until the front rim was touching her brow. She tipped her head back to see her eyes and gave the mirror an approving nod. "There! That's better."

Eva scribbled a note and left it on the kitchen table. She walked softly around the creaky spots on the floor and slid sideways and silently out the front door. The morning air was damp and cool and the woods were dimly lit in hues of greenish-blue. A thin patch of ground fog hovered above the front lawn where thousands of crystal-clear dew drops hung heavily from arching blades of uncut grass. When Eva glanced skyward she noticed the very tops of the tallest trees were glowing fiery-orange by the first light.

Before entering the woods she paused and lent an ear toward the witch's home. She stood squinting in silence for many seconds, her breathing the only sound. She was about to start off when a loon's repetitive cackle echoed up from the lake. A relieved smile relaxed across her face. Pushing a small branch aside she bolted down her path and didn't stop until she was standing on Cyril's porch.

She tipped her hat straight up and leaned her forehead against the cool glass while knocking gently on the door frame. Her eyes roamed the quiet interior of the small room. Not a sound. She saw that his red-checkered bed was made up perfectly and she realized he was not home. Leaning back she eyed his birch-bark sign on the door. The acorn was sticking out of hole number two. She turned around quickly to face the lake and instantly spotted the back of his snow-white head down by the beach.

Cyril was sitting on a stump with his hands resting on his knees. The sun had just peeked over the treetops, and just beyond him was a diamond-strewn sun lane that cut across the misty lake and ended at his feet. His body was arrow-straight and statue-still. Eva didn't want to startle him so she walked down slowly and quietly. She thought Cyril would hear her feet any minute, but he remained motionless.

"Cyril?" she said quietly from a few feet away.

There was no answer, so Eva poked her head around and saw his eyes were closed and he was wearing a very tranquil grin. "Cyril?" she said a little louder.

"Oh, Eva! I didn't hear you. Good morning!" Cyril said, spinning stiffly around to face her.

"Good morning ... what were you ... I'm sorry, were you sleeping?" Eva asked timidly.

"No, I was just taking a moment to empty things out," Cyril said, casually tapping his forehead. "But the best part is after, when I get to fill myself up!" he said boisterously, this time tapping his chest.

Frowning slightly, Eva's head tilted as she watched a placid smile stretch across Cyril's face.

"Fill yourself up … with what?" she asked.

"God," he said simply. "And peace. Can't have one without the other," Cyril said, chuckling.

"Oh, is that like praying?" Eva asked. "Because I can come back later."

"No, no, I'm all done. And yes, it's a bit like praying, but much easier, mainly, because you don't have to do very much. You just have to get your mind very quiet, like it's frozen, and then, in that perfect stillness, God will come and visit you. I've just never been able to find God in my noisy head, but He sure is in here," Cyril said with his hand lightly thumping his chest.

Eva gave Cyril a nodding, yet unsure smile and turned her head slowly and looked out over the lake. She was used to Cyril occasionally talking about God, but it never bothered her. His words sometimes confused her, but as long as he remained the same, reliable Cyril that she had always known, she didn't care what he talked about.

Cyril slapped his hands together heartily. "And you, Eva dear! What's on your agenda today?"

"Well, a whole bunch of things. First, do you feel better?"

"Yes, I feel much better today, thank you."

"Good! Second, did you find the yoke cleats on the porch this morning?"

"I did! And what a surprise. 1904! The boat's older than me!"

"And last, did you have any plans for today? Because Jared said we could use his father's guide boat while he's working on yours. He's coming back sometime today," Eva said quickly.

"Well that's very nice of him … but you know, Eva, I was just thinking of my hike this morning and how much I miss it. I thought I would take a handsaw and do a little cleanup work along the way, but mostly I would just like to take a nice slow walk, all the way around, if I feel well enough. You're welcome to come. Oh, wait a minute! I probably shouldn't go too far. It just occurred to me that Jared might need something ... and I'm not sure if his tools require electricity."

"Oh ... yeah," Eva said, turning away deep in thought. "Um ...hmm ... you could still go on your walk. I could stay here. I know where all the lead cords are if he needed power. I don't mind, really."

"Are you sure, Eva? I don't want to interfere with any plans you have today."

"It's no problem at all," Eva insisted.

"Thank you, Eva. It's going to be so nice to get back on my walk. And the best part is I finally feel better. Sleeping for two days straight sure did the trick."

Cyril leaned forward and stiffly raised himself from the stump. Eva heard a few cracks and pops as he twisted and stretched.

"I guess I've been sitting there longer than I thought," he said, arching backward.

"Were you down here in the dark?" Eva asked.

Cyril reached in his shirt pocket and pulled out a small flash-light. He grinned at Eva, blinking the dull beam twice in her eyes. "Yes, it was pretty dark when I arrived, but the moon and stars were out; beautiful morning, just magnificent!"

Eva looked around and saw that he was right. The lake looked like dark-blue glass and the woods were as still as a painting, and the only sound she could hear were the echoing voices of two fishermen sitting back-to-back in a tiny aluminum boat close to the opposite shore over a mile away.

"It's so still and quiet," Eva said, amazed.

"Yes it is!" Cyril agreed. "It's going to be a perfect day! Well, I'd better get packed up and hit the trail. As you know, it's much more enjoyable to hike in the cool morning air."

"It's the best time to hike; as you always told me, the woods are just waking up and everything is new and fresh."

They walked back up to Cyril's camp in silence. When they came to the porch, Cyril invited Eva inside so he could show her where the toolbox was kept. Sliding the big box out from under the bench, he sorted through the bottom and pulled out two huge lead cords. Eva noticed the letters "W.B." stamped deeply into the long wooden handle. She was just about to ask what they meant when Cyril interrupted her thoughts.

"If these aren't enough, there are two more lead cords hanging on the porch. I can't think of anything else Jared might need, but the camp will be open, and you know where everything is so you should be all set," he said, giving a last look around the bench.

"Yeah, and he's bringing a lot of tools with him. You should've seen the bucketful he had yesterday. It looked heavy," Eva said. "Oh, I almost forgot! Jared said your boat really needs a complete restoration and the sooner the better. He also said it shouldn't leak when you put it in—something about the water slowly rotting the wood away."

"Yes, yes I know," Cyril said glumly. "I've been very delinquent in the care of my boat. It's time. I won't put it off any longer. This fall I'll bring it in for a full restoration, or maybe Jared or his father would like the job?"

"I can ask Jared for you," Eva offered excitedly. "I mean ... if you want me to ... or you probably want to talk to him yourself," she said, slightly embarrassed.

"That would be fine. You can ask him today and then he can talk it over with his father later."

"OK," Eva said brightly. "Um, Cyril?"

"Yes," he said, looking up from loading his basket.

"I'm going to go back to camp for a while. It's so early, but in an hour or so can I come back and sit on your porch, just in case—"

"Of course you can! My house is your house. You know that. You make yourself right at home here. If you weren't here to help Jared I wouldn't be able to take my walk today," Cyril said, winking.

"You're welcome. Well, I guess I'll get going. Mom asked me to mow the lawn today, but most likely she's already finished the job. She can't sit still for a minute, except when she's reading one of her five-pound novels. That's the only thing that slows her down."

Cyril followed Eva to the porch. She jumped all three steps, then whirled around and waved.

"Goodbye, Eva."

"Bye Cyril."

Eva was in a hurry to get the lawn mowed and return back to Cyril's porch, where she could keep an eye out for Jared. She really liked the idea of the porch. That way she could see Jared first and it didn't look like she was waiting for him by the lake. She went up her trail with long, quick strides, head down, in deep concentration. When her racing thoughts stopped at her hair and clothes, her pace slackened and she grimaced, wondering what she could do about them. She really didn't want to change anything, but she couldn't help thinking that Jared viewed her as just another tomboy.

And then Eva got mad, thinking, *Why do I have to change for anybody?* She really wanted to be strong and free like Cyril and not need anyone. Suddenly she was talking out loud as she poked along, picking at the foliage. "Everything was fine before he got here. I like my hair just the way it is, and anyway, he'll be leaving in a few weeks and I'll probably never see him again."

She shuffled along, head even lower, with eyebrows almost touching each other in a frown. A few steps later, she was mentally arguing with herself. *We both like camp and the woods and guide boats, and his family seems nice, and he's so easy to talk to—how could he not have a girlfriend? He probably hates freckles and red hair...* When she reached the paved road, her jumbling thoughts disappeared and she was left with one very clear vision: Jared smiling at her as he held up the yoke cleat.

"Well, there you are!" Ann called through the screen door. "What time did you get up, Miss Early Bird?"

"It was dark, that's all I know, and speaking of birds! It sounded like they were singing into a megaphone. They were so loud! And since when do they sing in the dark?" Eva asked, breezing by her mother and into the camp.

Ann backed away and crossed her arms.

"What's wrong, Eva? What are you mad at?"

Eva was nosing around in the refrigerator, staring at a milk carton when she yelled back, "Nothing!"

After a minor argument with her mother about waiting for the grass to dry before mowing, Eva gave in and told her mom she would wait and mow it later. Eva was turning to go but her mom pushed a spray can in her hand with a soft white cloth wrapped around it.

"You dust and I'll sweep. I need your help pushing this furniture around anyway," Ann said, gliding around the room with her broom in overdrive.

"Mom?"

"What?" Ann said, not looking up.

"You know how to do French braids, don't you?"

"Yes, I can do them. Why do you ask?"

Ann's broom downshifted into low gear.

"I was just wondering, that's all," Eva said, shrugging her

shoulders.

While Eva turned away and sprayed the white cloth, she heard the broom and her mother's quick footsteps suddenly stop. When she peeked back at her mom, Ann was staring at her with an odd look on her face and Eva knew more questions were on the way.

"Did you want to learn how ... for yourself?" Ann asked.

"No, but I was just thinking that maybe I'll do something different with my hair, you know, besides my ponytail."

"Really?" Ann said, lifting herself into a big smile. "Eva! I think that's wonderful. Your hair's beautiful when it's down. And French braids! Can we do it now? I'll get a brush." She darted toward the bathroom.

"MOM! Whoooaa! I just asked if you knew *how*. I didn't say I wanted them *now*."

"Oh, sorry, Eva. I just thought it would be nice. But of course, only when you're ready. You just let me know, okay? Anytime you want French braids or anything else, I'll be happy—"

"Mom! Okay ... good ... thank you," Eva said, rolling her eyes.

Ann slowly walked past her daughter, wearing what Eva thought was a very goofy-looking smile. Her eyes stayed locked on Eva's until she bumped into a small table and knocked a picture off the wall with the end of her broom handle. Frowning, Eva shook her head, turned away quickly and started wiping. She had one thing on her mind right now, and that was dusting very fast so she could get back down to the lake. She was also arranging the right words to tell her mom about her plans.

"I'm going to be at Cyril's most of the day," Eva said nonchalantly. "Cyril has someone coming to work on his boat today and I told Cyril I would be there in case he needs electricity or tools."

"Oh, look! There goes Cyril now," Ann said, tapping on the window.

Eva walked over, and Cyril waved back at both of them.

"He wants to do his walk, says he really misses it,so I offered to stay and help," Eva said with her chin held high.

"That's very nice of you! I'm proud of you, Eva. It feels good to help others, doesn't it? Especially someone like Cyril. He's been so good to us."

Eva felt a tinge of guilt settle in, and while she smiled innocently back, she watched her mother's face change from proud to that all too familiar worried look.

"Now, Eva, just who is this *repairman* that Cyril is leaving you with for most of the day? Have you met him? Has Cyril known him a long time?"

"Yes, I've met him. He's very nice. His name's Jared and he knows a lot about guide boats and Cyril likes him too. Mom! Cyril wouldn't leave me with some lunatic. You know that."

Eva was smiling hopefully at her mom's squinting eyes and tightly folded arms. When Ann slowly slid her hands down to her hips, Eva could tell she was softening ... slightly.

"No, no. I suppose you're right. Cyril would never leave you with someone he didn't trust," Ann admitted, rubbing her chin. "But you listen, if this Jared person says something weird or makes you even a little uncomfortable, you hightail it straight back to camp, understand? And bring your phone. I bought that mainly as a safety measure for you and all it does is collect dust."

Eva thought about telling her mom more about Jared just to settle her down but she didn't want her mom teasing her about finally liking a boy. And she sure didn't want her mom to push the hair issue and start talking about different clothes. And then of course, she'd want to meet him.

"I'll bring my phone, and don't worry Mom, he's really nice."

"Hmm, I think I should meet this person, just to make sure," Ann said. "He's a stranger, Eva. How old is Jared anyway?"

Eva's face fell and she took a long, deep breath. "He's about my age," she said sternly. "He has a little sister named Wendy. His father, who is almost as strict as *you,* taught him how to build and repair boats, and they're staying at a camp down the lake for the next two weeks—that is, if his mother likes it and wants to stay. There! Now you can rest easy. He's not some deranged serial killer."

"Ooooookay. That'll be fine, Eva," Ann said, straightening up her face and grabbing the broom. While Eva braced herself for more questions, Ann turned away and started whisking around the kitchen, whistling at full volume. Eva just stood there holding a dirty dustrag, feeling confused, but mostly relieved. She was just opening her mouth to say goodbye when her high-speed mother stopped abruptly and looked toward Eva with a very casual expression.

"I'll be going into town for groceries in about an hour," Ann said. "I should be back about noon. I think I'll pick up one of those frozen pizzas we like so much. Why don't you come up from Cyril's around noon and we'll have lunch together? And of course Jared's welcome to come too, that is, if you'd like to invite him."

Eva put on a false smile, gritted her teeth and growled internally. "Um, he's probably bringing his own lunch, Mom. I don't know. We'll see. I don't even know when he's arriving."

"Okay, well, just let him know he's welcome," Ann chirped cheerily. She grabbed her broom and started humming to the rhythm of her sweeping.

Eva slammed the door to quickly drown out her mother's cheerful voice. That last thing she heard from behind the door was a muffled, "Have a nice day!"

Relieved to be outside and away from her mother, Eva headed straight across the front lawn, high-stepping over the tall wet grass. Eva knew her trail by heart now. There were three land-marks that she always looked for and knew exactly when they would appear. The "carpet rock" was first. It was a waist-high boulder completely covered by green moss. Next were the "twin tamaracks" with heaving roots that locked together, and last was the "snow log," a large pure-white birch log that lay across her trail, half of it sunk in the soft earth. When she jumped over it, she knew she had exactly five giant leaps before Cyril's burgundy roof appeared through the foliage.

Eva was just about to fly over the snow log when an un-known voice echoed through the woods. She hunched low, skid-ding to a halt just before the log. Staring intently at the ground, she tried to quiet her breathing to listen better. She could hear voices down by the lake. Relieved that one of them sounded a lot like Jared's, she stood up straight.

When she heard the other voice she mentally said to her-self, *That's definitely not Wendy.* Eva stole down the remainder of her trail, but at a more relaxed pace. At the same time the wildflowers brushed against her left leg, she looked to the right and Cyril's beach came into full view. Her stomach did a little flip the moment she saw Jared. She wasn't used to that feeling, so she reached up and pushed against her abdomen, trying to make it go away. Jared stood on one side of Cyril's boat while a much taller, larger man stood on the opposite side. There were two other boats on shore. One looked like the guide boat Jared had arrived in yesterday. The other was a purple wooden pram, appearing only big enough to carry one person. Attached to the back of the boat was a very small plastic-looking white motor.

Jared's father, Eva thought, walking down the small grade.

She wasn't even halfway down the hill when Jared turned to face her. "Hi, Eva!" he shouted.

Eva smiled and waved back at Jared, her stomach taking

another tumble. She barely lowered her hand and Jared shouted again.

"This is my dad!" he said, pointing. "Is Cyril home?"

"No, he's gone on his walk. He should be back in a few hours though."

She felt like all eyes were on her as she walked the last few yards of sand that brought her standing right next to Cyril's boat and Jared.

"Hi, Eva. My name's Tom Cole. It's very nice to meet you."

With the same smile as Jared's, Tom walked around the boat and extended his plate-size hand out toward Eva. She watched his huge grip wrap around her little hand and most of her wrist.

"Hi, it's nice to meet you too," Eva said, blushing.

Tom looked like Jared, except three times bigger, and his voice was the deepest she had ever heard.

"Jared's not stopped talking about this guide boat or you for the past two days now. Says you like to row—"

"Dad!" Jared interrupted.

Eva's heart jumped and she felt even more heat creeping into her cheeks. She caught a fleeting glimpse of Jared's scowling face as he backed away from his father and started fumbling through his tool bucket.

"What?" Tom said, looking from Eva to Jared. "Well, anyway, I was just saying, Jared, that you thought it was really neat to meet someone who knew about guide boats and also liked to row them." He held his large hands out questioningly.

Tom cleared his canyon-deep throat while Eva slid her hands deep into her jean pockets.

"I don't know that much about guide boats," Eva confessed. "I've just been rowing Cyril's since I was about five, or maybe younger," she said, twisting her feet in the sand.

"I think that's great!" Tom bellowed with his right hand flying up over his head. "Most young people today want something big and motorized and those damn jet skis! How can you watch a family of loons when you're whipping by at fifty miles an hour in some noisy, polluting powerboat?"

Eva thought his voice could not get any deeper, but it did.

"And besides, the waves from those boats raise perfect hell with the loon's homes. You've probably seen them, Eva. They build big stick nests right by the water's—"

"Dad! Please! Please don't get started on the loons," Jared begged.

Jared looked at Eva apologetically, shaking his head. Eva just smiled back, content to see someone else arguing with a parent.

"I'm sorry, I just feel strongly about that, and, well, it's just nice to see young people taking an interest in these beautiful mountains," Tom said, sweeping his long arms passionately about the lake. "And you know, Eva! It's mind-boggling,the damage we've done to this earth, and almost all of it in just the last century."

"DAD!" yelled Jared, glaring.

"What, Jared?"

"You're doing it again! We're here to talk about repairing the guide boat, remember? And look at the time, Dad. Didn't Mom say she wanted you back at nine-thirty? You know how she gets when you're late!"

Eva spun her heels in the soft sand and grabbed the brim of her hat. She slowly pulled it down, trying to shield a big smirk.

"Oh, yeah, let's see. What time is it, anyway?" Tom said, fumbling with his shirt sleeve.

"Nine-fifteen," Jared said instantly.

Tom frowned at Jared, checked his watch and walked over to Cyril's boat.

"Well, you've made a good guess, Jared. Parsons! They made

a fine boat. Now let's see what we've got here," Tom said quietly and seemingly to himself.

Tom single-handedly flipped Cyril's boat over and gently put it down on the rickety sawhorses.

"What a beauty! And still holding its lines. Yup, just as you said, Jared," Tom said studiously. "But I think you left one thing out."

Jared frowned and began shifting confused looks between his father and Eva.

"What?" Jared asked.

"How are you going to keep the gunwale from getting permanently glued to the top plank?" his father asked casually.

Eva watched Jared's face magically relax into a relieved, confident smile. Reaching around to his back pocket, Jared pulled out a piece of plastic and held it up toward his father.

"Excellent!" Tom said. "I was a little worried there for a minute. But remember, Jared, no gluing until you talk to Cyril about moving the boat, okay?"

"Yes, I know. You told me already. I'm going to get started, okay, Dad? I'm all set. You don't have to worry—"

"Now, take your time," Tom interrupted. "This is a rare antique. You want to keep everything authentic and if you find yourself getting into a snag, you'll give me a call, right?"

"Right!" Jared said loudly.

"This Cyril, I would really like to meet him. Sounds like an interesting fellow. When did you say he'd be back Eva?"

"It all depends on his pace. It's a five-mile hike. Sometime between eleven and one, I would think."

"Well, I guess I'll have to meet him next time."

Tom glanced at his watch and then cast a big grin toward Jared.

"Keep an eye on him, will you, Eva? If you hear any swear

words, write them down and we'll give them to his little sister. She has quite a file on Jared," he said, chuckling.

Jared scowled at his dad but when he looked at Eva, she watched his face brighten into a glowing grin.

"My mom's going to Lake Placid for the day," he explained to Eva. "Dad and Wendy are going to have a tea party and play with all seven of her dolls and take them on stroller rides and feed them—you should see my dad wearing a bra."

"JARED!" Tom said thunderously.

Eva jumped and Jared cowered slightly, but his huge smile never left his face.

"I'm just kidding, just kidding," Jared said, struggling not to laugh. "Wendy's the only one who wears a bra."

Eva cupped a hand over her mouth and was trying hard not to laugh while Tom stood glowering at his son. But in a matter of seconds, he began to laugh, and so did Eva.

"I guess I had that one coming," Tom confessed, taking a step toward Eva. "Wendy," he continued, shaking his head, "she makes things very interesting at our house. Well, Eva, Jared is right about *one* thing. His mother *is* very punctual. I'd better get moving. It was nice to meet you, Eva."

"Nice meeting you too," Eva said.

"I understand you've met Wendy?" Tom asked, shaking her hand.

"Yes. She's very cute and has such an imagination," Eva said, casting Jared a quick glance.

"Jared's mom and I were talking and we were wondering if you might be interested in babysitting Wendy this Friday?" Tom asked. "It would only be three or four hours."

"Ah, sure," Eva said brightly. "I'll just have to check with my mom, but it should be no problem."

"Terrific!" Tom said. "Jared's going to ask Cyril if we can

repair the boat over at our camp. There's a garage there and it will be much easier to work on it under cover, out of the weather. Our regular babysitter, although he's very upset about losing precious time with his little sister, will be working on Cyril's boat."

Tom flashed Jared a split-second grin and then refocused back on Eva.

"I wouldn't trouble you, Eva, but I told Jared once he starts this boat repair he'll have to work on it every day until it's finished."

"It's no trouble at all, really," Eva insisted.

"Thank you, and you know you're welcome to use my guide boat anytime. Jared's already offered, right?"

"Yes he has, but it's so shiny and new, I'd be afraid to damage or scratch it," she said shyly.

"NONSENSE!" Tom roared.

Eva flinched, swaying backward slightly.

"Sorry, Eva, I didn't mean to shout. It's just that you don't have to worry about that. Wooden boats are meant to be used, no matter how new they are. They much prefer the water, instead of some overheated garage, and scratches give them character and besides, like I've always told Jared, there ain't nothing you can do to that boat that I can't fix."

"Okay," Eva said, smiling and nodding at Tom.

Jared was measuring a section of the boat and whistling innocently when suddenly he stopped and cleared his throat. Tom and Eva looked over at the same time and found Jared tapping his wrist with his finger.

"Yes, yes I know. Your mother is waiting," Tom said, turning to go.

Lifting the bow of the little purple pram, Tom easily slid it out into the lake. He waded along its side until the water was close to the top of his knee-high rubber boots. Tom sidled in heavily, making the tiny boat shift and rock steeply. When the little boat finally settled, there were only three inches of boat showing above the water.

"Bye you two. Be careful, Jared, and follow the plan we went over ... *closely,*" his father ordered.

"Bye," Eva said, waving.

Jared nodded lazily and waved without looking.

Eva watched the big man turning with great effort on the little seat. A low buzzing sound of an electric motor broke the silence, and at a snail's pace, the half-sunk boat putted away from shore.

"Well," Jared said, turning toward Eva, "that's my dad! He'll probably be back in an hour with my darling sister, just so he can check on me. He'll make up some excuse, just to return, if I know him."

"You really think so?" Eva asked.

"I just never know what he's thinking," Jared said, shaking his head. "One minute he talks to me like I'm sixteen and then ten minutes later he treats me like I'm five years old."

"Well, he can't be any worse than my mother. She's the same way with me. She'll give me a little space and then, without any warning, she gets all panic-stricken." Eva lowered her voice and added, "She doesn't know it but I call her 'the blonde bundle of nerves.'"

"That's funny!" Jared said. "You know what I call my dad?"

"What?"

"The jittery giant; but I like yours better!"

Shaking their heads and looking at the sand, Jared mumbled, "Parents" at the same time Eva mumbled, "Grownups." They laughed easily and walked off in the direction of Cyril's boat.

Chapter 8

Eva could not believe how much her summer changed over the following weeks. She also couldn't believe there were only twelve days left before she had to go home and back to school. After Cyril's boat was repaired, Eva and Jared spent every day together, their interests being almost identical. Some days they ate lunch at Cyril's, other days it was at Eva's or Jared's camp. They hiked Cyril's trail three times, twice together and once with Cyril.

On a cold, rainy Tuesday they helped Cyril stuff and sew balsam pillows in the morning, and in the afternoon, as the rain drummed heavily off the metal roof, they washed and bagged two quarts of blueberries they had picked the previous day. When it was time for Jared to leave, he declined a ride from Cyril and insisted on rowing home in the chilly downpour. While Jared collected his things, Eva made her way across the room to

Cyril and asked him a quiet question. When she walked back to Jared, a navy-blue wool sweater rested in her upright hands, the same as if a soldier was carrying a precious, folded flag.

"*This* is a special sweater," Eva announced, glancing toward Cyril. "You won't ever get cold wearing this."

Jared smiled and reached out to take the sweater. When his hands slid under hers, his smile fell and their eyes locked. The connection lasted only seconds before Jared nervously looked down, took the sweater and pulled it over his head. He filled it out more than Eva had, but it was still a couple of sizes too big.

Many evenings were spent at Jared's, where they would build a big fire by the lake. Roasted marshmallows and chocolate pressed between graham crackers became the nightly after-dark treat. When the sugar overload made them lazy, they'd lie on the blanketed sand close to the fire, staring in wonderment at the billions of stars twinkling back at them. Wendy, never wanting to be left out, always managed to wiggle her way in, most often in the middle, wedged safely between the two big people. Wendy's little voice would prattle on while the two non-listening teenagers stared straight up. On the starriest, warmest night of the summer, while the fire danced in an easy breeze and tiny waves rolled musically at their feet, Eva glanced over through the talking hands of Wendy and stole a peek at Jared's relaxed upward smile. When her eyes returned to the diamonds in the sky, she suddenly felt weightless and she wiggled deeper and snugger into the soft sand. With the firelight glowing warmly on one freckled cheek and with every star brightly reflected in her smiling brown eyes, Eva thought for the very first time in her life, if there was a Heaven, this is what it must be like.

Just about every day they were in the guide boats. Sometimes they shared one boat, but mostly they rowed side by side in separate boats, mainly because neither of them liked being the passenger.

On a cool, overcast Wednesday, they packed a lunch and made big plans to row the entire shoreline of Union Falls Pond. The day was windless and an unusual stillness hung above the silvery, smooth lake. Being the middle of the week, the water was mostly theirs, having only to share it with a few of its true owners—rising fish, a pair of slinky otters and a lonely loon that was rarely out of sight all day. Over the creaking of slow, rhythmic rowing, their young voices echoed softly over the shallows as their little boats skimmed along in tandem, exploring every hidden bay and estuary.

As they were about to pass the big black rock that Cyril and Eva had hid behind, they pulled up on shore and had lunch. Without leaving any detail out, Eva told Jared all about the big storm. She showed him where they sat behind the boulder and explained how the hail was coming at them like it was being fired from a gun. She even demonstrated how Cyril woke up yelling from a nightmare and made her jump "about ten feet."

Rowing back to their camps and just before their boats separated, they made more plans, this time to climb Mount Marcy, the highest mountain in the Adirondacks. After Jared begged Tom, and Eva pleaded with Ann, they were eventually allowed to go. It was an all-day, fourteen-mile trek, and when they returned, they were exhausted and speckled with mud from the waist down. The next day, Eva's legs were so sore she had to go down the stairs sideways. Jared was in the same condition but it didn't stop them from spreading maps all over Eva's kitchen table so they could plan their next hike ... which never came.

******

"Eva, you have to keep your head still. French braids are

hard enough to do without a moving target," Ann scolded evenly. "But they're coming along beautifully!"

Eva was sitting on the edge of the kitchen table resting her feet on top of a tippy three-legged stool. Her tall mother was busy on Eva's left side, tucking and twisting her just-washed hair. Eva started fidgeting again and then sighed, looking out the windows nervously.

"You know, Cyril gets up super-early and I don't even want *him* seeing me like this," Eva said tensely.

"My God, Eva! The birds are still sleeping. You got me up so early, but it's okay, I'm not complaining. You're going to love this. I just can't wait."

Eva grimaced and rolled her eyes.

"Mom, I told you I just wanted to see what it looked like. I'm not planning on keeping them in today, it's just a trial sort of thing, remember?"

"Yes, but once you see for yourself, you might really like it and then you can just keep the braids in. Oh, Eva, you have such beautiful hair! And besides, you don't look that much different."

Eva noticed her mother's voice cracked and sounded odd when she said *look that much different*, so she tried to turn around, but her mom took Eva by the chin and turned her head away.

Eva sat round-shouldered, staring at the front door with a bored look on her face as her mom excitedly worked off to her left side, out of sight.

"Do you have a cold, Mom? You keep sniffing. Maybe you should go blow your nose," Eva mumbled.

"Allergies, dear. This always happens at the end of August."

Eva frowned and tried to turn around again. "Allergies? You don't have—"

"You're right, Eva. I do need a tissue. Now don't move! I'll be right back."

Sighing heavily with nervous excitement, Eva ran her hands over the thick, damp braids on each side of her head. Eyeing the bathroom, she abruptly kicked the stool off to one side and pushed off the table.

"WHOOA! Whooa!" Ann shouted, coming out of her room. "Eva, let me finish first. I just have another minute or two and then you can see."

Eva skidded across the wood floor in her socks and then sulked back to the table, patting her new hair. With the snap of the hair tie, Ann quickly centered herself in front of Eva for a closer look.

"We can look together, Mom, in the mirror," Eva said, side-stepping around her mother.

Eva stood in front of the mirror with a dazed stare and said, "Wow!"

When Eva glanced at the top of the mirror, she saw her mom's face grinning from ear to ear.

"Well, what do you think?" Ann asked giddily.

"I ... think ... I look ... totally different," Eva said slowly. "And I don't think my hat's going to fit over these braids."

"You look like a queen, Eva. You're beautiful. You don't need a hat."

Expressionless, Eva just kept staring and turning her head.

"Mom, I'll let you know. I want to look at it by myself, okay?

Ann's face fell and she slowly walked out of the bathroom. She dropped in a kitchen chair, and the silence lingered while Eva kept turning her head and looking. A slight smile was just creasing the corners of Eva's mouth when she heard a car coming down the hill and rumbling over the little red bridge. When brakes squeaked in the front yard, Eva stuck her head out the bathroom to see her mother walking briskly to the front door.

"Who's here?" Eva whispered nervously.

"I don't know. It's so early," Ann said, her head bobbing from window to window. "Oh, it looks like Jared's van. And the boat's on—"

"Mom! I'm not here! Or tell him I'm sleeping or something," Eva said sternly as the bathroom door snapped shut.

Ann made her way onto the porch and was out the door standing on the lawn before Jared was fully out of the van. Tom and his wife, Jessica, were waving under a dimly lit windshield as Jared walked toward Ann with a sheet of paper in his hand.

"Good morning, Jared. Everything alright?" Ann asked.

"Um, well, we have to go home. My mom got a call in the night, and my grandfather's in the hospital. It's his heart. I guess it's pretty bad," Jared said solemnly.

"Oh, Jared. I'm so sorry, dear."

"I was going to leave this note for Eva, but I won't have to now. Is she sleeping?"

"I, um, I'll see. I'll be right back," Ann said, darting up the stairs. "Oh! I'm sorry, Jared. Please come in. Why don't you wait on the porch and I'll see about Eva, okay?"

Jared entered and shut the porch door just as Ann shut the house door and disappeared behind it.

Ann leaned against the bathroom door with her mouth touching the casing. "Eva!" she half-shouted into the crack.

"I'm not coming out!" Eva said sharply.

"Eva, listen to me. Jared's grandfather is very sick. They're leaving for home right now. He stopped by with a note for you and he just asked me if you were up. He wants to talk to you. Eva, this isn't the time to be worried about your hair."

Eva stared at her big brown eyes in the mirror. Her heart sank and her mind started racing. *He's supposed to stay four more days. We're going hiking tomorrow. He can't be leaving.*

Maybe he can stay with us ... or Cyril, and then we could bring him—"

"EVA! He looks sad. It sounds like his grandfather had a heart attack. He just wants to say goodbye! Now open this—"

Click. The door squeaked steadily open. Ann looked exasperated as Eva calmly walked by without a word, heading straight for the front porch. She opened the door, entered the porch and turned around to close the door, all without looking up. Wishing she didn't have to move, she fumbled with the doorknob with her head down.

"Eva?"

Eva took a deep breath and slowly turned around with her eyes stuck on the floor just in front of Jared's feet.

"I'm sorry to hear about your grandfather," Eva said, starting to look up.

When she saw Jared's expression she quickly found the floor again, this time closer to her own feet. Jared's mouth was slightly open and he was looking at Eva with a frozen, blank stare. Crinkling noises were coming from a balled-up piece of paper in his right hand.

"I, um, thank you," Jared said, snapping out of his daze. "I wish I didn't have to go. I really like it here, but of course I have to. My grandfather needs us."

An awkward silence followed as their eyes kept failing to connect.

"It's been a really fast week," Eva said quickly.

"Nine days," Jared corrected. "But it was the best! This is the most beautiful lake I've ever seen and all the things we did ... I had a blast!"

"Me too," Eva said, smiling at Jared's excited face.

"My mom liked it here and a few days ago she was talking to my dad about coming back in the fall, on weekends. Do you ever come back in the fall?" Jared asked, taking a step forward.

"Sometimes, but it's usually just to close up camp for the winter; but I can ask my mom, she loves it here."

"OK! Well then, I'll call you, and maybe I'll see you this—"

Clunk! A side door on the van slid open and out jumped Wendy clasping a piece of yellow paper between two little hands. She ran right up the porch steps and opened the door with a loud bang.

"I made you a picture," Wendy said, handing Eva the paper, but still holding onto one edge. "That's me. I'm little and you're the big one. See, yours has red hair."

Eva stared down at the two crayoned stick figures that were holding hands. Feeling a sudden tightness in her throat, Eva swallowed hard and said, "I love it, Wendy! I'm going to put it right above my bed, in my room so I can see it every day. Thank you."

Wendy was rocking toe-to-heel and looking quite proud when her father's tremendous voice suddenly rang out and startled everyone: "Wendy!"

Wendy was out the door in a flash. She stopped on the stairs and looked back at Eva through the rusted screen. "Bye," she said, waving and smiling.

Eva wanted to grab her little arm and pull her back for a hug, but she hesitated too long. She mouthed a faint "Bye" as she watched Wendy skipping across the yard, her long black hair dancing with each carefree stride.

"Well, I'd better get going," Jared said dryly. "I know my parents are in a hurry." He reached for the edge of the screen door and pulled it open halfway and stopped.

"Hopefully this fall," he shrugged.

"Hopefully," Eva said. "I'll talk to my mom."

Jared looked toward the van and back to Eva. The paper in

his hand started crinkling again. The door didn't move. Eva felt a flurry of wings in her stomach, but there was a strange emptiness deep in her chest.

"Um, I'll walk out with you … so I can say goodbye to your parents," Eva suggested.

"Okay," Jared said, opening the door wider. Eva walked out first and Jared followed. When the screen door snapped shut, the house door opened, and a blond head peeked round the door frame. Ann walked across the porch and opened the rickety door.

"Bye, Jared," Ann said, waving from the porch steps.

"Bye, Mrs. Robinson. Thank you for the food … I mean all the great lunches," Jared said awkwardly.

Tom and Jessica stepped out of the van with Wendy on their heels. Jared hopped in the driver's seat, grinning innocently at his dad. Hands were shaking, future plans were being discussed and everyone said goodbye at least five times. Tom was just about to lift Wendy into the van when she broke free and ran full steam right at Eva and flew into her arms. Eva got her hug.

They piled back into the van and Jared slowly backed up onto the main road. Tom and Wendy were waving out the same window and with a couple of toots from the horn, the guide-boat-laden van slowly pulled away. With the back of the car still in sight, Eva turned sharply around and marched back into the cabin. Seconds later, Eva's bedroom door slammed shut.

In her room with her back against the door, Eva stared down at Wendy's present. As her eyes followed the lines on the drawing to the holding hands, she could feel an emptiness settling in like she'd never experienced. It was a hollow, painful feeling that started in her stomach and went all the way up to her throat. She flopped on her bed, pressing the drawing to her chest and fought back the tears. She lay there, determined and silent, but every time she blinked a droplet of water ran down the side of her face and into her ears. She heard her mother's footsteps come up to her door. *Please don't knock, please don't knock,* Eva repeated over and over in her mind. After what seemed like a long time, Eva listened to the footsteps walk away.

For the next couple of silent days Eva left her room only to eat and shower. Very early on the third morning, as she lay in bed, she decided she'd go see Cyril. She couldn't stand another day cooped up in camp with her mother's questioning eyes following her. She knew Cyril couldn't fix things, but as usual she was drawn to him, knowing that just being around him would somehow help.

Eva looked out her bedroom door to find her mother hovering over one of her giant novels, clutching a cup of steaming coffee at the kitchen table. Eva walked out lazily and started talking before her mother could.

"I'm going to Cyril's today," she said flatly.

Ann whirled around but Eva had already disappeared into the bathroom.

"I think that's great, Eva," Ann shouted at the closing bathroom door.

When Eva came out her mother was turned around in the chair waiting for her. "I was thinking we'd leave a few days earlier than planned," Ann said, standing up. "Is that okay with you?"

"Don't care," Eva mumbled, returning to her room and closing the door.

Eva shuffled across the pebble-paved road and dipped under her arch. Pushing a soft pine branch aside, Eva walked heavily down her trail, kicking every small rock she could get her foot on. About midway down, she stopped and listened in the direction of the bus. She thought she heard a grating noise and, after a few seconds of standing perfectly still, a door squeaked open and slammed shut.

"BUTCHER! BUTCHER!!" screeched an old woman's voice.

Chains rattled and Hazel's voice mumbled through the woods.

"BUTCHERRR! BUTCHERRR!!!" the raspy, desperate voice rang out in all directions.

Eva stood perfectly still and wondered what the witch was yelling about when her eyes suddenly grew big and her heart took off in her chest.

"Butcher's a dog! And it sounds like it's ... loose!" Eva's terror-filled eyes scanned in every direction and in a split-second she took off like a jet toward Cyril's. She flew across the stream, up the slight grade, past the waving wild flowers, and skidded up against the side of Cyril's cabin just as he was stepping out onto the porch.

"Eva! What a wonderful surprise!" Cyril said, opening the porch door.

Eva was breathless and bent over. When she straightened up and looked at Cyril, he stepped closer and put a hand on her shoulder.

"What's the hurry? Is everything alright?" he asked, concerned.

"I ... think ... one of Hazel's ... dogs ... is loose!" Eva said between fast breaths.

"It's okay, not to worry," he said, patting her shoulder. "I saw the dog just moments ago, a big brown one. It came pretty close to me, wagging its tail and looking friendly ... almost playful. It was probably thrilled just to be running free."

"Oh," said Eva, relieved, but still looking around. "I've just never ... I mean, her dogs are always tied up. I didn't think they ever got loose."

"That's the first time I've seen one. I'm relieved to find out they're not ugly—at least, that one wasn't," Cyril said with a reassuring smile.

Eva returned a tiny smile and looked out over the lake. It was just dawning on her that for the last five minutes and for the first time in several days her thoughts were not of Jared. But when she glanced at Cyril's beach, clear visions of last week started playing through her head and that familiar pain slipped back in. Looking away from the beach and focusing far out on the water, Eva also realized that her brief distraction felt ... good. She looked at Cyril and stood a little taller.

"Do you want to do your hike today or maybe pick some blueberries, or ... or something?" Eva asked, her voice trailing off.

"Certainly," Cyril said. "Nice cool day. Perfect! How about the hike? At least to The Cone Stone, if not all the way around. How's that sound?"

"Sounds good to me," Eva said, trying to look enthused.

They went inside, and while Eva slumped on a kitchen chair Cyril quickly threw a few things into his basket. Eva noticed he was moving faster than usual and she wondered what his hurry was.

With slow, long steps through the birches, Cyril commented on the beautiful late-summer day. For the first time all summer, Cyril led the way while Eva lagged behind with her head down, hypnotically watching Cyril's heels go back and forth until she spotted a bright leaf along the trail. When she picked it up she heard a noise to her left and was startled to see a blur of dark movement disappearing behind a huge pine tree.

"Cyril?" she said in a loud whisper.

Cyril stopped and turned around and looked in the direction Eva was pointing.

"What is it?" he asked, concerned.

"I saw something move over there, behind that pine tree—the biggest tree, the one in the middle."

"Are you sure? What did it look like?"

"It looked like, well I don't know. It was just a dark, fast movement."

Eva watched Cyril look through the woods in all directions but she mostly noticed he was looking toward the bus. She too looked toward the bus and wondered if someone was behind the tree. She walked up closer to Cyril.

"I've never seen Hazel along my trail, have you?" Eva asked, still whispering.

"I haven't. It was probably just a bird landing behind the tree, maybe just a big black crow. I see flashes of movement all the time in the woods."

Eva looked around one more time before returning back to her thoughts of autumn, and Jared.

"Fall's not far away, is it?" Eva asked, spinning a large bright-red leaf by the stem.

"No, it's right around the corner," Cyril said, turning toward her. "Now where did you find that?"

"Back there, behind that rock," Eva said, pointing. Her arm dropped slowly and she turned with big eyes. "You didn't see it?"

"No, I didn't," he said, slapping his knee. "Missed it completely."

Cyril looked up and pointed to the top of a tall, spindly sugar maple.

When Eva looked up she saw a patch of glowing red leaves at the top of the tree. The crimson colors looked out of place against a background of blue sky and the many dark greens of late summer.

"That's where it starts, Eva, the sugar maples. In three or

four weeks, the amazing autumn show will be in full force." Cyril started rubbing his chin. "You know, Eva, if it's alright with your mom, I could come and pick you up on a Friday and you could spend a weekend here, during the color change. Would you like that?"

Eva's face transformed into a sparkling smile.

"Really? Would you? I would really like that, but it's such a long drive. Are you sure?"

"Absolutely."

"I was going to ask Mom if we could come back this fall, but she always visits my dad on weekends. So I didn't know what she'd say, but now ... this is great!" Eva announced loudly to the surrounding woods.

When Eva's beaming smile returned to Cyril, he smiled back at her but his eyebrows were raised and he looked a little confused.

"Oh, I forgot to tell you. Jared had to leave early, a few days ago. Anyway, his parents said they might come back this fall and he said he'd call me and maybe he's coming for two weekends, but I better find out which one," Eva said all in one breath.

"Well that's just wonderful!" Cyril said. "We'll have plenty of time to figure everything out."

"Okay!"

Grinning, she bustled past Cyril with her reminder of autumn still twirling in her hand. After about ten steps the leaf slipped to the ground. When she picked it up she turned to find Cyril still in the same place. He was bent over tying his boot, but looking intently toward the bus.

Eva walked back quickly. "Did you see something?"

"No. Nothing. I was just tightening my boot," Cyril said casually. He stood up and patted Eva on the shoulder. "Ready?"

"Ready."

She started up the trail to the sound of his whistling, glad to be close by him, but she couldn't help looking at the pine tree one more time.

They made good time to the bench in the pines where they rested for quite some time before a much slower walk to The Cone Stone. While Eva waited by the great boulder for Cyril to catch up, she lost track of time daydreaming about seeing Jared again in the fall. She also wondered, for the hundredth time, if Jared's funny way of looking at her on the porch was good or bad. By the time she decided it was bad, Cyril was coming up the trail but moving much slower than usual.

Eva walked over to The Cone Stone and brushed off The Ruby Seat. "Cyril, you're winded again. Here, come and sit. We can head back. We don't have to make the whole hike if you're tired."

"I guess that would be a good idea," Cyril said, sitting heavily on the boulder's shelf. "It's just so confusing, Eva. Some days I feel perfect, others, I feel very old."

"When you're rested and ready we'll just take our time getting back. Deal?"

"Deal," Cyril said with his usual bright smile.

On the long, slow hike back, Eva was confused too. She kept thinking how strong he was last summer, and how he never was out of breath or tired. Last summer he was the strongest man she knew. But when her camp came into view her thoughts jumped to Jared and how she had to get back here in the fall to see him again.

"Well, hello you two!" came a voice from an open window.

"Hello, Ann," Cyril said, looking from window to window.

A screen slid up and Ann's head appeared through a small rectangle.

"I made some soup—chicken noodle—and I have a loaf of

bread that's just about ready to come out. I was hoping you'd stay for lunch, Cyril. I've made so much—"

"I'd love to, Ann," he said, glancing over at Eva. "I think we're both pretty hungry."

"Mom, Cyril offered to come and get me on a weekend this fall, during the color change, and Jared said he might be coming then, and you wouldn't have to drive, you could still visit."

"Eva, we'll have to see. That's a long drive. Cyril and I will talk about that later."

When Eva sadly looked up at Cyril, he gave her a reassuring wink and her expression instantly lit up.

******

Lunch went by with a lot of talking and an unusual amount of it was from Eva, who was very excited about autumn coming. Next to Eva's bowl of soup was a red leaf that she would occasionally run her fingers over. Try as she might, Eva could not seem to keep her mother on the subject of coming back to camp in October. When lunch was over, Cyril offered to help clean up but Ann insisted on him staying in his seat.

"Me too, Mom?" Eva asked hopefully.

"Nice try," Cyril whispered to Eva.

"That's right, Eva. Nice try," Ann said, stacking and picking up dishes.

While Eva and Ann cleared the table, Cyril quickly stationed himself in front of the sink.

"I'm washing," Cyril announced, rolling up his sleeves. "Now no arguing with me," he commanded. "You never let me help."

Eva looked at her mom, expecting her to tell Cyril to sit down, but instead Ann was pointing at Cyril's arm.

"There's blood running down your arm," Ann said, alarmed.

"Did you cut yourself?"

"Oh, not again," Cyril said impatiently. "It's nothing. I just tore a bandage off, that's all. I have another one in my pocket."

Cyril ripped off a paper towel from below the cabinet, and as Eva and Ann looked on curiously, he rolled his sleeve up higher and dabbed and wiped until most of the blood was gone. He then reached in his pant pocket, then the other, then all four. When he started to check his shirt pockets, Ann noticed he was bleeding again.

"I *thought* I had another Band-Aid," Cyril said.

"Come with me," ordered Ann.

She took him by the arm and led him to the kitchen table and calmly, but firmly, said, "You sit here. Get that shirt up a little higher. I have plenty of bandages, but first we're going to get you cleaned up."

When Ann disappeared into the bathroom, Eva laughed and leaned toward Cyril.

"Watch out, full nurse-mode is kicking in. You'll be lucky to leave here without a cast all the way up to your neck," Eva whispered with big eyes.

Cyril chuckled quietly while rolling up his shirt sleeve. When Ann returned she was carrying a large plastic box that looked like it belonged in the back of an ambulance. Cyril lay his arm out on the kitchen table while Ann rummaged through her medical supplies, pulling out white tape, gauze and antiseptic.

"Well, this is where I leave," Eva announced, looking disgusted. "I don't like blood. I'll finish the dishes."

Cyril acknowledged Eva with a warm smile as she walked by. After the kitchen water started running, Cyril leaned a little closer to Ann.

"She and Jared really hit it off. I didn't know he had to leave so soon. But she seems to be taking it fairly well, don't you think?" Cyril asked.

"I'm not sure. She's so closed up," Ann said, looking at Eva's back. "But her happiness is now hanging on the hope of seeing Jared this fall, and you know how it is … a million things could change from now till then, and—"

Ann glanced at Cyril's arm.

"How did you say you injured your arm again?"

"I didn't. It just bleeds once in a while, usually when I bump it. It's a mole that I've always had," Cyril said casually.

Ann started wiping the blood off his arm, but when she got to the mole she patted gently and wiped very slowly. With each wipe she leaned in closer.

"I need a flashlight. I'll be right back, Cyril. I need to get a better look at this."

When the bathroom door shut, Cyril got Eva's attention with a sharp, quick whistle.

"I guess you're right, Eva. I'm going to be here awhile," he whispered across the table.

Eva nodded knowingly in agreement and went back to her dishes.

Ann returned, all businesslike, with her flashlight nervously flickering on and off. She sat down, slid her reading glasses on and moved in for a close look.

"What do you think, doc?" asked Cyril. "Probably should just cut the whole arm off."

Ann slowly raised her head and looked right at Cyril's ever-present smile.

"Now, tell me, Cyril, when did this first start bleeding?"

"I, hmm, last winter sometime, maybe even the last fall … I think."

Ann's right arm fell to the table with a thump.

"CYRIL!" she yelped. "You don't let something go that won't

heal properly."

When Eva glanced over she felt bad for Cyril. He looked like a little boy who did not understand.

"I'm sorry, Cyril. I didn't mean to snap at you, but these different colors, how long have they been there?"

"What colors," he said, taking a closer look at his arm.

Ann drew the light in closer. "The red and brown and purple."

"All I see is a fuzzy dark mark, Ann. I've never looked at it with my reading glasses, and never with a flashlight. I've always just thrown a Band-Aid or two over it. It just won't heal because it's always getting caught on something."

Cyril studied her face, but Ann diverted her eyes to the mole and began washing it with antiseptic. In the lingering stillness, a clock ticked loudly above the table while Ann put gauze over the bruise and wrapped it with a wide cotton bandage.

"Ann? What's the matter? Why all so serious?" Cyril asked, still smiling.

"Moles can turn into cancer. Now, I'm not saying this is cancer, Cyril. I don't want you to worry."

"I'm not," he said, shrugging his shoulders.

"Well," Ann said cautiously. "It resembles a type of skin cancer and since it's been there so long, you'll need to get it checked out by your doctor, and the sooner the better."

"Next Friday when I go to town, I'll stop at the hospital and get it looked at," Cyril replied with a smiling nod.

"I think you should make an appointment with your doctor today," Ann said rigidly.

"I don't have a doctor."

"You don't have a doctor? Who do you go to when you're sick or you need a checkup?"

Looking at Ann sheepishly, Cyril rubbed the back of his hand over his mouth. "I haven't been sick. I always feel good, well except for this past summer, I've felt kind of tired, but I'm getting older, Ann. Can't feel like twenty-five forever," he said, glancing over at Eva and chuckling.

"Cyril, when was the last time you saw a doctor and had a checkup?"

"Let's see," Cyril said, scrunching up his face and looking at the ceiling. "I've never really needed a checkup, but let me think. Oh! Yes. I broke my arm falling in French Brook in 1981 or was it—"

"CYRIL!" Ann shrieked. "You haven't seen a doctor in twenty-six years?"

Cyril's eyes widened and he tipped back in his seat.

"I've been very healthy—no problems."

Ann shook her head, looking dumbstruck.

"Well, anyway, Cyril, this," Ann said, pointing at his arm, "needs to be seen, tomorrow. I'm calling a doctor I know in town and hopefully he can see you first thing. Now where did I leave my phone?"

"Ann, there's no hurry. It's been like this a long time. I don't want to trouble a busy doctor for a special appointment. It's just a silly mole."

Ignoring Cyril, Ann stood up and marched toward her room.

"We're going to have that looked at tomorrow, even if I have to take you to the emergency room," Ann commanded over her shoulder.

Cyril raised his eyebrows, looking like a scolded child. He took a deep breath that settled into a big grin.

"Eva warned me about you."

When he turned around, Ann was pacing back and forth in her bedroom, her phone cupped in one hand while her thumb punched at the numbers.

"Is the surgery over?" Eva asked, pulling out a chair next to Cyril.

"I love your mom," Cyril said, leaning close to Eva. "But I see what you mean. I kind of wish I had found one of my own Band-Aids."

"Why. What did she do now?" Eva asked, flipping her eyes to the ceiling.

"She wants me to see a doctor tomorrow about this little bleeding mole, but she's a nurse, so I really should obey."

"Oh," Eva said, looking from his bandage to her pacing mother.

"We're all set. Ten-fifteen tomorrow," Ann informed. "Dr. Lucas. You'll like him, Cyril. He's a country doctor, and such a nice man."

"Well, that's that!" Cyril said. He clapped his hands together and stood up. "We have a date tomorrow. But if you're busy, Ann, I can go on my own."

"No. I'm going," Ann said flatly. "It's no trouble. If there's a lot of medical talk, and, well, if it gets confusing, I can help you sort through it."

"Thank you, Ann. Okay then, I'll see you in the morning. I'll drive, if you don't mind bumping along in my old truck."

"No, that'll be fine. "

Ann paused, focusing on her twisting hands as Cyril and Eva looked on.

"I'll be ready, Cyril, but I think we should leave a little early, you know, in case the traffic's bad."

At the same time, Cyril and Eva looked at each other and frowned identically.

"Traffic?" Cyril said.

"Mom! There *is* no traffic in Saranac Lake," Eva said, shaking her head.

"Oh, yes, um, let's see then, ten-fifteen, hmm ... we'll leave at nine-thirty," Ann said. "Is there anything you want to do in town, Eva?"

"No. I'm going to stay here," Eva said, avoiding her mother's eyes. "Is it okay if I take your boat out, Cyril?"

"Of course. I'll flip it over tonight and have it all ready to go; and I'll leave the spare binoculars on the table for you."

Eva grinned at her mother's serious face and turned to Cyril. "Thank you," she said.

Chapter 9

At nine-thirty sharp, Cyril pulled into Ann's yard. He was about to open the truck door when Ann shot down the stairs and beat him to the latch.

"Frigid morning!" Ann declared, sliding across the blanket-covered seat.

"Yes, indeed! September's coming, with its amazing color change. I just can't wait. It's such an amazing time of year," he said enthusiastically.

Ann zipped her fleece jacket right up to her chin and folded her arms in tightly. "How are you feeling today?" she asked, frowning.

"Just fine," Cyril said with a casual wave. "I'll turn the heat up for you—this old truck heats up really fast."

"Thank you."

They rumbled along the winding camp road for several miles

in silence while Ann held herself tightly and Cyril hummed and smiled at the beautiful passing scenery. When the truck squeaked to a stop and turned onto the main road to Saranac Lake, Ann suddenly turned in her seat toward Cyril.

"Have you lost any weight, Cyril?" she asked, turning down the heat.

"I don't have any scales. I really don't know how much I weigh. A hundred and sixty-five rings a bell. My clothes feel the same, so I must be the same weight. Why do you ask?"

"Oh, it's just a common medical question. They'll be asking that again at the doctor's office, plus many more questions, mostly like the ones I asked you last night."

"Alright, sounds pretty easy to me."

******

Eva awoke with two things on her mind. She was going to collect autumn leaves in the morning and take a long row in the afternoon. She hiked up behind the pole line and found three more maple leaves, two orange and one red. She brought them back to camp and carefully laid them next to Wendy's picture. Resting her elbows on top of the chest of drawers and her hands under her chin, she stared down at the crayon drawing. Only then did she realize that some of the pain she was feeling was also for Jared's family. She missed them too.

Her right hand slowly slid from under her chin and reached into her jean pocket. For the third time since she woke up, she checked her phone for messages and also to make sure it was working. She frowned and stuffed her phone back in her pocket and quickly grabbed a heavy sweatshirt off her bed and stuffed it to the bottom of her backpack. A water bottle landed on top of the sweatshirt and a hastily made lunch followed. Walking to the door, she zipped her pack tight and flipped it up to her shoulder. Swinging left at the end of the front lawn, she made a quick decision to go down Cyril's road. Yesterday's close encounter with Butcher was still fresh on her mind.

******

"Look over there!" Cyril exclaimed, pointing out Ann's window. "Just look at the fall color along Moose Creek! Isn't it beautiful? That wasn't there last week."

Ann looked just in time to see a cluster of red and orange maple trees whisk by. "Yes ... very pretty," she said distractedly.

"Along the wetlands the color always comes early. It's nice we always get a little autumn show in August," Cyril excitedly informed Ann.

Ann just nodded and kept staring at the oncoming pavement.

Ann helped Cyril fill out all the forms and questionnaires that were handed to him when he first walked in to the doctor's office. The big circular waiting room was full but they found one chair and Ann insisted that Cyril take it. She hovered over him, offering answers when Cyril pointed at certain questions.

"William?" Ann commented, pointing at the form.

"It's my first name," Cyril said. "I just don't use it except for legal things."

"Oh," she said, nodding, yet looking a little puzzled.

An hour later when his name was called, he stood up and looked at Ann.

"I can come with you, if you'd like," Ann said.

"I'd like that very much. I'm glad you're here, Ann."

The next stop was a small room where a nurse asked many of the same questions that Cyril had just answered on paper.

His knee was jerked, his finger was pricked and his blood pressure and weight were recorded. The nurse then led Cyril and Ann down a long hallway and into another small room, this one with an exam table and a countertop lined with medical supplies. Sitting side by side in small plastic chairs, they waited for Dr. Lucas.

"I have to admit, Ann, I feel a little foolish. All this fuss, and this doctor seems very—"

A soft knock on the door interrupted Cyril.

"Well, good morning Mr. Bankstrom, and hello, Ann."

Cyril stood and Dr. Lucas offered a hand. They each wore the same relaxed expression.

"Please call me Cyril, Doctor."

"Okay, fair's fair, Cyril. My name's Arthur," he said with a pleasant grin.

Except for the stethoscope draped around his neck, Arthur looked more like a hardware store owner than a doctor, wearing green cotton pants, a roomy flannel shirt and a gray wool vest with its breast pocket stuffed with pens and pencils.

"Now let's take a look at that arm and see what we can make of this," Arthur said, putting on his glasses and raising them with his eyebrows. "Please take a stool, Cyril, and slide over to that table where there's better light."

While Arthur leafed through Cyril's four-page chart, Ann helped unravel the bandage she had applied the day before. Cyril sat with his arm stretched out over a huge sheet of white paper that covered the vinyl exam table. The doctor clicked on a long gooseneck lamp and pulled it over Cyril's arm. His head kept slowly dropping until it was about eight inches above the arm.

"You say it's been bleeding about ten months?" Arthur asked.

"Yes, about that long."

Arthur glanced over his half-glasses at Cyril. "And how long have these different colors been present."

Cyril looked at Ann and then back to Arthur.

"I don't know," Cyril said, feeling a little embarrassed. "I've just never looked at it closely with my readers on."

Arthur rolled another stool to the table and sat down next to Cyril.

"Have you had any pain anywhere that wasn't there a year ago?" he asked.

"I've had pain in my side, right here," said Cyril, pressing against his lower-right ribs. "But not all the time."

"Anywhere else?" Arthur asked.

"No."

"How about your breathing, Cyril? Anything changed there in the last year?"

"Yes, I get winded easier. Some days I feel fine and others are not so good."

"And your energy level? Is that the same as last year?"

"Well ... no, it's not the same, but these changes are pretty normal for someone my age. Aren't they?" Cyril asked.

"Yes. They're very normal," Arthur said with a jovial slap on his knee. He pushed against the floor with his heels, rolling the little stool over to Cyril's chart.

"I'd like to do three things today, Cyril. A biopsy of that mole, a chest X-ray, which we can do right here, and I'll need to listen to your lungs and do a physical exam of your abdomen."

"Okay with me," Cyril said, shrugging his shoulders and grinning at Ann.

Ann forced a smiled and quickly looked at her purse. "I'll step out for this part. I'll be in the waiting room, okay, Cyril?"

Cyril smiled and nodded at Ann. When the examination was complete, Arthur walked over and put his hand on the door-knob. "I'll be back shortly, Cyril. A nurse will be in soon to get the biopsy tray ready. Don't worry, it's pretty simple. I'll first numb your skin with a tiny needle using lidocaine and then excise a small piece of the mole with a scalpel. The needle pick is the worst part. After that, you shouldn't feel a thing."

"No worries here," said Cyril.

Arthur exited and a few minutes later a nurse knocked and entered with an armful of sterile items.

After the biopsy, Arthur told Cyril the results would take about a week. The nurse then walked Cyril down to an X-ray room and introduced him to a technologist. After the X-ray was taken, Cyril joined Ann in the main waiting room, where they were told to stay until Dr. Lucas had read the results. After only a few minutes the X-ray technologist returned and called for Cyril. Ann jumped up nervously, but then waited to follow Cyril as he was led to a different room. It was Dr. Lucas's office and he was standing in front of a light box, staring eye-level at an X-ray with his glasses dangling from one hand. As Cyril walked in, Arthur gave him a tiny smile while nodding his head. When Ann peeked over Cyril's shoulder at the X-ray, her left hand flew up to her mouth and her body buckled slightly forward. Arthur caught sight of her and his tiny smile disappeared. Cyril just stood there, his non-medical eyes casually glancing from his chest X-ray to Arthur and back again.

"Cyril," Arthur said, his voice much softer than earlier. "I'm going to be very frank with you. I'm not one hundred percent sure, but these round spots here and here and here," he said, pointing, "Well ... your X-ray has the appearance of metastatic cancer—that means a cancer that has spread from somewhere else in your body. These spots might be something else, but in all likelihood I believe its origin is from the lesion on your arm."

"This little thing?" Cyril said, pointing at his bandage.

"There are many types of skin cancer, Cyril, and most are

benign and treatable by simply removing them, but melanoma, which yours resembles, is the kind that can spread to other parts of the body. If melanoma is caught early, before it spreads, the cure rate is usually excellent."

"I don't know a lot about cancer, Arthur, but I've volunteered for the hospice in the past and I've learned that when cancer spreads throughout the body there's not much that can be done, except making the person comfortable," Cyril said calmly, like he was talking about the weather.

Arthur suddenly looked confused and his eyes went back to the X-ray. Sniffing sounds were coming from Ann.

"It's okay, Ann," Cyril said gently. "I'm ready. I've been ready."

Arthur glanced over at Ann's confused, tear-streaked eyes and began rubbing his forehead wearily. Ann asked to sit and Arthur suggested they all take a seat. Bringing his hands tightly together, Arthur looked at Ann and then Cyril. "Now, let's not get too far ahead of ourselves. We'll get a better understanding of all this after a CAT scan of your abdomen and brain. I've called the imaging department at the hospital and they can scan you at one-thirty today. I've also ordered STAT blood work. Why don't you and Ann go have lunch and then come back to my office after your tests are complete?"

"Alright," Cyril said, nodding.

Chairs scraped across the wooden floor, and awkwardly they all stood up but only one of them looked content.

"We should have a much clearer picture of what's going on after you return," Arthur said, walking them to the door.

"Thank you," echoed Cyril and Ann at the same time.

With one last helpless look between Ann and Arthur, they left the office.

******

As Cyril had promised, he had left the boat upright and the binoculars on the kitchen table. With her ponytail and binoculars swinging in unison, Eva walked down the small grade to the lapping, almost white-capped lake. A high pressure system from Canada brought with it a deep-blue sky, but also a cool, stiff breeze that funneled down the lake from the northwest. With difficulty, she settled into the tippy boat and made her way across the choppy pond. Rowing clumsily in the tossing boat, she scanned every shoreline and hillside searching for a splash of fall color, looking for autumn, thinking of Jared.

When Eva finally reached the other shore, her right side was damp from the windswept mist caused by an oar that kept hitting waves on the return stroke. She was getting chilled, but she knew when she entered the sheltering woods the high sun would warm her up quickly. Landing the boat was going to be tricky, so Eva rowed hard and fast and at the last second, leaned forward to help the boat slide further up on the beach. Close to shore she spotted a patch of sun warming a thick layer of pine needles. Dropping her pack and herself at the base of the huge tree, she ran her hands over the glistening needles and leaned back against the bark. Eva then propped her elbows on her knees and pressed the binoculars against her freckled cheeks. One hundred yards away was Charlie's giant stick nest. Eva spent almost two hours waiting and looking for the bald eagle. She was beginning to feel like she was the only one in the universe. No squirrels, no birds, no deer, no animal sounds. *Too windy,* Eva thought.

When the wind started to make her shiver, she downed her lunch, packed up and trudged back to shore. As the boat skimmed away from Charlie's home, she kept the binoculars close at hand and her eyes on his nest. When Eva landed on

Cyril's beach she pulled the boat over a pair of wooden rollers as far away as she could from the now white-capped lake. With her head slumped down again, she plodded along back up to Cyril's cabin.

Laying the binoculars down on his table, Eva sighed and looked around. Her spirits, fairly high when she woke up, were now falling. Falling too, was any hope of ever seeing Jared again. School, which started next week, deepened her sadness. She didn't want to leave. She wanted the week she spent with Jared to go on forever, right here by the lake. Shuffling out the door and down the steps, Eva stopped on the last rung, wondering which way to go. The unceasing wind was racking the trees noisily.

Eva looked toward the woods and thought briefly of the dogs. Suddenly she didn't care about falling branches or biting dogs. She sighed after a deep breath and walked with heavy feet past the wildflowers, over the stream and through the birches. When she came to the snow log, she brought her right leg back as far as she could and kicked with all her might. The log didn't move and Eva's face twisted in pain. She wanted to scream something, anything, but she defiantly clenched her teeth and continued on, grimacing at the ground. As she neared the twin tamarack trees, Eva felt a sudden prickling sensation on the back of her neck. When she looked up she instantly drew a hand to her mouth and reared back. Her heart took off in her chest. Standing motionless, only twenty feet away, was the shabby, brownish outline of Hazel. She was bent over, leaning heavily on a tall walking stick, her tiny dark eyes glaring down the trail right through Eva.

"I saw you with him! You mother know you with him?!" sneered the hunched figure in broken English and a raspy tone.

Eva took a step back, and without moving her head, her huge brown eyes moved away from Hazel and scanned everywhere for dogs.

"I'm talking to you, girl! You mother know you with him?!" she demanded louder.

Who? Eva mouthed silently.

"Bankstrom! WILLIAM! His name ain't Cyril. Probably didn't know that, did you? There's a lot you don't know!"

As Eva inched backward and frantically scanned around, the old lady heaved to one side, and pushed off with her cane. Without taking her piercing eyes off Eva, she clumsily took a step forward.

"You not afraid of me, are you?" The woman's voice suddenly became unnaturally smooth. "I never hurt anyone, ever! But *him*—he murdered his whole family! While they was sleeping, burned them up, all five of them is what I heard! Nothing but a no-good drunk he was!"

A look of horror spread across Eva's face and from the very bottom of her lungs she screamed, "YOU'RE CRAZY!! YOU DON'T KNOW ANYTHING!!"

Eva glared at the old woman, breathing like she had just run a hundred miles.

A faint smile appeared on the old woman's face as she flashed her top teeth. Her eyebrows rose high and she let out a gravelly cackle. "Don't believe me? Find out for yourself then."

Eva spun around, but she only managed three giant leaps before she heard the witch yell, "IT'S FOR YOUR OWN GOOD YOU SHOULD KNOW! AND YOUR MOTHER TOO!!"

Eva rocketed down the trail. When she glimpsed Cyril's camp, she swung to the left and headed toward his dirt road. Her mind was exploding with horrible images. She stopped in the road, panting and looking, not knowing which way to go. She didn't want to meet the witch again and she didn't want to run into Cyril coming down his road. She ducked into the woods on the right side of the dirt lane and pushed and slapped at the branches, running at full speed until her hat flew off. As she scrambled back to pick it up, her terror-filled eyes searched for a follower.

She turned and headed for the stream, knowing that when she found it she would follow it up to the little red bridge close to her camp. When she was nearing the road, she hesitated for a moment, listening for cars or people. She then poked her head through the bushes and looked up and down the road. Seeing and hearing nothing, Eva bolted across the road and fought her way through the brush to her camp. Her mother wasn't home. She ran in and locked the door. Out of breath, scratched and sweating, she ran to her bedroom, slammed the door and started pacing. She couldn't believe what had just happened. It had to be a nightmare. Feeling dizzy, she started coughing and wondered if she was dreaming. She looked in the mirror. Her face was beet red. Glancing down, she saw Wendy's drawing surrounded by colorful leaves. She wasn't dreaming.

******

Ann jumped and started fumbling with the zipper on her purse. Bent over and digging through her canvas bag, she quickly surfaced with her ringing phone.

"Hello," Ann said quietly.

"Mom!? Where are you? When are you coming home?" Eva demanded in a shaky voice.

"Eva? What's ... just a minute."

Ann stood up and put a hand over her phone. She looked around the almost empty waiting room and then at Cyril.

"It's Eva. I'm going to step outside for a minute. I'll be right back," Ann said, patting Cyril's shoulder.

Cyril smiled and nodded and watched Ann hurry out the door.

"Is everything alright, Eva? You sound—"

"Mom! I just want to know when you're coming home! That's all."

"Eva, there *is* something wrong. This isn't like you. Now what's the matter?" her mother ordered.

"Where are you? Where's Cyril?"

"I'm standing outside the doctor's office. Cyril's inside waiting to see the doctor about some test results. Why? What—"

"The witch was on my path today and she said awful things about Cyril. Said he murdered his family and he was a drunk. But she's crazy. Why would she say those things?" Eva pleaded.

Ann's eyes widened and she looked back at the office door.

"Eva, this sounds absurd. Where are you now?"

"In camp. In my room. I ran away from her. I had to cut through the woods and come out by the red bridge. She can't be right, can she?"

"Did she chase you?" Ann asked sternly.

"No, she just stood there with a cane."

"Alright, you stay in camp," Ann said, pacing up and down the sidewalk. "Now, Eva, try to calm down. This can't be true. Some people stir things up or exaggerate things because they have nothing better to do. I should be back in about an hour. Just stay in camp and lock the doors, okay?"

"Alright," Eva said reluctantly.

Ann closed her phone with shaky hands and looked toward the doctor's office. When she walked slowly back into the waiting room, Cyril's chair was empty. She started rubbing her stomach when suddenly she heard a window slide open.

"You can go back, ma'am. Mr. Bankstom's with Dr. Lucas, in his office. Do you know the way?" the receptionist asked.

"Yes," Ann said blankly. "I was there earlier."

Dazed, she walked the long hallway unusually slowly. When she entered the doctor's office, there were no X-rays or CAT scans being looked at. The two men were sitting quietly, in tall, broad-back chairs. Cyril's hands were crossed over and resting comfortably on his legs. Arthur was sitting straight up with an open folder in his hands.

"Hello, Ann," Arthur said, shuffling papers. Both men stood up at the same time.

"Hi," Ann said meekly.

"Is everything okay with Eva?" Cyril asked.

"Um, yes she's fine," Ann said distractedly.

"Please sit down, Ann," Arthur said.

Ann glanced at Cyril with a swift smile and then looked away quickly.

"Cyril and I were just starting to discuss some of his test results, Ann, but he asked if we could wait for you," Arthur said.

"I hope that's okay with you, Ann?" Cyril asked.

"Yes. Yes of course. Thank you, Cyril."

"The CAT scan of the brain was completely normal. But the problem is the liver," the doctor said heavily while leafing through the papers on his lap.

"It's pretty conclusive that you have metastatic cancer, Cyril. The liver, well, it has the same problem as the lungs—many, many tumors. The biopsy results still need to confirm the diagnosis one hundred percent, but in all reality, I should talk to you about radiation and chemotherapy."

A long minute of silence went by as all eyes watched Cyril, who was looking out the window.

"I'd like to talk about hospice care instead," Cyril said, calmly turning to face the doctor. "I mean, I've seen quite a bit of this while volunteering for hospice, and, well, wouldn't I just be prolonging things?"

Arthur leaned back in his chair, took off his glasses and put the stack of papers on his desk. He then brought his hands together and smiled at Cyril.

"Personally, Cyril, it's the route I'd take. Hospice, it's a wonderful organization. They'll take excellent care of you. I believe radiation and chemo will buy you some time, but once cancer takes hold of the liver, well, you're in God's hands then."

"I can't think of a better place to be. I appreciate your frankness," Cyril said. "From what you've seen, how much time do I have?"

Arthur seemed much more relaxed now, almost as much as Cyril. Ann was focused on her hands, which were rolling in tight circles on her lap.

"From what I've seen today, I would venture to guess about three months. Maybe less, maybe a little more. When someone's ready and accepting, it doesn't take long. When an individual is not ready and willing to fight, it could take much longer, sometimes up to a year."

When they left the office and got in Cyril's truck, Ann sat rigidly, and for once, very still. She was staring straight ahead when Cyril broke the silence.

"Ann, everything's going to be fine," he said softly.

She took a jumpy breath and nodded her head. Cyril began to whistle and while fumbling in his pocket for his truck keys, he caught her glance and their eyes met.

"Cyril," Ann began slowly, "this news, and all in just one day, it's, well it's just devastating and you don't seem to be upset ... at all."

Cyril put his keys down on the seat and rubbed his chin. The rasping sound of his invisible white whiskers filled the quiet truck cab.

"In all honesty, the news *was* devastating, but I'm not afraid, Ann, of dying. The process and the pain frightens me a little, but in the end, nothing can ever have you; not cancer; not a car accident; not the murderer; nothing of this world can have or take you. Oh yes, they can take your body, surely, but the real you is untouchable and eternal and belongs to God forever."

Ann smiled timidly and patted his hand.

During the long, quiet ride back to camp, Ann talked Cyril into buying a cell phone. She reasoned that hospice would want to stay in touch with him and so would she. Ann then rattled off five or six more reasons why it would be important to have a phone.

When they pulled into Ann's yard, she turned toward Cyril and for several seconds just sat there frowning and looking at his feet.

"I'm going to visit John tomorrow, but I'll be down to check on you in the afternoon," she said quietly.

"That's not necessary, Ann. I'm feeling okay right now. And besides, you have a lot to do. And aren't you leaving in a few days?"

"In a few days, yes, but I'll stop by for a visit anyway."

Ann wiped the corner of one eye and sniffed.

"Cyril?" she said in a quivering voice.

"Yes."

"What should I tell Eva?"

"Tell her everything. But please explain that I'm not nervous or upset," he said gently.

Ann nodded her head and unlatched the door. Getting out slowly, she leaned against the truck and gave Cyril a shy smile through the window. When the truck backed away, Ann watched Cyril disappear and reappear as the woodland shadows flickered off the windshield.

Seconds later, Ann had barely made it onto the porch when suddenly, her daughter confronted her, looking for the truth, wanting her mother to tell her that the witch was wrong.

"MOM! I told you she's crazy. She's got to be!" Eva yelled. "Why would she say those things?"

Ann dragged herself past Eva with hardly a glance.

"Eva, I just need to sit down. I don't know why she would tell you those awful things about Cyril. I'm exhausted. It's been a terrible day."

Ann dropped into a big puffy chair and stretched out, half-lying and half-sitting. Her head flopped back and her eyes found the ceiling. Eva stood off to one side looking at her in disbelief.

"Mom! We have to find out if it's—"

"Eva, come and sit down."

Without raising her head or looking at Eva, Ann reached out and patted the chair next to her. Bewildered, Eva scowled her way past her mother and sat down on the arm of the chair with her hands held out in a questioning pose.

"What's the matter?" Eva asked irritably.

Ann let out a shaky deep breath. "Cyril's sick. Very sick."

Eva slid silently off the arm and into the chair. For several long seconds the room became very quiet. "What is it?" Eva asked tentatively.

"He has skin cancer that has spread to his liver and lungs. That's why he hasn't been himself this summer—the pain in his side and his breathing ..." Ann cupped a hand over her mouth and looked away.

Eva sat forward and watched her mom. Suddenly her palms became sweaty and she began rubbing them up and down her blue jeans. "What about the treatments for cancer? Can't they get rid of it?" Eva asked loudly. Before Ann could answer, Eva felt the truth creeping in and her eyes quickly filled with water.

"No, they can't get rid of it. It's in his liver and there's no cure. There is a treatment that could give him more time, maybe a year, but he's decided against it." Ann's voice suddenly cracked and wavered as she said, "Says he's ready." Ann reached over to Eva. "I'm sorry."

Eva slowly stood up. She looked at her mom with big watery eyes and then her hand flew to her mouth and she marched off toward her room.

"Eva?"

Eva wiped her face and nose on her sweatshirt sleeve. "What?" she whispered.

"We haven't talked about Hazel. Tell me everything that happened."

When Eva got to the part about his name being William, Ann shot out of her chair.

"William!!" Ann shouted. She walked over to Eva with a puzzled look. "Are you sure she said William?"

"Yes! That's what she said," Eva insisted.

Looking stunned, Ann walked away and sat at the kitchen table, followed closely by Eva, who also pulled out a chair.

"What's the matter?" Eva said, now looking scared.

Ann slowly looked into her daughter's fearful eyes but didn't say anything.

"What is it? Tell me!" Eva demanded.

"This might not mean anything, it might only mean she got one thing right about—"

"WHO?!" Eva shrieked.

"Hazel," Ann said wearily. "When Cyril filled out his papers today, he wrote down William as his first name."

Eva glared at her mother and shook her head back and forth in disbelief. When she stopped, tears were rolling down her cheeks. "You should've asked him about it today, all of it. He would have told you it's just a crazy lie. It has to be!" Eva said desperately. She slammed her fist down on the table and yelled: "He's the nicest person I know! I don't believe it, any of it!"

Eva stood up, sending her chair toppling backward. She was about to step toward her room when her mother grabbed her wrist. "I think you're right, Eva," Ann said gently. "And I think we should forget all about it. We know who Cyril is. He's never changed, he's always been the same and he needs us right now."

With shifting, confused looks between them, Eva pulled her hands free and stomped off to her room and slammed the door.

Chapter 10

Eva tossed and turned most of the night. Each time she woke up she had to rethink what had happened in just the past few days. None of it seemed real, except for Jared. Everything kept playing over and over in her mind, but mostly she could not get the witch's words or face out of her head. She refused to believe any of it, but she couldn't stop the scary images from creeping back in—her scraggly hair, her cane, her tilted glare. She also couldn't believe Cyril was that sick and knew that camp would never be the same without him. She thought that if anyone in the whole world could get better it would be Cyril. *He's always been so strong*, she would constantly remind herself.

Punching the pillow and smacking her head down, she forced herself to think of Jared and relive everything they did from the very moment she walked down Cyril's hill and met him. She finally fell asleep looking at Jared's blue-eyed smile on the other side of a camp fire. An hour later she awoke to a dark room and reality, but when she drifted off again, Jared was sitting on a boulder alongside a hiking trail, waiting for her.

******

Cyril listened to the swelling symphony outside his windows for a moment before rolling out of bed. Fire-gold sun shafts were dancing warmly on the west wall, but the cabin air had grown chilly during the night. Wrestling into a heavy sweater, he walked to the back window and checked the truck for hoarfrost. "Just a heavy dew," he said aloud to himself. It was the coldest morning of late summer and he decided to build a small fire. While kindling wood snapped and popped behind the deer-painted window of the cast-iron stove, a tea kettle started whistling from the kitchen. Carefully walking over to the table with a very full cup, he sat down and mused over what he had learned from Dr. Lucas. Deep in thought, he stood up and switched chairs to be closer to the warming stove. He extended his arms, resting them flat on the table, and looked longingly at the opposite chair as if someone was there. His eyes closed wetly, and in a shaky, hollow voice, he whispered across the table to the empty chair, "I've finished up, thank you so much."

******

Ann was the first one up. After starting the furnace in the living room, she sat slumped at the kitchen table watching the steam swirling from the top of her large coffee mug.

Cross-armed and shivering, Eva shuffled in and opened the refrigerator door without a glance in her mother's direction. A quart of milk hit the countertop with a loud thud.

"Seems like a horrible, bad dream ... yesterday," Ann said, clearing her raspy morning voice.

Eva zigzagged around the kitchen, gathering a bowl, spoon, cereal and sugar before sliding onto her cold seat.

"You're going to see Dad today, right?" Eva asked dryly.

"Yes, I was planning on it. Why?"

"Because I don't want to stay here."

"Oh! Do you want to come with—?"

"No! I don't want to go *there*," Eva said. "I just don't want to be here. Can I stay in Saranac Lake while you go?"

Ann blew on her coffee while intensely studying Eva, who was focused on her cereal.

"Why? What would you do there for several hours?" her mother asked.

"There are a lot of hiking shops and other outdoor stores and I could take that walk that goes around the village. I've always wanted to do that. And there's the park. You said there's always something interesting going on there, and it *is* a Saturday," Eva reminded. "After all that's happened, I just don't want to be here today," she added glumly.

Ann crossed her arms and skeptically watched Eva's spoon twirling around the edge of her bowl, pushing all the sugar back down into the milk.

"Well, I guess that would be alright," Ann said hesitantly. "Though you've never wanted to do that before, but considering what happened yesterday. But I was really hoping you could visit Cyril today, you know, keep him company."

"I can do that when we get back," Eva mumbled through a mouthful of cereal.

An hour later, Ann and Eva were sitting in their car in front of the Blueline Sporting Goods store. Ann was nervously going over all the rules and precautions every teenage girl should follow. Having heard them hundreds of times, Eva sat still and didn't argue. She knew better. While her mother rambled on, Eva smiled patiently and checked her phone.

They said goodbye, but before entering the store, Eva sneakily eyed the little yellow car as it turned right past the gold-domed town hall building and disappeared up a steep hill. *There, finally,* she thought, exasperated. She shot through the frosted glass doors of the store and headed straight for the counter. She quickly came upon a middle-aged woman folding rain jackets alongside the cash register. Her sun-bronzed face was framed by flowing long hair that was as white as new snow. A crumpled old man, fitted tightly in a low rocker, sat behind her idly twirling a cane and staring longingly at a fat, unlit cigar. Before greetings could be passed, Eva quickly asked for directions to the library. The old man, eager to help, righted his hunched back and flashed his perfect dentures, and the woman, who kept folding in an easy manner, gave Eva a warm, leathery smile.

"Just up the road a bit," the old man said, motioning with his cigar. "Right across the street from A. P. Smith Restaurant. Can't miss it," he said brightly with a few thumps of his cane.

The woman nodded reassuringly at Eva while reaching for the next jacket. Eva thanked them, turned and marched straight for the doors. Along the sunlit side of Main Street, Eva scurried by window shoppers and almost bumped into a pair of gangly teenage boys carrying a canoe over their heads down the wide sidewalk. Within a few lost minutes she was standing in front of the library. The red brick building was one story and looked as though it had been there forever. Large tightly paned windows reflected the shaded restaurant across the street. A tarnished brass plaque screwed to the foundation read *1892*. The walkway, paved with lumpy orange cobblestones, wound its way to a wooden bench just outside the entrance.

Eva sat for quite a while, nervously pondering if she should go in. From the moment she woke up she felt very guilty about lying to her mother so that she could secretly investigate the man she admired more than anyone in the world. While the witch's words echoed through her head, she agonized over her decision. Eva reminded herself that if the witch didn't know his name was William, she'd probably be sitting in Cyril's camp right now telling him all about her crazy confrontation with the old woman. Staring absently at a young couple laughing their way through the restaurant doors, Eva spotted a bright-yellow butterfly fluttering helplessly in a slight breeze. Her hand slid over her pocketed phone and in a frozen daze she remembered Cyril catching a moth inside the camp and running to the door to set it free. *He wouldn't ever hurt an ugly old moth. The witch is wrong, absolutely wrong and I'm going to prove it and tell her so,* Eva thought.

With an air of determination, Eva pushed through a massive pair of oak doors and met a frail old lady standing behind a counter, shuffling and stacking books, her bony hands struggling with effort. Perched atop her spindly frame was an oversized poof of sparkling hair, which reminded Eva of blue cotton candy. The air was musty and cool and heavily laced with the pleasant smell of old books. It was dimly lit and everything seemed to be made of polished dark wood.

"Good morning, dear," crinkled a delicate, friendly voice.

"Hello," Eva said, squinting.

A seemingly permanent smile etched the old woman's rouge-painted face and her ancient eyes had a youthful, mischievous twinkle.

Taking off her hat to see better, Eva glanced around the darkened aisles looking for other people. Her eyes quickly fell to a dust-speckled sun shaft that cut across the floor and lit up the polished black leather shoes of a tall, well-dressed man with his eyes only inches from an open book.

"Something we can help you with today?" inquired the woman, bringing her hands together as if in prayer.

"Um, right, yes. I was just wondering how I would find out something that might have happened many years ago, and I don't even know if it happened at all. Might there be some record of it somewhere, like microfilm or newspapers or something like that?" Eva asked nervously, in one long breath.

"How long ago, dear, and where did this incident take place?" the lady asked, smiling and slightly bowing.

"Probably forty years ago, and if it happened, which I don't think it did, it would be right here, in Saranac Lake."

"Ooooh, well now, that makes a world of difference," the old woman said, gleaming upward and tapping her chin. Turning stiffly with a few cracks from her neck, the little librarian shouted over her shoulder, "Lucy?!"

"Yes, Sister," croaked a muffled voice from behind a dividing wall.

Eva's head jerked toward the half-wall where the voice was coming from. Wheels squeaked loudly across the floor and another dome of blue hair appeared sideways from behind an oak panel. Groaning and scuffing sounds could be heard. Eva glanced at the floor by the panel and noticed the shaky movement of two shiny metal legs with little black wheels on the bottom.

"Lucy's the town historian. Sharp as a tack, her memory is," Sister said proudly in a leaning whisper. "If something happened worth remembering in this town, she'll have it all packed away somewhere in that great brain of hers! Mine? Oh my, my, I can't remember what I had for breakfast, and we're identical twins, no less! Well, like I've always said, someone had to get the good looks."

Sister raised her knobby shoulders and giggled like a school-girl, while Eva looked on stoically. When Sister caught Eva's eyes, she daintily cleared her throat and patted her standing hair several times before asking, "Now tell me, dear, what's your name?"

"Eva Robinson. Um, she doesn't have to get up. I could just go over there. I really just wanted a newspaper."

"Nonsense! Does Lucy good to get off her duff," Sister said, waving with an approving nod. "When she hears her name, she knows we're all stumped about something and she'll roll right over and save the day! Mind you, it takes her a bit. She'll be here soon."

Turning away from Eva with a comical wink, Sister started humming as she watched Lucy clunk and scrape across the eight-foot distance.

Each four-inch shuffle looked agonizing, but it didn't stop Lucy's big eyes from smiling behind thick yellow-tinged glasses. Except for Lucy's hunched posture, there was no question that the two were identical twins. Eva smiled back faintly, but winced with each forward strain of Lucy's flimsy arms. When the walker finally bumped into the counter, Sister took off like a flash and rolled a chair out from behind the wall. At a fairly good clip the chair hit the posterior of Lucy's knees and she fell back with a relieved thump. Rocking slightly, but still smiling, Lucy's magnified eyes never left Eva.

"Yes indeed, Lucy acquired an excellent memory!" Sister declared. And then Sister suddenly frowned mournfully and lowered her head dramatically. "But sadly the arthritis seems to have come with it." In a wink, Sister popped back to life, her cheeks aglow with rosiness, smiling at Eva. "Now let's see, Lucy, this is ... oh my, I've misplaced your name already!"

"My name's Eva Robinson," Eva returned quickly.

Lucy gave Eva a faint nod. Confused, Eva wondered if the old woman had even heard her.

Eva felt sweat forming at her hairline. She had only one question to ask but it seemed to be dragging on forever. She also wanted documentation from newspaper clippings or anything that would prove Cyril's wife had died during childbirth, and that the horror story the witch yelled at her was a complete lie. And no matter how sharp Lucy was, she didn't want vague recollections from two very old women.

Sister smiled at Eva and then bowed toward Lucy, who sat beaming in hunched stillness.

"Go ahead, dear. She's ready," Sister said, motioning toward Lucy.

Leaning over the counter on her forearms, Eva teetered on her tiptoes.

"I was just wondering—" Eva said loudly.

"No, no, child," hushed Sister. "Lucy has excellent hearing. No need to shout, after all this *is* a library."

"Oh. Sorry," Eva said shortly. She then began looking around, thinking, *there's got to be someone else here who can help me.* The patience she had walked in with was dwindling fast. She returned her eyes to Lucy, took off her sweatshirt and got right to the point.

"William Bankstrom, about forty years ago, used to live here and he told me his wife died during childbirth."

The twins stopped looking at Eva and lowered their heads slightly. Lucy's ever-present smile slackened into a somber reflection. The mood changed instantly and Eva felt her heart speed up.

"What?! What is it?" Eva asked desperately.

Lucy sighed and looked out a tiny window to her right. When her huge eyes settled back on Eva, her expression was solemn and serious.

"Is Mr. Bankstrom a family member or relative of yours?"

Lucy asked gently.

"No, just a friend. I … my mother and I have a camp close to his home. The other day someone told me awful things about him and I'm here to prove that she was wrong. He's a nice man, a really nice man."

Eva's throat suddenly tightened and her voice trailed off. Sister clasped her reedy hands together and tut-tutted several times.

"It was a very sad time in our town," Lucy said, shaking her head. "And those poor children—"

"Children?!" Eva gasped.

"Yes, dear. There was a fire, let's see now … 1967 it was, at the end of May, if my memory serves me. Although you are correct, dear, about Mrs. Bankstrom. She did die during childbirth and sadly too, her baby died at the same time, a girl, I think. That took place about a year before the tragic fire."

White-knuckled, Eva gripped the edge of the counter.

"I heard there were five people? That part's wrong, isn't it? Who were the children?" Eva asked quickly, her eyes darting between the sisters.

"Now, now, dear, rumors can warp the truth and the past can hide many, many secrets. There are a few gray areas that, to this day, have not been fully understood. I'm sorry to say, I've forgotten their names but I do know there were only two children that perished in the fire, a boy about seven and a girl, younger, maybe four or five. Now, as I recall, and the papers reported, well, Mr. Bankstrom had an awful time with alcohol, that was a known fact. Wrecked many, many vehicles and spent his share of nights in the town lockup."

Sister put a hand on Lucy's forearm, stopping her in mid-sentence. They watched Eva shaking her head in disbelief, her ponytail flopping from shoulder to shoulder.

"No, no, something's wrong," Eva said in a ragged whisper. "This can't be the person I know. There must be some mix-up. There has to be."

"I'm so sorry, dear. I can see you genuinely care for Mr. Bankstom. Last I heard, William Bankstrom was still residing on Union Falls Pond, alone, in a small cabin. Calls himself Cyril, I guess to avoid his past," Lucy said, nodding to Sister.

Eva stared blankly at Lucy's tall hair while the sisters shared confused looks.

"Would you like, dear, that we copy all the newspaper articles about Mr. Bankstrom? That way, you would have a much better understanding of the incident," Lucy said gently.

Eva's stare slowly left the shiny blue hair and fell into Lucy's thick glasses. Lucy's head was tilted and her giant eyes were full of concern. A heart-pounding stillness stole over Eva, and the little women slowly faded away and were replaced by awful visions of Cyril stumbling around, drunk. The terrible scenes continued behind her unfocused eyes, and now she was picturing a white house engulfed in orange flames. Suddenly, in a distant room, a chair rumbled across the wooden floor. Eva blinked rapidly and the questioning old faces returned.

Eva's eyes were flat and heavy and her voice followed just the same.

"Yes, please. I would like them."

"We'll take care of it, dear. It will take about an hour or so. We usually charge fifty cents a copy, but today they're going to be free. You're welcome, of course, to wait here."

"No. I'll come back ... later ... thank you," she said with a sigh of despair. With a vacant expression, Eva turned and walked stiffly across the entranceway and out the oak doors.

Slumped on a park bench in the village green, Eva stared aimlessly at a pair of mallards fighting over breadcrumbs. A few feet away, two little boys were running in tight circles, tossing pieces of bread high in the breezy air while their mother read under the shade of a maple tree. Eva's expression was lost and empty.

The wrinkled copies of Cyril's past lay strewn over the breeze-rippled grass, with Eva's right foot barely holding them down. After reading all of them, she threw them to the ground, knowing she would tear them up if she held them any longer. She kept the papers for only one reason: to show them to her mother, knowing she would never believe her otherwise.

Between numbness and relieving breaks of not caring about anything, bouts of anger would swell inside her and she could feel her face growing red and hot. Her depressed mind played on the overwhelming sadness and she welcomed in all the past hurt, letting it consume her. She was adopted, and right now it didn't matter how nice her birth mother was, someone didn't want her, including her real father. She hated how different she was from other girls. Her alcoholic father was in prison. Jared wasn't calling and if he did, it was unlikely she'd be able to see him this fall, if ever again. Cyril was dying and she'd just learned who he truly was. She used to idolize him and want to be just like him. Now she felt completely lost. Her future, which she used to be excited about, suddenly felt meaningless.

Startled, but then excited about her ringing phone, Eva flipped it open and glumly shook her head.

"Hello, Mom," Eva said heavily.

"Hi, Eva. I'm just entering Saranac Lake. Where are you?"

"By the lake, in the park, near the gazebo."

"What's the matter, dear? You sound so far away. Is everything alright?"

"Nothing. I'll show you when you get here. Bye"

"Eva? Um, bye."

Ann parked the car after spotting Eva's long red ponytail and green baseball hat.

"Eva. What's wrong?" Ann asked, nervously rounding the bench.

Eva stood up and looked sadly into her mother's eyes. She then bent over and reached for the crumpled papers under her foot and pushed them into her mother's hands. Without a word, Eva turned and walked to the car and got in. Standing, Ann sorted through the copies before slowly sitting on the bench. Eva watched as her mother would occasionally shake her head, but when she saw her wiping away tears, Eva would look away at the dashboard with a hardened stare.

******

Ann read one article, but only the headlines of the remaining seven: "Saranac Lake man responsible for the death of his children"; "Bankstrom children buried today, alongside their mother" ; "William Bankstrom to serve time." The next paper showed a picture of a house with burned siding and blackened windows, and next to that, a mugshot of Cyril's young face. The remaining clippings stated several felony DUI charges with pictures of wrecked vehicles.

It was a long, mostly silent ride back to camp—completely silent on Eva's part, but Ann kept trying to defend Cyril.

"Eva, it sounds like a horrible, awful mistake," Ann sympathized. "No one seems to know why he lit all those candles, and although he was very drunk, he did try to get back in the house to save them. That's probably why his hands are all scarred up, from trying to get back in."

Eva's arms were folded on her lap and her head was resting against the door window. With a glassy stare, she watched the trees whipping by and didn't care if she ever talked again.

Back at camp, just after dinner, Eva finally spoke: "I want to go home and the sooner, the better." As she walked away toward her room, she added firmly, "And I'm not saying goodbye to Cyril."

The next day, after the car was packed, Ann begged Eva to visit Cyril. She tried forcing guilt on Eva, saying that it might be her last time seeing him, but Eva didn't seem to care. Ann yelled, but that failed also. Standing by the car, Ann glared at her daughter with her hands on her hips while Eva sat on the porch steps stonily ignoring her mother. Ann threw up her hands, whirled around and headed down Cyril's road. She looked out over the lake and then down at the shore. The sawhorses were there but the boat was gone. She went inside the camp and left him a note, saying that she would call him tomorrow to make plans for a visit in a few weeks.

******

They drove home and a few days later Eva reluctantly started school. She wasn't softening a bit. She moped through each day, recounting her wonderful—and horrible—summer, sensing the wonderful part was lost forever.

Ann noticed that Eva's phone, which used to be in her pocket, was now clutched in her hand most of the time. Eva walked through each day in a quiet stupor. When Ann tried to talk to her, Eva would repeatedly say, "There's nothing to talk about," and then walk off to her room.

Chapter 11

On a Saturday morning in late September, well before daylight, Ann drove the winding four hours through the mountains to Cyril's. Over the past few weeks they had been staying in touch by phone and he always sounded like his old self.

The early morning mist was burning off in the fields and along the streams as Ann zoomed along a little over the speed limit, as usual. Driving deeper into the mountains, Ann noticed the rooftops and lawns were becoming whiter and whiter from the heavy overnight frost.

When her car rumbled over the little red bridge, she pulled alongside the road and for several minutes stared blankly at the dashboard. An oncoming logging truck snapped her out of her daze and she slowly turned left and drove right up to the back of Cyril's cabin, unlatched the car door silently and closed it with barely a sound. It was very early, and also very still. Out over the lake, a huge bank of misty-gray fog stole the morning sun. Colorful leaves were releasing all around her, spinning and twisting straight down from their summer hold.

As she approached the porch she could see Cyril wrapped tightly in a blanket, rocking slowly. He seemed to be sleeping. Ann stepped with a light thud on the first step and gave the wood frame a gentle knock.

"Well hello, Ann!" Cyril said warmly. "Come in, come in."

Holding the door wide open, he craned his neck outside looking for her.

As they hugged, Cyril asked, "Eva didn't come?"

Ann pulled away with a frowning smile. "No, she couldn't make it, but maybe next time," Ann said, looking away.

"Is everything alright, Ann? Is Eva okay?" he asked, concerned.

"Yes, yes, everything's just fine," Ann said with shifting eyes.

"Has Jared called her about coming to camp this fall?" he asked excitedly.

"Not yet," Ann said, sighing.

Cyril looked down and shook his head. "She hasn't tried to call him?"

"No, she won't. Says she doesn't have the number, but I think she's too stubborn or maybe she just doesn't have the confidence to call him. You look good, Cyril! How are you feeling?" she asked, quickly changing the subject.

"Not bad at all, feeling fine. It's so nice to see you, Ann! You can stay for a while, can't you?" he asked hopefully.

"Oh yes, I have the whole morning."

"Let's go inside," Cyril offered. "I know it's a beautiful morning, but we can sit by the fire and I'll whip us up some tea."

When they entered the warm cabin, Cyril went straight to

the wood stove and opened the squeaky door. A small puff of smoke escaped and curled lazily toward the ceiling. After he livened up the red-hot coals with the end of a beech log, he tossed it in and snapped the door shut. Ann went straight to the kitchen and busied herself boiling water and setting cups out on the counter. She then ordered Cyril to sit down and relax. Looking a little helpless, he walked over and sat down in one of the overstuffed lakeview chairs. With brimming mugs, Ann carefully walked over and put the steaming tea down on the small birch table that separated the two chairs.

"Thank you, Ann. You're a good friend. You don't know how much you and Eva have meant to me over the years."

Ann patted his hand and smiled. She then picked up her tea and wrapped both hands around the warm mug and looked out toward the lake.

"How have you *really* been feeling, Cyril?" Ann asked with a tilt of her head. "Are you having any pain, any at all?"

"No pain, honestly. I feel the same as I have all summer. You know, Ann, I should've sensed something odd these past few months," he said, shaking his head. "Why, just last summer I was so much stronger and I had no breathing problems."

Cyril smiled and added, "I never had trouble keeping up with Eva then."

Ann looked down and sighed.

"Melanoma," she murmured. "It's so treatable. They just take the lesion off your arm before it gets into your bloodstream. Oh, I wish we could have caught it earlier!"

"Oh, it's not that," Cyril said with a wave. "I'm not thinking in hindsight. I firmly believe everything, good and bad, has a reason and a purpose."

Ann took a shaky gulp of her tea. She set it down carefully and suddenly became very fidgety.

"Everything?" she asked.

Cyril looked at her questioningly.

Looking straight ahead, Ann slid forward on her seat and didn't stop talking until Cyril had heard all about Eva's run-in with the witch and her visit to the library. As Ann tried to dodge around Hazel's harsh words, she glanced Cyril's way and stopped in mid-sentence. He was sitting on the edge of his seat with his head in his hands. She hardly recognized him. His sadness overtook her and she began to cry. Cyril took a deep breath, rubbed his forehead wearily and sat back in his chair.

"Poor, Eva," he said in a whisper. "I'm sorry, Ann. I'm so sorry. I should have explained myself when we first met. Of course, maybe it wouldn't have helped ... I just—"

"Cyril, you don't have to be sorry and you don't have to explain anything," Ann said, reaching over to him. Her grip tightened on his arm, but her reassuring smile slipped away.

"Cyril?" she said in a strained, tight voice. "Eva—"

He began to turn, but he suddenly choked up and looked away.

"Yes, I know, but it's okay," he said.

"I'll try, Cyril, I really will. She'll change her mind and come and visit. It might take a little longer, but she'll come—"

Cyril stood up and put his back to Ann.

"It's not that, Ann. It's not her visiting me. It's what she thinks of me now," he said softly. "She must be going through a terrible time right now, between her father, and Jared not calling, and now this news about me."

"Eva knows who you are! That was long ago! Everyone makes mistakes."

"No, Ann!" Cyril said in a deep voice she had never heard before. "It was much more than a mistake. It was selfishness and stupidity in the worst form, and to this day I take full account for what happened. I ... I was a very mean drunk," he said quietly, looking away, ashamed. "They all deserved so much more."

Ann stood up nervously and then just as fast sat back down. Sniffing and wiping, she shakily sipped her tea. Cyril was very still and suddenly he started talking in a distant, lost voice.

"Eleanor loved candles. She made them herself. She would mail order different kinds from halfway around the world to get special fragrances, but pine and balsam were her favorites— anything to remind her of Christmas. That was her favorite time. She was no different than a six-year-old on Christmas morning, always so excited."

Cyril sighed lazily. Ann slid back in her seat, cupped her hands and stared at them.

"I was a drunk most of the time and hardly ever home," he continued. "I had everything right in front of me, but I just wouldn't give up the bottle. After Eleanor died, the only thing I focused on was my pain, my loss—*me*! I was drawn so deeply into myself that no one else mattered. That night, it had been almost a year since she died ..."

Cyril inched forward, sitting on the edge of the chair. He gently cleared his throat as Ann watched him swallow several times with difficulty.

"Caleb was seven. Ruthie was four," he said in just above a whisper.

"Cyril, please! You don't have to tell me this. It seems very hard on you."

"I'd like to, if you don't mind. I think it would be good for all of us."

Ann nodded and looked down.

"That night I missed her terribly. After putting Ruthie and Caleb to bed, I opened a bottle of whisky and started lighting Eleanor's favorite candles, something I'd done many times before. But on that night I just kept lighting them and drinking. I couldn't get enough of the pine and balsam smell, it reminded me so much of her. I don't know if it was the alcohol or the candles, but I was getting very hot. I brought the bottle with me, out on the porch, just to get a little air, and then go back in, or so I thought; but I must've kept drinking because they found me with an empty bottle, passed out in a porch chair."

Cyril took a deep breath. Ann, trying not to make a sound, sat motionless with tissue paper pressed against her nose and eyes.

"The sirens and the lights didn't wake me, but my neighbor did. He and the fireman shook me and started dragging me off the porch. When I saw the smoke pouring out the windows, I broke free, yelling and running at the door. My hands went through the door window. Blood was everywhere. That's all I remember. Days later I was told three policemen carried me kicking and screaming away from the house. They pinned my useless, drunken body down and wrapped my hands. I was wild and kept screaming for my children. They forced me into the ambulance where I was given a sedative. I woke up in the hospital the next day. I learned the fire was put out quickly. The flames never reached their rooms, it was the smoke ..."

Cyril slid back in his seat and rested his head comfortably against the puffy chair top. As he stared at the ceiling, Ann sat frozen, her face wet from tears and golden from the sun that had just burned through the lake fog.

"I'm so sorry, Cyril, but how did you ever get over something like that?"

Cyril sat forward and crossed his arms.

"I didn't," he said simply. "I never have and I never will, but my grandmother helped. She's actually the reason I'm still here."

Ann dabbed her eyes and turned in her chair toward Cyril.

The golden light was on him too, and as it moved and flickered on his body, she watched the tension leave his face as his voice took on a relaxed, peaceful tone.

"I don't know how to explain her properly, but she was the most serene, loving person I've ever known. My parents were ... well, let's just say I loved being with my grandmother. She was at our house often because things were usually pretty bad. I would follow her around wherever she went," he said with a fond grin. "She always had time for me. Peace seemed to emanate from her—her eyes, her movements, her voice ... especially her voice. Even my father's violent temper melted away when she was around. If I was near her nothing could go wrong. Just her voice could take away all your deepest fears. She was constantly talking to me about this door, and God standing right behind it. 'Everyone has their very own door,' she'd say. I didn't care about a door or God or any of that talk, I just wanted to be next to her, to look into her eyes and hear her voice. To an eight-year-old-boy, to me, she was God.

"The following year, when I was nine, she died. When I was older, my mother told me that just after she died I was inconsolable for weeks. She even took me to a doctor. I don't remember any of it. As the years went by, the importance of my grandmother all but faded away and I came to depend on only myself. I had all the answers and if I didn't, I would fix them by drinking."

Cyril shook his head as if disgusted with himself.

"I'm sorry, Ann. I hope I'm not talking too much, but strangely, it feels good to let it all out."

"No, no, I'm here, Cyril," Ann said reassuringly.

"After the fire, I had to spend a little time in jail. There I was able to give up drinking for good. Surprisingly it wasn't very hard—mainly because I seemed to have lost interest in everything. They really didn't know what to do with me. In the end the judge figured I'd suffered enough and that I would for the rest of my life. He was quite right. I came here to live as soon as I could, but after several months the depression became unbearable ... I just wanted everything to end, I wanted to die, to punish myself permanently. I hardly ate or slept. I just existed in a black fog. I thought of different ways to make the constant misery go away, but it finally got so bad the method didn't matter anymore."

Cyril stood up and leaned heavily against the window. The sun was gone, now hidden behind the lake fog that was swirling upward in a slow motion. In the clock-ticking silence, Ann nervously watched him as he stared out the window.

"That pine tree was about half that size when I moved here," he said, pointing. "It's hard to believe forty years have passed this fast," he reminisced. "One night, in the fall, I drove the truck under that tree and threw a rope over the thickest branch."

Ann put her hand over her mouth and looked away.

"I stood on the cab of my truck with the rope around my neck for hours, staring at the moonlit water. I thought it was going to be easy, but it wasn't. I took the rope off, promising myself I'd do it tomorrow. I went inside and lay on my bed, wide-eyed for most of the night, finally falling asleep toward morning. And then, I had a dream of her, my grandmother. We were sitting opposite each other at my kitchen table, right over there." He motioned with his hand. "She was just as I remembered, and I thought I was a boy again. We just stared at each other. She was glowing with peace and serenity but her eyes were sad, yet full of compassion. I recall feeling perfectly content to just sit right there forever. I felt weightless and all the pain and darkness was gone. She reached her hands out toward mine and I did the same. That's when I suddenly realized I wasn't a boy. My hands were big and scarred. I pulled them back, ashamed, remembering what I'd done. I was about to get up and run, but her voice. She only said a few words but I've never forgotten them, nor have I forgotten the intense tenderness that radiated from her voice and eyes."

Cyril's voice thinned and stumbled as he suddenly became very emotional.

"She tilted her head slightly and said, 'You should finish up. Open your door, Willie. It's the only way.'

"She barely finished the last word and my eyes flew open. Panic-stricken, I jumped out of bed and raced to the table. It was so real, she had to be here, somewhere, I thought. I ran around the cabin, frantically yelling her name, but she wasn't there. I went back to bed and tried with all my might to fall asleep so she would come back and visit me again—I had so many questions. I never fell asleep, but as I lay there I realized something had changed. It was miniscule, but *something* was different. The misery that was crushing me before somehow didn't feel as heavy, and I knew, Ann, I knew right then that somehow my life would never again be the same."

Cyril's voice suddenly lifted and became clear and smooth.

"I struggled terribly through the first few weeks, and at certain times I never thought I'd make it, but I clung to the peace of her voice and relived my vision of her over and over, almost all my waking hours. In the beginning I begged and yelled at the sky for forgiveness and a clearer understanding of what I should do, and then, thankfully, several months later, I began noticing peaceful, quiet breaks that interrupted the endless noise in my head.

"This unexplainable stillness seemed to surround me and follow me, and the more I let that wonderful silence take me, the further my door opened. And somehow, during the quietest moments, mostly when I lay in bed, crystal-clear words would gather and flow effortlessly through my motionless mind—words of peace and healing and forgiveness, words and answers that I alone could never think of. But when my thoughts drifted back to guilt and fear and worry, my door would close completely. It didn't take me long to realize that I held the key to this door, and the choice was mine to make: live with God, or live alone in darkness."

Cyril sat back down and turned toward Ann. He rubbed his chin and looked her straight in the eyes.

"Ann, I know it's hard to understand, but in that wonderful stillness, life becomes a dream and God becomes real."

Ann smiled weakly and nodded. Cyril patted her knee, stood up quickly and walked into the kitchen. The paper towel rack spun several times as he coughed and cleared his throat.

"Thank you, Ann. Thank you so much for listening," he said hoarsely from across the kitchen.

Ann swiveled in her seat, bringing a wad of tissue away from her face. "You're welcome," she mumbled.

Cyril walked back to Ann and stood before her. He lifted his tea and took a long drink. When he put the cup down, his eyes were red but he had a calm, serene smile, one that Ann was so familiar with and couldn't help smiling back at.

"I feel much better, Ann," Cyril said, nodding. "I'm so happy you're here."

He dropped back in his chair and they talked about the beautiful fall morning. To Ann's amazement, Cyril told her he was still taking his walk, not the whole distance of course, and only on good days, which came about twice a week.

Ann offered to make lunch and Cyril readily accepted. Before she stood up, Cyril leaned forward and put his hand on hers.

"Can you stand to hear one more thing that's kind of bothering me?" he asked in a soft tone.

"Of course," Ann said. "Go right ahead."

"My belief in the dream of my grandmother has never changed or faltered. I've never doubted or questioned it, ever. But ... I ... well, I believe God forgives anything and everything, and several times over the past four decades I have felt His absolute immensity. It is something I'm unable to explain. It is very powerful and real, but sometimes I can't help thinking ..."

Cyril swallowed hard and paused for a moment. He leaned forward, brought his hands to his forehead and looked down.

"Caleb and Ruthie—their lives hadn't even begun. How could *I* ever deserve forgiveness ... especially from them?"

"Cyril," Ann interrupted quietly. "You've made amends. You've told me many times that God forgives everything, you just need ask."

"I know," he admitted, shaking his head. "But it's just so hard sometimes."

Ann patted Cyril's knee and gave him a comforting smile. He leaned back, folded his arms and gazed out the window while Ann hurried off to make lunch.

A few hours later, Ann clomped halfheartedly down the porch steps, telling Cyril she felt terrible about leaving him alone. She all but begged him to come home with her where she could take care of him.

"Thank you, Ann. I'll be fine right here. I'm in good hands. When the cancer advances, I plan on moving into the hospice rest home in Saranac Lake, where I'll have round-the-clock care."

When he walked down the steps, Ann fell into him, hugging him tight.

"She'll come around. You'll see," Ann whispered into his ear.

"Maybe, Ann, but maybe not. I completely understand if she doesn't."

Cyril broke off, looking lost in thought with a growing, tired grin. Ann just squinted back at him, perplexed.

"I could write to her. It probably wouldn't help, but there's one thing I'd like her to know."

Ann's eyes brightened. "Yes! That would be wonderful! Thank you."

With a quick smile, Cyril leaned in toward Ann. "I'll take care of that today."

Linked arm in arm, they strolled toward Ann's car, crunching noisily over layers of colorful frost-rimmed leaves. She speedily reminded him what to do and what not to do in the event that certain health problems arose. Cyril nodded dutifully and walked along, but when they reached her car, Ann stopped in mid-sentence and took his hands. After a frowning glimpse at the pine tree, she smiled bravely into his blue eyes, squeezed his hands and turned quickly to get in the car. Through the open window they said goodbye and Cyril watched and waved until the little yellow car rounded a tight bend and disappeared into a tunnel of autumn colors.

******

Over the next several days, Cyril noticed that he had extra energy, almost feeling like his old self. He didn't know what caused it, but he knew one thing for sure: He felt much better after talking to Ann. He decided to use this time wisely, figuring his energy surge wouldn't last very long. After writing to Eva, he walked outside and started down the trail to Datus's camp.

Cyril had only made it halfway when Datus appeared with a shovel over his shoulder. They both stopped in a thick stand of young pine trees, the light-green branches rubbing their shoulders and arms.

"Bringin' yer shovel back," Datus said, swinging the tool off his shoulder and offering the handle to Cyril.

"You can have it. I've got two," Cyril said, pushing it back.

"Naw, ya might break one. Here, take it. Besides, if I keep it I might use it on Flossie."

Cyril took the shovel, wrapped both hands around the wooden handle and planted the spade in the earth. He leaned comfortably on the shovel and smiled broadly at Datus. Datus frowned and reached in his shirt pocket, took out a pack of cigarettes and smacked the bottom several times with the palm of his hand. "What ya smilin' at?" Datus asked while lighting a cigarette.

"You. You make me smile. I'm going to miss you."

"Going somewhere?" Datus asked, blowing a thin stream of smoke over his lit match.

Cyril shifted the shovel to one hand and his smile fell. "I've come to ask you a favor. I'd like you to put my ashes in a certain place after I die."

Datus chuckled and spit a piece of tobacco on a pine branch, then planted his hands on his hips and smiled his crooked smile.

"Okay. Ya plannin' on soon?"

"Well, yeah, probably before Christmas," Cyril said softly.

Datus's smile vanished and he looked around uncomfortably. "Ya serious. What's wrong?"

Cyril explained everything and Datus promised to take care of his ashes. When it was time to part, Datus reached out and awkwardly took Cyril's hand. Cyril looked at Datus's tight grip and then into his eyes. Datus shook hard, throwing Cyril off balance and then in one fluid motion, Datus released his hand and turned and walked away, his short body sweeping silently through the soft pine branches.

******

Back at the cabin, Cyril made a short list of the things that needed to get done. The next morning he drove to town. After arriving too early for his appointment with his lawyer, he stopped at the post office and then walked across the street to the bank. He then spent an hour with his lawyer and another hour at the funeral home. At the end of his meeting, he half-jokingly asked the director if there was such a thing as a multifaith service available. The director was curt. "No," he said simply. Cyril paid the polite, yet austere man for the simplest service available.

On the drive back he felt tired and the back of his ribs were aching on his right side, but he forced his mind to the present moment, and started looking and admiring—the autumn colors were close to peak and he was having a difficult time keeping his eyes on the road. As always, he looked in awe at everything, as if seeing it for the very first time. For some reason, he could never get enough of the changing seasons and the beauty brought with each one.

The past two days of unending tasks taxed him heavily. He rested and slept straight through the weekend. From his bed, at sunrise, with a chorus of honking geese flying low over the cabin, he was deep in thought as he watched the many colors of autumn dancing and reflecting off the walls of his cabin. Suddenly, he sat bolt upright and said out loud, "Yes! That would be a beautiful place, near The Cone Stone or maybe even French Brook."

He was up and showered in no time. After a big breakfast, he laced up his "old leather friends," as he called them. They were custom-made Limmer hiking boots that were at least fifteen years old. The bottoms had been replaced many times. He stared down at the smooth black leather and wondered how many miles had passed underneath them. Thirty or forty miles a week for fifteen years; *it is a big number*, he thought. Grimacing slightly, he also wondered if this might be their last trip on his cherished walk. Instinctively, he turned in his seat and glanced out the back window at a pair of wild apple trees that almost always had a deer or two standing underneath them.

On this perfect fall morning, a spike horn buck was munching contentedly, and off to the left, sitting in a sun patch, a velvet-brown rabbit was nibbling on a lone clump of emerald grass.

With his mind lost in the beautiful scene, Cyril walked out on the front porch and around to the back of the cabin, all the while thinking, *I sure hope I'm strong enough for this ... and all the way to French Brook, I'm not so sure—*

Suddenly, but as Cyril expected, the deer whistled sharply through its nose and bounded off, its white tail flashing its way through the colorful woods. Sitting statue-still, the rabbit decided to stay.

Leaning against the camp with one hand, he reached up with the other and freed the long wooden handle of a shovel that was pinned between two rusty nails. Resting it over his shoulder, he turned and headed straight for Eva's trail. When he crossed the stream and entered the stand of birches, he was taken by a sudden urge to stop and look back. Leaning on his shovel, he closed his eyes meditatively and almost immediately Eva's little face appeared: She was two or three years old, running through the wildflowers, plucking the tops off and throwing them straight up. He remembered sitting on his basket, unable to stop her fun, watching the colorful flowers fly through the air. Holding the beautiful vision, he flipped the shovel back on his shoulder and continued on across the road, past Eva's camp and through pines.

The trek was slow with many rest stops, but after an hour

the top of The Cone Stone became visible. From Cyril's vantage point it looked as though someone had thrown a bucket of red paint all over the boulder. A tall, lone maple tree stood naked and hovering a few yards from its base, and last night's hoarfrost had stripped it of its foliage, leaving a blanket of scarlet leaves covering the rock and surrounding earth. Cyril stood ten feet away, admiring the scene. Shuffling through the florid landing, his right hand set the shovel against the boulder while the other rode over the knobby rock surface just to watch the bright red leaves tumble to the ground. He then walked a few steps and brushed the soft, damp leaves off The Ruby Seat. As he rubbed the smooth surface clean, the rubies grew brighter and once again he thought of Eva.

Suddenly, a chill ran through him and his body felt very heavy. His arms and legs became stiff and his head was cold. He wiped his forehead and looked down at his hand. Sweat was dripping off of him. He turned slowly and sat down heavily on the cool granite seat. His breathing changed to quick puffs and an odd, dull ache made him rub his left shoulder. He looked up to the sky. *What's happening to me?*

When his eyes settled back to the forest, he squinted and peered back down the trail. The woods seemed blurry and strangely lit up, like a sunbeam had settled in just one area. He rubbed his eyes, trying to see clearer, but when he looked again, the light seemed to be getting brighter. He glanced up at the sky to see if the sun was doing something strange, but his head snapped back quickly. Quite a ways down the path, he caught a flash of glowing movement. A tingling sensation inched its way up his spine. He squeezed his eyes tightly shut and when he reopened them, a little boy with black hair was bobbing up the trail with white light dancing all around him. Cyril's face twisted in confusion. The little boy stopped abruptly, almost stumbling forward. His arms waved in excitement and his mouth was moving very fast. He was pointing a finger right at Cyril, when suddenly, from behind the boy's waist, a lovely little face with two blond pigtails peeked out. Wearing a light-blue cotton dress, a beautiful little girl sidestepped out into full view and took the boy's hand.

Cyril reached up with shaky hands and rubbed his eyes again, trying to see clearer. When he brought his hands down, he thought he must be dreaming—his fingers were glowing and surrounded with the white light. He shook his hands in disbelief and returned his eyes to the children. He wanted to move or yell out to them but was terrified they would go away. With a smooth sweep of the little boy's hand, the fuzziness between them lifted, and Cyril's vision became crystal clear. His heart starting hammering out of control and his eyes twitched and squinted in confusion. Just as his quivering lips whispered *Ruthie,* his arms buckled up. Pain like a lightning bolt seared through his chest and shoulder. At the very instant his eyes slammed shut, he felt a complete release—from himself.

Now standing a few feet away, he watched what had contained him for seventy-four years twist in clutching agony and fall to the ground. Looking on, there was no pain or fear, just an overwhelming sense of freedom and wholeness. He felt light as air but solid in everyway. "Truth" was the only word he could think of, and he kept repeating, "This is the real me! This is the real me!" He glanced sadly at his fallen body but all he noticed was an old hand that was creased with ugly scars. He quickly raised his new hands. The scars were gone. His hands were perfect. When he anxiously turned to look for the children, a flood of sparkling light enveloped him, bringing with it a strange yet tranquil pulling sensation that swirled deep inside him. Mesmerized, he could not take his eyes off the light that was now

shifting and gathering into a single beam of shimmering bril-
liance. He sensed the children were close by, but the wondrous
light held him, drawing him deeper into the greatest peace he
had ever experienced. His trance was suddenly broken when a
tiny hand slipped into his and began swinging back and forth.
An explosion of both panic and joy swept through him. From
the corner of his eye he saw her dazzling blue shirtsleeve and
her graceful little hand cupped in his, and as the swinging settled into a soothing rhythm, his fear melted away and he slowly
turned. Tears welled in his eyes and spilled down his cheeks as
Ruthie's perfect little face and glowing smile gazed up at him.
Still smiling, she shook her head "no" and reached out to dry his
trembling chin.

From his other side a small, clear voice broke the stillness.
"We've missed you so much." Cyril turned quickly and met Caleb's warm crystal-blue eyes beaming serenely into his.

When he thought he could bear no more, Ruthie embraced
his arm in a full hug. "Don't be afraid," she said softly. "You've
never been alone." She then rose to her tiptoes and excitedly
pointed into the brightness. "And the wonderful pulling you feel
... is God."

Chapter 12

He ain't been here. I've not seen him in ..."

Datus yanked his pants up a notch and scratched at his bare chest.

"... three ta four days, I reckon."

"He hasn't been home or answered his phone in the past three days. Can you think of any other place he might be?" the nurse asked.

Two state troopers and a hospice nurse were standing in Datus's doorway. Heat from a very full wood stove was pouring out the door as Datus stood there peering suspiciously at the three strangers.

"His boat here?" Datus asked, pulling a shirt over his head.

"Yes, his boat has been accounted for. His cabin is cold with no indication of his wood stove being used," said one of the officers. "It appears he has not been home for at least forty-eight hours. Has he had any company in the past few days that you know of?"

"None that I heard, but as far as seein', his camp's too far from here. Did ya bother checkin' his acorn sign on the front door?" Datus asked, frowning at the officers.

"We saw it, but nothing indicated—"

"His walk!" Datus exclaimed. "Gotta be where he's at. I can't think of no other place."

"Could you please show us where it is?" interrupted the officer.

"Suppose I can git ya started, but I ain't makin' the whole trip. It's about five miles through the woods, ya know."

"Is there a good trail we can follow?" the other officer asked.

"Yeah it's a good one. It starts behind that camp on the main road," Datus said, pointing up through the woods.

On the way to their cars, Datus leaned toward the nurse and whispered through last night's cigarettes and beer. "He told me he wasn't checkin' out for a few months—maybe even make it 'til Christmas. Whatta ya suppose happened?"

"Mr. Datus, we're hoping he's off visiting friends or relatives, or something like that," the nurse said evenly.

"Oh! Yeah, right. Could be visiting Ann and Eva."

"Ann Robinson? Is that who you mean?" the nurse asked.

Datus rubbed his forehead and frowned.

"She's got a camp on the road, above Cyril, but I don't know her las' name," he said, frowning.

"Must be the same," said the nurse. "But Ann Robinson has not seen him. We called her this morning."

******

The funeral service was held in a little white church in Saranac Lake. Ann talked with many people who knew Cyril, mostly employees from the two local nursing homes and hospice volunteers and nurses. The Cyril that Ann knew was the same Cyril they talked about. Alone among strangers, Ann drifted over to Datus. "You must feel honored, Datus. Cyril really liked you."

Standing stiff and out of place in a mismatched suit of brown, gray and red, Datus grinned and stood a little taller. He was holding a little pine box that contained Cyril's ashes.

"Cyril liked everyone, Ann. You know that," Datus said, shrugging and looking round. "Where's Eva? Thought sure she'd be here."

Ann's face tightened with anger and she shook her head. "Eva's having a hard time with many things right now. She just couldn't make it."

"Oh, I see," said Datus, peering up at the vaulted ceiling. "Well, I'm gonna get goin'.These places make me nervous. Bit musty in here. I need some fresh air anyway. I'll be seein' ya."

Ann's face relaxed and she reached out and patted Datus's arm. "Take care, Datus."

Datus's fast footsteps echoed loudly through the church. Ann watched him until the large wooden doors creaked open and shut behind him. She then walked over to the altar and picked out four red roses from a large bouquet.

Walking slowly out of the church, holding the four roses, Ann turned left and followed the leafed-in lane that led into a small graveyard running alongside the church. She saw their names earlier, through an open stained-glass window from her pew. At a brisk pace, with dry leaves crunching underfoot, Ann was soon standing before their headstones, reading every word. Gently pushing the autumn leaves away, she laid two roses in front of the large stone and one on each of the smaller stones. Taking a deep breath and swallowing hard, Ann shivered as the wind blew.

When Ann got home, she fought with Eva about Cyril's letter. The day it arrived, Eva ran in her room and stuffed it under her mattress, unopened. Eva did notice, however, that it was thick, like it had more than one page. She stubbornly told her mother that it was her letter and she would open it when she was ready. And then she told her mother that she might never open it, because, according to Eva, "It didn't matter." The following week, when Eva's dark mood remained the same, Ann tried one more time to talk to her. The talk ended quickly, as usual, by Eva slamming her bedroom door.

******

At the very end of October, on a raw, windy morning, Ann and Eva motored through the dark mountains. Ann told Eva that she had to go, no matter what. She needed help closing down the camp and she couldn't do it all alone in just one day. What she didn't mention was that she had to close Cyril's camp down too. Eva brought her pillow and slept, stretched out on the backseat for most of the four-hour ride with her phone white-knuckled in her hand. She thought of Jared constantly now. She felt that was all she had. Everything else was gone. When the car hit a pothole on the camp road, she awoke in a fog, stretching and yawning.

"After I get the furnace fired up, I'll whip us up some breakfast before we get to work. How's that sound?" Ann asked cheerfully.

Eva grunted and fell back on her pillow.

When Eva stepped out of the car she looked up just long enough to realize that the fall had transformed to winter. Gone too was Jared's phone call that was supposed to have come during the color change. The woods were gray and brown, which mirrored her mood and added to her misery. Turning away from the open, windy woods, Eva zipped her coat up to her neck and trudged stoically into the cold camp.

After a quiet breakfast, Ann cleared the few dishes from the table and then walked over and stood in front of Eva, who crossed her arms and frowned at her mother.

"Eva, there's something I haven't told you. I was going to wait, but ..."

Eva's eyes widened and she looked up. For some distant, hopeful reason, she thought it was about Jared.

"Cyril loved you, Eva," Ann said softly.

Eva locked her jaw and looked away.

"Eva? He left you the camp, the land, the boat, everything. When you turn twenty-one."

"I don't want it! Any of it!" Eva said bitterly.

"EVA!" Ann yelled. "How can you hold so much anger? I knew I shouldn't have told you."

Unfazed, Eva just sat there, arms locked together with her eyes fixed on a distant wall. Ann took a deep breath and pulled a chair out from the table and dropped into it, slamming her elbows down on the oak surface. She cradled her forehead and looked straight down into her empty coffee cup.

"Eva, he never did anything to hurt you," Ann said almost in a whisper. "He was always so good to you."

Eva shot out of her chair, startling her mother. She went to turn away, but quickly grabbed the top of a chair and glared directly into her mother's eyes. Ann just stared up at her daughter's stony expression.

"Their names were Caleb and Ruthie!" Eva said fiercely.

"I know their names."

"They were seven and four!"

"I know, Eva."

"He got drunk and lit candles in the house and then walked out! How stupid was *that*?" Eva said, her voice growing deeper.

"Look Eva, you don't—"

"Why do people drink?!! They have a choice and they *choose* to get drunk, not caring what stupid things they do or who they hurt ... or kill!!"

Ann wearily shook her head and slowly stood up.

"Drinking is a sickness, a horrible, horrible disease," her mother said softly.

"You're making excuses for him, just like you make excuses for Dad."

Eva quickly broke off and began pacing and pushing the chairs in and out from the table as Ann looked on helplessly.

"He acted like they were never alive! No talk of them, ever! And he was the happiest person I ever knew! It didn't bother him one bit," Eva said in a low growl.

"Yes it did!!" Ann shouted. "It tormented him his whole life. I told you all about it!! Where's the letter he wrote you?"

Eva jammed her hands into her back pockets, her left hand clutching the thick letter and her other hand on her phone.

"I don't have it. I told you it doesn't matter anyway! And you know what's really idiotic!? He thinks God's his best friend! Well how can that be?!! After what he did?!"

Ann locked her jaw and watched her daughter's brown eyes grow small and dark. Eva threw her hands in the air and hysterically yelled out, "HE'S NO DIFFERENT THAN ... THAN *YOUR* HUSBAND!!"

"EVA !! HE'S YOUR FATHER!! DON'T YOU EVER—"

SLAM!! Eva smashed her hand down against the table, forgetting her phone was in it. Several pieces of plastic flew in different directions. When Eva looked up, Ann was glaring at her with a fury that Eva had never seen before. Leaving her phone spinning on the edge of the table, Eva sprinted across the living room and burst through the front door.

"EVA! EVA!" Ann yelled at the slamming screen door.

Eva had no idea where she was going. She only knew one thing: She just wanted to run forever. But where? Cyril's? Never. The road? Her mother would drive up and pester her. She swung to the right and ran up Cyril's path.

Ann's shaky hands were pressed into her cheeks and she was slumped over at the table. For a long minute, the silence was overwhelming until she heard a buzzing noise and felt a vibration under her elbows. She looked up and Eva's phone was an inch from pulsating off the far edge of the table. In a flash, she was up and throwing chairs off to the side. She dove, catching the dancing phone in midair.

"HELLO! Hello!" Ann said, leaning over a chair.

"Eva?"

"No, this is her mother. Is this Jared?"

"Yes. How are you?"

"Fine. And you?" Ann said, smiling weakly.

Wiping her eyes on her sleeve, Ann hurried out the front door in hopes of finding Eva.

"I'm okay. I just heard about Cyril. I'm sorry. I was calling to see how Eva was doing."

"Can you hold for just a minute, Jared? I'm going to see if I can find her. She just stepped out."

Ann ran down to the road with her thumb pressed tightly over the receiver end of the phone and yelled Eva's name in four different directions. Not a sound returned.

"I'm sorry, Jared. She's not here right now, but if you'd like I can have her call you back," Ann said, biting her lower lip.

"Okay. She has my number, I think, but I'd better give it to you just in case. Are you ready?"

"I will be in just a minute. I have to get back inside."

Ann dashed back through the yard and into the camp. She skidded across the kitchen floor and grabbed a magnetized pencil off the refrigerator.

"There! I'm ready, Jared," she said, panting.

Between one-hundred-yard sprints, Eva was walking, holding her chest, coughing and trying to catch her breath. She thought her lungs were going to explode at times, but the pain didn't matter; nothing mattered. The agony felt good, and she thought when she ran the full hike and hit the camp road, she would just run all the way home. The Cone Stone was coming up and she began to slow down. It was where Cyril died, and she felt strange going near it. She passed by, sidestepping and gasping for air. When she saw the shovel leaning against the stone she stopped and stared at it, confused. She took off her sweat-soaked baseball hat and wiped her brow on her sleeve. The wind was rattling the branches overhead and swirling the leaves in tight eddies around the great boulder.

Feeling relief from the cool breeze, she glared down at the shovel. It had long rust streaks running down the blade. As her breathing slowed, she remembered something Cyril had told her years ago when she cut her finger on a nail. *We're all rusty on the outside, Eva, but on the inside, the real you is glowing like the sun.* Eva thought it was stupid and made no sense. Frustrated, she shook her head, wondering why she remembered his words so clearly. She reached back for her letter, wanting to throw it at the shovel and bury it, but her hand never made it to her pocket. She whirled around and raced down the back line and didn't stop until her boot caught a raised tree root and sent her flying through the air. She landed arms out, flat on her front, with her face in the dirt.

When she opened her eyes, she was staring down the leaf-covered trail that went up West Mountain. She quickly stood up, slapping the dirt and pine needles off her pants and arms.

"I'll run up that stupid mountain!" she spat, wiping dirt from her mouth. Eva put her hands out like she was diving into a pool. She pushed and squirmed through the soft balsam greenness, keeping her eyes down to follow the narrow trail, which was getting wider with each small shuffle. About twenty steps later, she emerged into an opening and stopped instantly. Frowning, she slowly surveyed the ensconced setting. It was a circular clearing about fifteen feet wide. Off to the left stood a pair of pine trees separated by a leaf-covered bench. Balsam and birch trees had been planted all around the opening, spaced every foot or so. Golden ferns lined the entire edge of the circle. The earth in the middle was worn down to the tree roots. It was beautiful and serene. Eva could almost feel what she was seeing. She also felt more anger right alongside it. *Another secret of his*, she thought, scowling to herself. *Why didn't we ever stop here?*

Before stepping in, she watched the ferns bending and swaying with the swirling air. Turning her head side to side and taking in every detail, she slowly walked over to the bench. The front edge was shiny, appearing as though it was glass-covered. Frowning deeper, she knelt down and laid the length of her arm over one end of the bench. Wobbling on her knees sideways she cleared all the leaves off with one long swoosh. The top was the same as the front, displaying many layers of glossy, hand-brushed varnish. The wood was dark brown and very old, but meticulously cared for. When she sat, the calming sensation continued to ease in.

Fifteen minutes passed as she held the edge of the bench and unknowingly rocked back and forth. *Where is this strange feeling coming from?* she wondered. For one brief moment she pictured Cyril sitting there, praying about the awful thing he did, but she quickly dismissed it. While her anger fought the peace, she forced herself off the bench. When she leaned forward, her heels went backward and clunked into something hard and hollow. Sliding off the bench and resting on one knee she pushed the ferns aside. There was a green metal box sitting on a wooden rack above the ground. Eva held the ferns and didn't move. She looked behind her and then all around. She felt like she was trespassing; suddenly, she didn't feel alone. The only thing she saw was what the wind was doing; the ferns were waving calmly while the leafless branches were clinking eerily overhead. She swallowed hard and lifted the small but heavy box onto the bench. She sat next to it for a moment and just looked at it. *United States Marine Corps* was faintly stamped on the top. The green paint had faded, especially on one side, and the heavy, single hasp that opened the box was worn down to the metal.

When Eva pulled on the shiny lever, the top abruptly sprung open. She squinted into the darkened container and then glanced around again, feeling oddly watched. Slowly she reached in and pulled out a neatly folded pink blanket. Confused, Eva held it out at arm's length. And then suddenly her breathing began to speed up and she started squirming and shifting on the bench. The blanket was faded and threadbare, but the soft pink edging was intact. Lifting it straight out in front of her, the little blanket slowly unraveled in her hand. She noticed stitching in one corner and pulled it in close. Hand embroidered in faded yellow thread was the name "Ruthie." A prickling sensation ran up her spine. She slammed the blanket down on her lap and began pushing the metal box away until it toppled over with a loud clunk, sending something black and white silently tumbling across the bench. Lying on its side, a little stuffed penguin stared back at her. She slowly reached over and picked it up by the good arm. The other arm was hanging limp, looking as though it had been mended several times. She pulled it in close and blinked to clear her eyes. "Mr. Penguin" was stitched on the front in the same yellow thread. She quickly spun the penguin around, searching for his name but found nothing. Gripping the penguin tighter, she looked up through the wind-whipped treetops and closed her eyes. She wanted to scream, but her voice was buried under a growing lump in her throat. A quiver ran through her stomach and her eyes began to fill. She couldn't understand what was happening, and she was becoming very afraid.

Eva exploded into loud, gasping sobs. She slammed her hands up against her mouth trying to force it back in but she couldn't stop it, and her hands fell to the bench with a surrendering thud. While she rocked back and forth, heavy tears slid down her face, dotting her faded blue jeans from her hips to her knees. When her rocking finally eased to a gentle sway, she felt an unfamiliar warming sensation filling the cold, tight places in her chest and abdomen. As she allowed the soothing relief in, she finally let herself think of Cyril; and for once, she didn't try to stop.

Forty years I've taken my walk. I hardly miss a day. His voice was clear inside her head and so was his face and she missed him so much.

While sniffing and wiping, Eva took long, jumpy breaths and looked around the woods in a daze. She was surprised to find the wind had completely stopped. Not realizing what her hands were doing, she glanced down and found they were pressing the blanket and penguin tightly against her stomach. She released the tension, and as she started caressing the silk edging on the blanket, a snowflake landed on her knee and melted just as fast. Her eyes slowly moved upward and met a mass of large flakes drifting straight down through the wooded stillness. The beautiful scene added to her peace, which now seemed to be settling into her whole body, her whole being.

When her body shivered with a quick jerk, and the snow-squall began to thin, she knew she had to go. She knew she had to talk to her mother, but she was afraid to leave. She thought the understanding and peace that filled her would go away when she left the circle.

Eva was just about to sit up when she remembered Cyril's letter. Pulling it out, she tore at it with trembling hands. Inside was a single sheet of heavy, yellowed parchment. When she unfolded the stiff paper, she was surprised to see only a few small words, written in the center. Her eyes clouded up again as she read out loud, "*I just love you, Eva.*" She turned the parchment over, thinking there had to be more, but it was blank. She wiped her wet face with her sleeve and slowly folded the letter and slid it back into her pocket.

She put the penguin and blanket back in the box and closed the lid. Standing up with wobbly legs, Eva cradled the metal container tightly with both hands and walked to the balsam-border of the circle. Stopping for a moment, she looked back at the bench one last time before sliding through the evergreens and out onto the main trail. Pressing the box close to her chest, she started down the back line. When she reached The Cone Stone, she carefully sat the box on The Ruby Seat and picked up the shovel.

Sixteen years later …

BOYS! HALT RIGHT THERE! Nathan, Jason, you said
you'd take Kristy!"

"Aw, Mom! It takes her forever and she always has to bring
her stupid dolls, and then I always end up carrying them," Nathan whined.

The boys, ages eight and nine, were standing on the other
side of a narrow stream in a small birch grove. Eva folded her
arms tightly across her chest. She couldn't decide whether to be
strict or let them go.

"Let them run free, Eva. It's camp week. They're so excited
to be here. I'll bring Kristy up later," John said out of the corner
of his mouth.

When Eva glanced over at her father's solemn expression,
her motherly tension slowly drained from her face and was replaced by an acknowledging smile.

"Alright, you can go. But stay on the trail and when you get to Grandma's call me, okay? And save some cookies for your sister," she added a little louder.

"Yup, we will," Nathan shouted unconvincingly, spinning on his heel.

"WAIT!" Eva yelled, stepping out of the wildflowers. "No throwing rocks at that old bus. If I hear one window break, that's it for the path. You'll be hanging close to camp for the rest of the week."

"We learned last year, Mom. We wouldn't do that," Nathan said innocently.

Jason put his hands behind his back and nodded in agreement.

"Bye, boys. Tell Grandma I'll be by later."

Nathan and Jason disappeared in a flash. Eva shook her head, wondering if they had even heard her.

"Did I see Jason drop something?" John asked quietly.

"A rock," Eva said sighing heavily. "*Jason* ... that one needs constant surveillance."

Eva laughed and turned to face her father, but he was gone. He was still standing next to her but his eyes were suddenly empty and avoiding. Eva could always tell when the darkness of his past cloaked him and took him away.

He slowly turned and put his back to Eva. Like many times before, when he retreated inside himself, Eva wanted to help somehow, but her caring words never seemed to make a difference. Frustrated, she thought of Cyril and as always her anxiety melted away. Focusing on a bright-white flower in the garden her face relaxed into a serene smile. While her mind blanked and the flower blurred into a dazzling sparkle, Eva closed her eyes and for some wonderful reason, Cyril's voice began in her head. *Perhaps dear, your father's life—the good and the bad—*

is unfolding perfectly. Might it be that our idea of perfection is vastly different than God's perfect plan for each of us? Eva shook her head and looked around. Confused, she peered up at the sky and then back down at the flower. With a growing grin she reached for its stem.

Eva walked over to her father. John was standing tall and rigid, staring glassy-eyed across the lake.

"Dad?"

Startled, he turned quickly to find Eva's arm extended and her compassionate eyes staring into his. After a frown and a shy glance at his daughter, John's heavy eyes locked on the flower, and after a moment's hesitation, he reached out and took it.

"Thank you," he said in just above a whisper. He cleared his throat and added, "I think I'll take the long, roundabout walk to the lake. I know you want to get going on your hike so I guess I'll see you when you get back."

"OK, and thanks for helping out with Kristy. Now, don't let her wear you out," Eva said, trying to reconnect with his eyes.

"I won't," John said with a half-grin.

Eva watched her father walking slowly along the path until he was out of sight. She then turned into the garden and was soon lost in thought, strolling through a rainbow of colors. It was their first day at camp since last fall and it was always the hardest for Eva. Memories of many past summers spent with Cyril would tumble through her mind. Simple memories, but to Eva, great memories, and then she would do something Cyril had taught her long ago. She would block the sadness by being very thankful, believing somehow, sometime, everything would come back, full circle.

"MOMMY! MOMMY! Daddy's almost done with the dock ... thing," Kristy yelled.

Kristy was running through knee-high grass, up from the

lake. There was a doll tucked under her right arm and her left hand was busy pushing her long red hair out of her eyes.

"Kristy, honey, why don't we tie your hair back so it's not in your face?"

"No! I like my hair like this," Kristy said, all out of breath.

And Eva knew why. Someone else wore her hair down and Kristy thought that person was just about perfect.

"Where are they? Where are Nate and Jay?" Kristy asked, looking all around.

Eva's phone rang and she flipped it open. Noticing the number, she smiled.

"Hi, Mom, are the angels there yet?"

"Yes, they've arrived. They asked me to call you because their faces are full of cookies," Ann said, laughing.

"Mom, not too many sweets, and no soda, okay?"

"They'll be fine. They're at Grandma's camp! Bye, dear."

"Ah ... bye," Eva replied, scowling at her phone.

Eva slid her phone in her pocket and knelt down in front of Kristy. She reached out to fix her hair but Kristy pushed her hand aside.

"I let your brothers go to Grandma's, but don't you worry. Grandpa said he'd take you. I think he's down by the lake," Eva said, looking toward the water.

Kristy lifted her doll in the air and slapped it against her leg. Her lower lip doubled in size.

"Mom! They said they'd take me. Now they're gone. They don't ever want to take me. They're mean to me always! I hate them!" Kristy said.

"Whoa, Kristy. You don't hate your brothers. We have to work on them being nicer, but that—"

"What am I going to do now?!" Kristy interrupted.

Eva was still kneeling at eye-level with her five-year-old.

Kristy's hurtful brown eyes were staring into her mother's identical ones, looking for comfort. Without thinking, Eva pulled her in for a tight hug. When they parted, Kristy's expression was unchanged, but a growing smile was stretching across Eva's face as she decided to cheer up her youngest.

"Kristy? I have a surprise for you. I was going to save it—"

"What? What is it?" Kristy interrupted.

"Someone's coming to camp for the whole week. Now let's see if you can guess. She's tall, has long dark hair and likes to wear it down. Just like—"

"AUNT WENDY!!" Kristy yelled.

Eva smiled and nodded at Kristy, who was now jumping up and down.

"REALLY?!! WHEN?!" Kristy shouted.

"Tonight, about dinnertime."

"And for the whole week?" Kristy screeched.

"That's right, for the whole week," Eva said happily. "And she told me she wasn't coming unless she could share a bunk bed with someone." Eva looked up and tapped her chin. "Let's see, what was her name?"

"ME! ME! She meant me! Aunt Wendy always sleeps with me in my bunk bed. And for the whole week! I'm gonna tell Daddy! Does he know?"

"Daddy knows," Eva said softly. "But Grandpa doesn't."

Kristy looked down by the lake at her grandfather, who was standing in the sand staring out over the water.

"You can tell Grandpa. I bet he'd like to know. He thinks Wendy's so funny. You can be the one to surprise him," Eva suggested.

Kristy looked down, frowning, and Eva could tell she was thinking hard.

"Grampa John looks sad again. But Papa Tom doesn't ever

and he's loud and funny! Is he coming to camp this week?" Kristy asked excitedly.

"Yes, honey, later in the week."

Eva took Kristy by her little hands and glanced toward the beach at her father.

"Kristy, you're right. Sometimes Grampa John is sad. But did you ever notice when he sees you he always smiles?"

"No, well maybe," Kristy said, still frowning.

Eva shrugged her shoulders, smiled and said, "It's you, Kristy. It's your smile. I think it's magic! Every time I see it I feel all good inside!"

Kristy's face slowly relaxed. She turned away and Eva watched her studying her grandfather on the beach.

"He does think Wendy's funny, doesn't he?" Kristy asked with a full smile.

"Yes he does."

"OK! I'll go right now," Kristy said quickly.

Singing "Aunt Wendy's coming to camp," Kristy took off down the hill. Eva watched lightheartedly as Kristy's red hair bounced and shimmered in the June sun.

Eva went inside the cabin to fill a water bottle and grab her pack. She was heading down the porch steps when a familiar "Hello" rang out from the edge of the wildflowers. Eva jumped a little and then, smiling, walked over to the garden.

"Didn't mean to scare ya, Eva," Datus said shyly. "Just thought I'd come over and say hello. You know, kinda welcome ya to camp."

"Thank you, Datus," Eva said wide-eyed. "How are you?"

"Fine, just fine," Datus said, looking a little sheepish.

Eva hardly recognized him. He was standing almost straight, wearing a clean buttoned-up shirt. His salt and pepper hair was combed off to one side, somewhat neatly, and his belly looked smaller.

"You look wonderful, Datus!" Eva exclaimed.

Datus scratched his head and bashfully kicked at a nearby tree root.

"Been dry for nine months," he boasted with a full chest.

"Why that's fantastic Datus! Just fantastic!"

"Doc said ma liver was going to implode or explode or some-thin', if I didn't stop drinkin'—said once your liver goes, that's it, it's all over. Anyway, it's been hard, real hard, but I'm gittin' it ... slowly."

Eva stood, glowing with amazement.

"Congratulations!" Eva said. "I hope it gets easier and easier for you. Be strong, Datus."

"Oh I will. Still got my cigarettes though. Ain't givin' those up, not yet anyway. Gotta have somethin', for God's sake!"

Eva followed Datus's eyes over to the swaying wildflowers.

"Still miss him, don't ya?" he asked casually.

Caught off guard by Datus's usual bluntness, Eva's stomach did a little flip.

"I ... yes I do," she said softly, reaching down and stroking the dancing flowers. She spotted another white flower and said, "Seems like he's still here sometimes."

"Good neighbor, Cyril. Liked him a lot. Sixteen years," said Datus, shaking his head. "Why it seems like only yesterday I sprinkled his ashes over them flowers, but ... 'course it would be for me. I've been drunk most of my life."

Datus sighed heavily and looked at Eva.

"I've missed out on so much ... so much," he said, frowning and shaking his head.

"But now you have a new start!" Eva said. "And Flossie, she must be so happy."

"Thrilled. Says her prayers been finally answered, and her

voice is back to normal, she don't scream no more, well, hardly as much and believe me, that's a big plus! It's a wonder I can even hear! But I deserved it though. It's just plain amazing she put up with me all these years."

Eva smiled warmly and walked over to Datus. As she patted him on the shoulder, he gave her a crooked smile and then dropped his gaze to the ground.

"I'm so happy for you, Datus."

"Well, me too, I guess," he said, pulling a pack of cigarettes from his shirt pocket. "I'll git going now. If you need anything, some help or something, you know where to find me," he shouted, waving and walking away.

"Thank you, and if you need anything at all, don't hesitate to ask," Eva said. "And please say hi to Flossie for me."

Datus was striding down the hill when he raised a waving arm straight up in answer to Eva's favor. Eva smiled, crossed her arms and proudly watched him walk away without one wobble.

When Datus disappeared into the pines, she unzipped a pocket on her backpack and pulled out a multi-knife. It was big and heavy and had everything from scissors to a toothpick folded in its many slots. Tossing it up and down, she strode easily through the tall grass toward the lake. Stopping about halfway, she raised her arm and waved in a circular motion.

"JARED!" she yelled evenly.

Jared was standing in the water up to his waist, tying heavy rope around one end of a small dock. He stopped what he was doing and waved. Even though he was far away, Eva could see and feel his understanding smile. He then motioned in the direction of her path, indicating for her to go.

Eva glanced over to the left and felt very content. Kristy was sitting on her grandfather's lap in Cyril's Adirondack chair. After voicing a sincere "Thank you" skyward, she walked back up the hill, stopping briefly in the wildflowers before continuing on.

As she did every June for the past sixteen summers, Eva took a slow hike up Cyril's trail. When she reached The Cone Stone she dropped her pack to the ground and took a long drink. After carefully brushing the golden pine needles and last year's sun-dried leaves off her ruby seat, she sat down and almost immediately a familiar peace settled in as she immersed herself in the sights, sounds and smells of the summer woods. The serenity Eva felt here was beyond words. She couldn't explain it to anyone, not even her husband. It was her place, her healing, and at times, an almost tangible connection to the unknown.

When it was time to go, Eva slid off the smooth seat, took a few steps and carefully laid an armful of wildflowers over the brown leafy earth that covered a little green box.

Acknowledgments

A very special thanks goes to my very first readers, my daughters, Emily and Alyssa, who inspired me to never stop moving forward on the story. Another special thanks goes to my wife, Kathy, for putting up with my hundreds of disappearing acts with my laptop. I also wish to thank the many first readers who prompted me onward: Kathy Rector, Dana Cross, Ron and Marianne Rector, Nancy Strack, Beth and Richard Jaques, Ann Hough, Jack and Jean McMartin, Julie Rogers and Sarah Ferro. On the publishing side, I am deeply indebted to the Koehler Books team: acquisitions editor Terry Whalin for believing in *The Ruby Seat* and taking me in; my publisher, teacher and now friend, John Koehler; Joe Coccaro for his seamless and expert editorial guidance; Cheryl Ross for her superb copy editing; and Margo Toulouse for her help with the finer details.

CPSIA information can be obtained at www.ICGtesting.com
Printed in the USA
BVOW07s1004131213

339066BV00003B/151/P